Winkle and Aster

A NOVEL

DEREK CORSARO

First Published in the United States
BISAC: Fiction. Fantasy. Urban.
Cover art created by, goodCoverDesign.

PUBLISHER'S NOTE

This is a work of fiction. Names, characters, businesses, places, events, and incidents are either the products of the author's imagination or used fictitiously. Any resemblance to actual persons, living or dead, or actual events is purely coincidental.

Imprinted by, SleepKingdom Press

ISBN-10: 0-9996877-2-7
ISBN-13: 978-0-9996877-2-7

E-Book ISBN: 978-0-9996877-3-4

This novel received the Readers' Favorite 5-Star Medal

For quiet people.

Only stay quiet while my mind remembers
The beauty of fire from the beauty of embers.

—John Masefield,
"On Growing Old"

Winkle and Aster

Chapter 1
Phthalo Blue

In the morning the red even consumed the figs and the plums where she played when she was younger. It spread out of control so much faster than she expected. They replayed footage of the incident all day. Periwinkle dimmed the light on her phone and counted the survivors in the broadcast. One—two residents in the first home and a family of four that she knew in the second. Her palms tingled. The fire engulfed two homes; it did not move like the first one. She hid her phone and went inside.

Periwinkle Dalisay sat at the table nearest the doorway. She chose the seat two weeks ago when they switched her classes. Something about sitting by doorways kept her from feeling constrained. Her brown complexion reflected her silhouette against the black table, and she shrunk into the seat. Winkle's hair crinkled against her shoulders and bounced away from the rim of her chair. Curls shifted around her cheeks into the façade she prepared for the school. *Other students in these classes always looked the same.*

The door swung open when one of the upperclassmen arrived. He wore a blue letterman jacket decorated with patches from the school. Winkle never at all felt small for her age, but now she wondered if it was worth it; her success with academics made her feel insecure. In this class, even more than others, her gifts and accomplishments made her feel strange.

Some of the other students talked about the fires in the news, but they soon ran out of things to say and moved on to talk about video games, or shoes, or other students, and sports.

The boy with the letterman jacket bellwethered their conversation. "Those fires were bad," he said. "But did you see these shoes I'ma wear at the next game?" He pulled a pair of red and yellow high-tops from his bag, and the admirers swooned.

The group hovered beside her desk, and the boy with the letterman's jacket bumped her chair. Winkle twisted the corners of her lips. Most people liked him because he ran well with footballs and drove a blue mustang.

"Hello Mrs. Oublier," he said to the teacher. The boy matriculated through class and found his seat at one of the tables in the center. Students jostled to sit near him before class started. He lived across from the school and learned to twirl a mean wooden gun in tempo with his ROTC troop. That was one reason they let him attend—and football. And debate. Also good grades.

Winkle crumpled into her seat and sketched the golden shield which adorned the classroom wall. The words, *Oasis Desert Shields*, underlined the school's emblem. The words took up as much space as the shield. Someone had ripped the award poster next to the shield—not on purpose—not at this school. Maybe it was a backpack buckle or a pen tip from an unwary student that slashed the announcement poster about achieving the third highest test scores and the third highest graduation rates in the district, but the photo of her school's building on the poster remained intact. Winkle drew the school.

Oasis High looked like a brown brick of a school, and it

was created to improve the county's performance with S.T.E.M. subjects like science and math.

Mrs. Oublier handed Winkle her test from the previous week, and Winkle slipped it in her folder before anyone else saw the grade. There were two ways to attend this high school: live no more than a mile away while maintaining a 3.0 grade-point average or score high enough on standardized tests. Winkle did both. Her home was in the neighborhood across the street; they moved when her mom and dad both earned their promotions, and at fourteen, she was in her sophomore year. Last year she tutored the boy with the letterman jacket who was two years her senior. She finished the sketch of the school building and added a slash through its roof and windows, along with some crumbled bricks.

"What'd the new girl get?" one of the students behind her asked. "That quiet girl."

"That brown girl?"

"Yeah, I don't know what she is."

"Isn't she Mexican?"

"Nah, she's Hawaiian, or Indian, I think."

The students started to play her favorite game: *what is she*, and Winkle pretended not to hear. She was not a new girl.

Her first science class grew a little too big, so she was one of the Advanced Placement students moved into a class that included almost all neighborhood kids. She didn't mind so much because she already scored high enough on the AP exam, and Mrs. Oublier was her second favorite teacher in what had become her third favorite school of the six she's attended.

Today they focused on information about the hydrologic cycle and how water moved through the lower atmosphere. Winkle used her colored pencils to draw and detail the cycle, and it fascinated her that no matter how the environment changed, the water always remained the same molecule. Winkle drew a gold log with water evaporating from the surface of the log while the teacher lectured. Then she added arrows to depict the water's journey. It was its very own palindrome. The relaxed pace of the class let her focus more on the sketch than the content, and she kept herself busy by thinking of some real palindromes while she sketched her notes before she had to repaper her binder.

Other kids in class chittered and played games on their phones whenever the teacher looked down or turned her back, but once the lecture and examples ended, students had to talk with their peers about their evaluation of one molecule's effect on the environment. Winkle shared her illustration and her descriptions with the boy beside her, who was both intimidated and aghast with its content compared to his own, and he did what other sixteen-year-olds do when presented with her work in comparison to their own; he pretended not to see it.

Winkle looked at the clock. Her partner swung his chair around to talk to the kids behind him.

"Ok, what have we learned?" Mrs. Oublier asked. "I expect an answer that exemplifies the acumen of an Oasis scholar before I dismiss class."

Winkle appreciated the teacher's intellect and kindness, but her hands started to sweat when Mrs. Oublier's attention gravitated in her direction.

"And you?" Mrs. Oublier smiled at the boy who sat beside Winkle. "What have we learned about transitioning from one stage to another and its effects on the planet?"

The boy flipped around and grabbed Winkle's drawing. He held it in the air to show Mrs. Oublier. "These are my notes." He read from the colorful paper as the dismissal bell rang.

"Very well," the teacher said. "The class may go."

The boy dropped the drawing, and it slid off the table. Chairs rubbed across the floor and the students trampled toward the exit. After the other kids pushed past her out the door, Winkle picked up her notes. *Everyone here was the same.*

She put her head down, then squeezed into the hall where students talked again about the recent fires in the neighborhoods—two occurrences in the last two weeks. The news mentioned arson, but the police had no proof.

"It's just the law of large numbers," one girl said. She smiled at her friends. "We learned about it in math. It's all Occam's Razor."

Winkle and the girl had the same English class, the same math class, and they used to have the same science class until Winkle's schedule changed for rebalancing. No homework assignment ever remained unassigned in a class with that girl, and she made sure to smooth and stroke her hair with every enunciation and smirk.

The girl turned and whipped her hair across a boy's mouth. "It's not arson. It's the law of large numbers. Like I said, all of it is just coincidence and that is why the same neighborhood had two fires in two weeks. It can happen." The girl stared at her conversationalists to allow the concept to worm through before she broke into an explanation.

Winkle thought about the girl's idea as she squirmed her way out of the hall. The law of large numbers—an assertion that in any system even improbable coincidences—like a coin that lands on heads fifty times in a row or a teacher that spills coffee on the same blue shirt every Wednesday in April is possible because over time, the system averages itself out. The other students thought it was just coincidence the fires started in the same neighborhood.

Winkle heard a click from her backpack. She backed against the wall and pulled the bag from over her shoulder and rummaged around for an extra pocket she had sewn into the inside of her bag. She pushed aside her books and art supplies and found the pocket, reached inside, and then snapped the object shut. Winkle fingered the brown metal lighter her dad had given her, then traced the etchings on its side that outlined the image of the hotel where he used to work. Sometimes its cover flipped open, and the mechanism sparked. She wondered if her dad knew that the souvenir he chose, out of however many the shop displayed, was the one with a broken top.

Winkle didn't think the fires had anything to do with coincidence. Fires near the school—what would it be like to solve a problem that helped everyone and then bring calm to a system instead of chaos—to try and accomplish something notable from beginning to end. This is what she wanted for herself, but she wasn't special. Is that what it's like as an adult? Maybe she'd surprise everyone. Winkle checked again to make sure the lighter stayed secured in her backpack. Over the years, all the students in the halls must look like equals to adults.

Water splashed on the ground outside, and once school ended, Winkle sat on the wall and waited for the rain to subside. She watched leaves swirl above her classmates like mosquitoes that breed over a swamp and credited the rain for making her shadow bend in unnatural angles as it refracted through the water. She listened to the boy from her science class talk about the law of large numbers with his friends as he waited for his parents, and she watched a rain puddle rise in the gutter amongst a small bank of sand and napkins on the sidewalk. Their conversation spread to the next group.

Winkle rested her head in her hands and hoped that the downpour would end before walking home. Her shadow ran through one of the puddles where the water drained itself into a crack in the curb.

A white Mercedes pulled up, screeched into the curb, and when her discussion-partner from science stepped into the puddle and reached for the door handle, the puddle swelled. He slipped, then crashed into two other students. His lips split open against the curb, then his mom ran out of the white Mercedes. She screamed at the two other kids. "I saw you! You pushed my son on purpose." She grabbed her son by the arm. "You will all tell me your names! My husband is a lawyer. I am a lawyer!"

One of the other boys yelled at the woman, and a crowd converged. They all argued. Winkle tried to gather her backpack before someone asked her what happened— before someone demanded her name. No one pushed the boy. He was a klutz and his mom couldn't control her car, but that's all everyone ever does in this place, argue or laugh at something. Winkle huffed. Did they ever get tired of it? Her thoughts turned dark. She felt like the darker she got, the less anyone cared to listen.

She left when the assistant principal who stood near the busses noticed the crowd. The assistant principal squawked into her handheld like a drill sergeant. She was serious. She was going to handle this.

Winkle slunk away before the administrators had a chance to see her and ask witnesses to write a statement and waste time in an office being intimidated while counselors and administrators tried to modulate their "I care" voice while dusting their Jimmy Choo's and Fendi's and saying "Thurrrrrssdayyy" into a compact. Winkle walked home in the rain. She remembered it was October.

Parents and students gathered and argued in the distance. It was the same all the time. The routine turned her thoughts dark once again. Winkle's mood felt like charred flesh. She was umber in a forest, darn near mahogany. It made it easier to shy away from everyone. Besides, she wanted to get home soon, not just to get out of the rain, but she had an important project to plan and finish.

Her thoughts materialized into a Bob Ross lake of phthalo blue. She saw phthalo blue in the blurry part of the sky and the darkest part of 6:00 pm. It colored the inside crease of a wave, and she bought a pack of all phthalo blue colored pencils to interpret it.

Winkle walked faster. She wanted to work on her comic strip before her mom and little sister got home. She called it Barnen and Pistasho.

"Barnen," Winkle muttered. "It was time for you to break out of your shell and get those baddies out of your home." *You're bigger and stronger than them anyway because you're the hero.*

If she could get home before her mom, then Barnen's fur was about to become a little wilder today, and his claws would be a little sharper. He would not be an amiable bear in today's comic strip. Maybe even Pistasho, his rabbit friend, would undergo a change.

Winkle modeled Pistasho after her little sister, and she wanted to lay out their next adventure. This time it would take place by a mysterious lake and it would be the perfect chance to use her new phthalo blue pencils.

Her house resided just under a mile from the school, and she darted inside to get out of the rain. No car. No sounds. She made it home first. Her mother had to pick Aster up from school, and they hadn't returned yet. Winkle rummaged through the art supplies under her bed. She grabbed her drawing pad, pencil set, and two of her new phthalo blues. She packed it in her bag. The rain let up outside.

Winkle had this idea to represent her two characters with colors. She mulled it over. For Barnen—brown—because he was steady, natural, and strong. She tried to make Pistasho like her sister, and her sister was wild and always in motion. She imagined her like the color a person sees when they close their eyes tight. It's that flash with no discernible color at all—just points and brightness that lets a person know the outside world exists. She couldn't get a handle on the color, but her little sister moved like that.

Winkle scuttled into a large bush with a hollowed-out center that grew in front of her house. She used the hideout when she wanted to get away and just work, and she played inside the shrub even as a kid, to build dirt castles and watch the neighborhood people walk by. She crawled into her shrub, sat to view the neighbor's house and their gray breaker box on the side of the wall, and got to work drawing Pistasho.

Pistasho liked to wear clothes, and Winkle drew her with one of her pant legs pulled up. Aster always had something uneven about her clothes—one sleeve crinkled on her elbow and the other uncurled over her hand, or two different colored socks and a pant leg stuck above her calf with the other cascaded over her shoe. The face was important too. She gave the rabbit chubby cheeks just like her sister and exaggerated the eyes to encompass most of Pistasho's face. She continued with the ears. One straight and one folded down like the pant leg.

With today's adventure, Barnen and Pistasho would discover a hidden source of water. The water would conceal something mysterious, something life changing. Winkle just didn't know what yet, but she figured it'd come to her now that she worked in her hideaway. She wished something mysterious or life changing would happen to her.

She heard her mother's car roll up the driveway. Winkle saw Aster jump out of the back seat with her too-big backpack and ramble through a one-sided conversation. Her little sister was small for a nine-year-old. Aster Dalisay was so small that she wasn't even on the growth scale.

The pediatrician called it failure to thrive. As a result, Aster got to eat things like marshmallow, peanut butter, and margarine sandwiches. She plopped gobs of ice-cream right into her cereal and ate half-sticks of butter with her vegetables—anything she could do to gain calories, but her sister was so flighty, talkative, and active that the girl never budged an inch upwards or gained an ounce of fat—not in her legs, not in her belly. Aster walked in circles around their mother, narrating something that no one could follow with any semblance of sense.

Their mom carried jackets, bags, and groceries and yomped to the house. She fumbled her keys into one of the grocery bags. This gave Aster all the encouragement she needed to spin off into some tangent that had something to do with an avocado and electric guitars.

Winkle wanted to finish before lunch.

The new pencils worked, and they blended into transitions of color much better than her older set. She detailed the scenery first and finished a lot of the backgrounds for her comic strip. Winkle drew faster when she heard the front door slam and heard footsteps gambol toward the bush.

Winkle saw Aster's elbow poke through the leaves. Her sister continued to multitask through bare branches until she finally pushed her way into their cubby, camouflaged from the world.

"Mom says you have ten minutes, then we have to eat. She's inside working on the ofrennnnda, and Ah made feeenger sandwiches with maahshmallows and jelly. I only touched them with my feengers."

Aster sometimes talked like she just spent a lifetime milking goats, raising chickens, or trying to grow turnips in the south; she had a speech impediment and had trouble sometimes saying 'R' or 'I.' Maybe it was her broad front teeth. Maybe it was her chubby cheeks, but whatever it was, Aster didn't sound like anyone else who grew up in the west.

It was a good time for her and her sister to get out of the house. Their mom always got a little withdrawn around this time of year. She looked like she had everything together, but Winkle knew October was difficult.

"Did you wash your hands this time?" Winkle asked. "You gotta stay clean if you're making food."

"Ahh don't know, Periwinkle! Ah guess ah washed my hands."

"How could you not know? Did you even take a shower today?"

"I took a mawning shower. Ah washed my hands but didn't wash my feet." Aster ran in place and performed her full body run. Her head dropped. Her arms chugged. Her entire torso shook into performance. "I got new shoes and don't need to wash my feet. The shoes contain the stink."

Winkle winced. "Aster, you have to wash everything or people will smell you. You'll be the smelly kid in school."

"Why is anyone going to try and smell my feet? Do people do that in your school? I don't want no one to touch me."

"No, we don't do that in my school. Nobody does that."

"Then I don't need to wash my feet if no one can smell them."

Winkle shook her head. "Aster…no. Look. Fine. Ok, sit down. We have ten minutes. I said I'd teach you to draw."

Aster smiled. Her cheeks beamed, and Winkle decided she needed to change Pistasho to a chipmunk.

Aster's drawings looked much better than the amoebas she used to make. They focused on the basics: guidelines for scale, basic shapes for a face and eyes. Aster practiced, and Winkle watched a neighborhood cat meander across the neighbor's yard. The gaunt creature wore a funny tortoiseshell pattern. Half its face was a dilute gray and the other half orange and black. Its irregular pattern continued across its body in shades of black and orange. Its tail remained solid gray, but Winkle swore she detected tinctures of blue.

"I always wished we had a pet," Winkle said. "Maybe a puppy. Dad said we could get one from the shelter once."

"How do I make hands?" Aster asked.

"Just concentrate on the shape. Don't think of them as hands. A shape connected to a shape and…" Winkle smelled the smoke before anything else.

The heat seared through next. It reminded her of a grill when her family visited one of her mom and dad's friends. Her dad's friend used a silver cooking torch. The flame burned so hot that its colors turned invisible. She knew the torch worked because the smell of propane burned her nose, and the heat in front of the torch's nozzle made the air quiver. The skin of the meat in the invisible fire crackled, then formed a sort of shriveled crust.

Heat crept up Winkle's back. She saw Aster drop one of the new pencils and look up at her. The bush behind Aster caught fire, and her sister's eyebrows arched and pressed together. Aster tried to pick up the pencil. Flames whipped against her sister's clothes. The yard outside the hollowed bushes disappeared behind the flames and dark cinders.

Winkle grabbed her little sister's hand. She heard screaming. Aster's new shoes and then her pants caught fire. She saw their house reflected in her sister's brown eyes and flames reflected in her sister's brown hair. She wanted to hold on to Aster. Winkle felt as if she burned from the inside out. It did not take long.

Chapter 2
Seaweed and Pickle

It felt like pressure against her ribs and back, or like an ill-intentioned hug. Then her thoughts felt as if they separated from her head because the sensations did not match the image of seeing her own body consumed in an inferno.

Something stung her ribs again. Not quite a bee sting, more like a jagged stick jabbed into her side, and the weight of whatever it was pulled on her ribs. A hand materialized in front of her, and she ignored the jab against her ribs. Periwinkle grabbed for the little fingers, but they burned away until a golden point of light remained. She wondered if the same thing happened to her.

Her head hurt, and everything in the shadows showed tinctures and colors of seaweed and pickle. She had never been concussed before; she imagined it felt like this. Maybe she didn't survive. A hammer to metal din of pressure against her temples brought dizziness. *Why was it so blurry?*

Winkle gasped for air. She shot up on her knees. Her sister? Winkle spun around. Leaves blanketed the ground. Everything looked so blurry. "Aster?"

Her sister's little body curled over a rock on the ground. Aster's face looked pale, and dirt crumbled away from her cheeks and lips. "Aster!"

She pulled her sister into her chest. Aster's body felt warm, and she started to move. Winkle felt her sister's heart beat against her shoulders, and then Aster coughed out dirt.

"Where am I?" Aster asked.

Winkle looked around. The dizziness subsided. She saw trees—some type of forest. Was it almost night? The forest sounded quiet.

Aster wiped the dirt from her eyes and looked around. "Where are the houses?"

"I don't know," Winkle said. She let Aster rest, then stood up to get her bearings. Trees crowded her vision. The light that illuminated the forest didn't look like the light in daytime or starlight at nighttime. Winkle felt cold as if she stood in a wintertime shadow. The light breached the trees from the sides more than from the top, and it left everything in the forest with a hue almost like a snow-cone with the color sucked away.

"I don't know if it's morning or night," Winkle said.

"It's daytime," Aster said. "We can still see. If it's night, there should be stars."

"Where is the sun?" *Where were the stars?*

"It's not night," Aster repeated. "If it were night, I'd be even more afraid."

"We should go," Winkle said. "I think it'd be wrong to stay here. We need to find our house." Winkle helped Aster up, brushed off her clothes, then smoothed her sister's hair from her face before tucking it behind her ears.

"What was the last thing you remember?" Winkle asked.

"Hmm." Aster grabbed Winkle's hand. "I remember drawing, and then I think I had trouble breathing." She pursed her lips. "That's it."

"I remember…" Winkle thought of black fires. She remembered her ribs hurt, and she saw a spot of light that she thought was her sister. The flames burned closer and closer to the light. Winkle's arm tensed. The hair along her forearm stood up and her skin felt cold and bumpy. She imagined the fire growing closer. "We were outside. It was almost lunchtime."

Winkle felt Aster stagger against her hip. Her sister kept looking back and to the sides. "Do you think we'll have to sleep in this forest? I can't see a way out."

"Let's just keep going a little more, Aster. We need to find someplace safe and we should look for water. We have nothing."

Winkle's arm yanked back. Aster stood in place and pointed to a tuft of plants that stood at least three-feet high. They had frizzy bulbs at their tips. However, two of the plants bore a pair of gray spots at their ends, like the large irises on a peacock's feather. An array of blacks and brown circled the spots.

"It's following us," Aster said. "I've seen those plants before. Those same plants. It's been following us since we started walking. I thought they were different plants, but it's the same two all the time."

Winkle's stomach turned. She didn't know where they were. She didn't know what happened to their home or their mom. She's read many books about predatory cats and snakes that live in forests. She knew camouflage was a common adaptation for predators and prey. Her arms shook and her legs felt heavy. Aster looked even smaller as she curved inward and trembled.

"I know they're following us, Periwinkle."

Winkle wanted to sound calm, but her voice and her stomach did not cooperate. She whispered to Aster, "I don't think we could outrun it, not if it's a predator. Most predators have evolved to be capable of bursts of speed."

"Like a cheetah or a shark." Aster said.

"Yes." Winkle's legs felt rooted to the ground. "Animals

at watering holes mix all the time. Don't run. Keep walking. We'll try to make sure there are trees between us."

A blast of thunder ripped branches off the tree behind her, and then Aster screamed. Winkle's body shook. She squeezed her sister's hand, pulled her close, yanked her along, and ran.

The forest sped by. Aster screamed louder, and her eyes darted back and forth.

"Keep up with me, Aster. I won't let you go. We'll be fine. It's fine." Winkle said.

Up ahead, something stood in their path. A person. A shadow. They needed to change directions.

"Don't run!" it said. "You'll get lost."

Winkle slowed down, but her heart raced. Her throat felt dry. Aster, too, must feel dehydrated by now.

"I won't hurt you," the creature said. "But you two need to keep quiet in this forest. We're in a safe spot, but if you keep going, you'll run into a pack of nekrouns. That wouldn't be good. Mostly, they're scavengers, but they're still deadly."

Winkle wanted to feel at ease. She pushed Aster behind her.

"What is she?" Aster asked.

The individual in front of them stood on two legs but moved like a cat. Bony, scorpion-like plates lined her body. A brown carapace grew over her elbows, forearms, and legs, as well as her back and torso. Two sinewy tails trailed from the creature's back and curled around her legs below her knees. The tips of each tail flared out into the two eye-like markings they saw in the forest.

The girl stood with her hands on her hips. Splotches of gray covered her arms, and a chalk white sword hung from her side. "My name is Hooyip. I saw both of you enter. You fell out of the fire, which means you come from someplace strange. Do either of you need water? Do you know water? I have some, but we'll need to get more." Hooyip held out a leather flask.

Winkle kept her hand from shaking and took the flask. They needed to drink. She took a sip, handed the water to Aster, then, once her sister finished, Winkle helped her sister dump the rocks out of her shoes.

"Your names!" Hooyip said.

She didn't look that old. If she were human, maybe she would be four or five years older than her. She could grab Aster and try to run, but they were both so tired, and Hooyip moved faster. How did she move so fast?

Hooyip smiled and stood with her fists on her hips, but Periwinkle saw the corners of the creature's mouth tremble. Maybe she felt scared, too.

Periwinkle thought for a second to give fake names, but she did not even know where they were or why it would matter. "I'm Periwinkle Dalisay, and this is Aster, my sister. It's late, and we need to get home."

Hooyip fought to keep her smile. "I'm not sure where home is for you two, but this isn't the place to travel alone. Not unless you know these parts like I do. I am a great alakdan hero, and I'm on a noble quest." Hooyip lurked toward a tree, then scoured the forest. "But I can take a break to help you and your sister if you like. I might not be able to get you home, but… hey." Hooyip looked around. One of her tails unwound from her legs and twitched up. She crouched and her other tail shot up. "You two should get down. Something's coming toward us."

"Get down Aster," Winkle whispered.

"So," Hooyip said. "Periwinkle, Aster. Like I was saying, I'm a great hero, and I'm on a quest—hey. We should go somewhere else. Follow me. You drank all my water. I'll pass out if I don't drink anything."

"This is fun, Winkle," Aster said. "It's like hide and seek. We're land sharks nomnomnom." A blush of red returned to Aster's cheeks.

Little kids had this way of turning everything into a game. Maybe her sister thought they were asleep, and they somehow shared a dream. The smell of rot wafted in the air. It stung Periwinkle's nose and smelled like the stew of banana peels, bread crusts, old potatoes and whatever else her dad used to scavenge from dinner plates to throw into compost for their garden.

Hooyip pressed her stomach to the ground and prowled. She skittered below the tops of the foliage. Aster, too, scuttled across the forest floor. Winkle felt stiff and altogether unnatural, stumbling through the fallen branches and dead leaves in the forest. Her back felt sore.

Now she heard it—*whatever it was*—rustle through the trees toward them. It did not sound as if it moved too fast, so maybe it didn't notice them yet. She almost gagged from the overripe smell of decay, but Winkle forced her throat to keep everything down as she bumped into Aster.

Every time the sounds moved closer, Periwinkle saw Hooyip's tails twitch in response to the vibrations created by the creature's approach. The smell grew stronger. The beast remained at least 40-yards away, but near enough for Periwinkle to see its outline through the gray and pickle colored forest. It walked on four limbs, all swollen with muscles, and its shoulders undulated higher than the full height of any man she's seen or met. It turned its head, and Winkle wanted to scream. She looked at her sister. Aster continued to follow Hooyip. Her sister hadn't seen the creature yet.

Skinless bone made up the monster's jaws, snout, and eyes. Blood stained its face. Was this one of the nekroun that Hooyip mentioned? Its tongue curled over its teeth.

Winkle tried to block her sister's view of the creature. If she were to see it, she'd yell, or worse. Aster might freeze and they'd make easy prey for this new beast. The trio crawled. Winkle heard water. The beast disappeared into the gray tinge of the forest, and the cool dampness from the wind blanketed Periwinkle's face.

Periwinkle felt Aster pull at her sleeve. "It's like we're alligators."

"Yes. We're alligators, Aster." If her sister needed to make this a game to cope, then that was fine. Winkle knew her sister was smart—maybe the brightest kid in her school ever since the second or third grade. She had a strange knack for knowing the right thing to do. Maybe pretending this was a game was the best way to figure out where they were and how to return home.

Hooyip stopped below a bed of grass which kept most of her body hidden. Her two tails stood up, and she waited.

Winkle felt Aster grab onto her hand again.

"It's getting darker," Aster said. "Our home isn't here, and I don't think anyone is looking for us in this forest."

"We'll be ok. Maybe she knows a place we can stay. I'll get you home, Aster, I promise."

Hooyip hopped up. "It's safe. We need water, and we need food. Then I can finish my quest."

"What is your quest?" Winkle asked.

"Well, you are part of it. Remember, I saw both of you come out of the fire. You are in the Ember Lands. At this point I want… well, I'm going to fix things here. The black fires that surround our world are unstable." Hooyip stared at Winkle and Aster.

"Look, as long as I can remember, the black flames have burned at the edge of the world, but they've moved inland now, and sometimes when they appear, something comes through the fire." Hooyip pantomimed an explosion.

"You see…" Hooyip wrenched her lips and shrugged. "Sometimes it brings nothing, but sometimes the fire brings *something* from its abyss. A fire opened up by my home once." Hooyip waited. "It would be easier to show you."

Periwinkle looked for places where she and Aster could hide or run. How hard would it be for them to escape?

Hooyip's lean muscles outlined her skin whenever she gestured or stalked through the forest. Periwinkle sighed. *You have no chance, Winkle.* She felt Aster's grip tighten around her hand.

"Us alakdans don't use a lot of magic," Hooyip said. "It's not clear when or how we first learned, but I know this one thing—well, two. We use it to tell stories. If you help me get some water, I can show you. I can't do too much, but if there's just a little water, it should work. But it has to be at rest." Hooyip cleared the leaves, rocks, and sticks from the ground.

Winkle looked at the pond. It almost spanned the limits of her sight, but she saw it terminate before its border disappeared into the dark. It formed what looked like an irregular circle and was small enough that she figured she could walk its complete length in 15 or 20 minutes. Its current rippled, but other than the flow of water, Winkle heard no other sounds.

"Come on, Aster, help me dig." Winkle kicked the heel of her shoe into the ground and dug a small canal between the area where Hooyip worked and the pond. Aster helped, and she kicked at the ground and swung her little arms with every kick and stomp.

Winkle figured her sister must be tired or hungry or both. This was the sort of job where Aster would make up some nonsensical song to sing as they tried to link their ditch to the pond, but now Aster just concentrated on the work.

Hooyip finished clearing the ground and created a small

ditch, and Winkle broke away enough dirt so that the water filled in her little tributary and flowed toward the excavation into a pool.

"Ok, give me a moment," Hooyip said. She concentrated on the smaller pool of water. "I have to match my breathing to ripples in the water. I can do it with small amounts like this. It just takes time." Hooyip flicked the edge of the pool, which sent a ripple from one end to the other. "I was better at this when I was a kid." She closed her eyes and steadied her breath before opening her eyes again and repeating the process of flicking the water and breathing in tempo with the reverberations. "This is one of the few things I've learned." Hooyip twisted her lips. "Ok, I think I've got it."

Bits of light—colored purple, blue, yellow, and white—fell from Hooyip's hands and sparked across the water. The colors stretched apart until they made discernable shapes.

Within the pool, Winkle saw a cliff carved with stairways and crevices that connected it to both the sand and the ocean. She saw the strange black fires burning further away at the edge of the ocean, and many of the alakdans bustled along the shore and along the face of the cliff in what must have been Hooyip's city and home. The surface of the sand smoldered. Black flames crackled to life. They shot up to the top of the cliffs. The alakdans did not have long to prepare. A strange creature preceded splatters of gray and red that tore through the fire. The lower half of the creature's body looked tattered from the abdomen down as if it ripped itself away from its waist and legs. Torn, leathery wings held the creature aloft. Its sharp tongue trailed in the air and stretched the length of its torso. It seemed to say something to the people in the city. Then it attacked.

Winkle realized this was Hooyip's manipulation reflecting on the pool. Someone must have pulled her away when a second behemoth, then a third, entered through the flames.

"We split up when the manananggals attacked," Hooyip said. "There were three of us away from our home. I went into the forest. The other two traveled south. The elder who survived told us that there's a game those creatures play to try and be the first to find a vine from the Abyss. Whichever one finds it first is reborn into the land as a perfect version of itself and receives the world as its gift, but it's as if something is making it easier for them to come through. It's different from our older stories this time. The fire bursts are so erratic, and there are so many. Before we parted, the elder, she told me that the Vine must have made its way into our lands. It grows in a different spot every time it is born, and the manananggal and any other creature that comes through the flames would destroy everything just to find any information about its location."

Hooyip threw a stone into the pond. "The first creature to find it and return it to the Abyss lives forever. Then the Vine sprouts again somewhere else, and they repeat the cycle. The manananggals destroyed my home. I'm going to find the Vine before them and use it to close the portals so it can never grow again. The sylphs are one of the ancient races in the Ember Lands. Their history stretches back further than the alakdans. If I can find them, maybe they'll know where to find it."

"What happens if the manananggals reach it first? Do you think this Vine can help us get home?" Winkle asked.

Hooyip's tails flicked around her waist and legs. "If they get the Vine first, then I'll be their gift, just like everyone else and the rest of the Ember Lands. If the manananggals find it, then they'd just use all of us as food. It is their nature, and I won't be anything's food or gift. The Vine is supposed to rebirth whoever returns it, so maybe it can rebirth you into your home. If you help me find it, I'll help you return home."

Aster's stomach growled. Winkle felt hungry as well.

"There're snails here and toads," Hooyip said. "There's fish, but they're hard to catch. Do you eat fish? I can cook them, but we would need fire and I don't have any with me."

"I've never eaten a toad," Aster said. "The time I ate a snail, I wasn't supposed to, and I was little."

Hooyip smiled and stretched her arms. "We'll catch some! The ones here are so meaty. And this time when you eat them, it'll be on purpose. It might take us a while to get enough, though."

Winkle watched the water and wondered how she could help. She wished she had something to eat. Her stomach felt cold and empty, and her hands grew clammy. She knew how to swim—barely. Maybe she could tie some of the thinner twigs together to make a net. Winkle watched Hooyip and Aster move closer to the bank of the pond, and she felt the same ill-intentioned hug and sting in her ribs as when she first woke up in the forest. She heard the breeze whip by her ears and almost mistook it for a whisper. Her eyes itched and teared up, and the world around her disappeared. Something dark and strange waited in front of her.

Winkle could not tell if she was asleep or awake, as if a gray scrim materialized in front of her, and the water in the pond almost hissed away.

"I must be asleep," Winkle whispered.

Ripples on the surface fell still, and the water receded. Soon, dry land appeared to replace the water. Droplets of moisture fell from Winkle's eyes and hands into her shadow. She heard toads croak in the mud and fish flop around on the exposed land. Was she responsible?

A voice echoed to Winkle through the scrim, "I knew you could help! Anything that comes through the fire is magical somehow. Even though you're human but don't look human… Can everyone control magic like this where you come from?"

Winkle saw the alakdan take Aster's hand.

"I didn't know this was something you could do," Aster said.

Winkle wondered who Aster and Hooyip were speaking to.

Her sister's voice sounded like an echo, "I wondered how we could get food from the pond without knowing how to swim, but I guess I could help if it's like this." Aster edged toward the pond. "You and Hooyip shouldn't have to do everything. I can collect food, too."

Periwinkle saw Aster sit on her backside and slide into the pit that once held a pond. She grabbed one of the larger fish with both hands and it wiggled in her grasp. Periwinkle knew that Aster never liked water. Not the way Periwinkle did. She never even ventured into the shallows much when they visited their relatives in the Philippines. If a pool had a wading area by the stairs, then that was as far as Aster preferred to go. Sometimes with floats on her arms and an inner-tube to lounge on, Aster trailed the walls if someone was there to pull her about, but not often. She almost drowned when she was younger. She did, however, always want to show her worth.

"I got one!" Aster tossed the fish out of the pit to Hooyip. She moved further away to scoop up a second and a third.

Winkle's arms felt cold, and a spasm of pain shot into her back. Was she awake now? Her head hurt. "Aster, I-I don't know what's happening. You need to get out." She saw Aster at least twenty feet from the edge of the bank. Water burst from Winkle toward the pond. Her sister's voice disappeared. Instead, Winkle heard the flood of water spray forward. Her arms and legs remained fixed in place, and all the water returned to the pond. She lost sight of her sister beneath the torrent.

Winkle collapsed. She heard splashes and screams. Then she saw Hooyip emerge from the water. The alakdan carried Aster under one arm, and then she pulled herself from the water onto the bank of the pond.

Aster choked. Water spilled from her nose, and she gasped. Her little body quivered. "Why did you do that to me, Periwinkle?"

Chapter 3
Astronomy

"You tried to drown me," Aster said. Her voice quivered as she huddled into a ball beside a tree. "You don't do that to people. You saw me. I was getting food for us, and you dropped all the water on me. You looked like you were helping, but you did this on purpose."

"I didn't," Winkle said. The pain from her back disappeared. She didn't know why the pond flooded. She didn't know why the water vanished in the first place.

"You waited for me to get away from the edge."

Aster had a way of arguing. As smart as she was for a nine-year-old, she had a way of latching on to an idea and letting it consume her.

Aster paced as she wrung out her clothes. "When I was far enough away, you made all the water return."

Even at four years old, if Aster felt she was somehow wronged, she would follow Winkle around their home for what seemed like hours, yelling at her. Winkle knew nothing about this place. Her fingers bent into a fist. She wanted to go home. She wanted to work on her drawings in the hollowed-out bush. What had happened? She tried to remember. *The fire. Did she really survive?*

"You tried to drown—"

"I didn't! It wasn't me! I didn't even know the water disappeared or how it came back. If you can get us home, then get us home. If you know how to find food or water, then go in that pond and get it for yourself. But I bet you don't know how to do any of that stuff, either."

Hooyip stepped in front of Aster. "Well, someone who could do all that stuff you said would be a tremendous help. Just like someone who could make water vanish or appear. At least we're all safe now, and we should have enough to eat."

Winkle stood back and watched Hooyip take care of everything. Being lost in the woods would be easier if Aster weren't here. Winkle sat in the dirt and threw rocks into the pond and waited for Aster's grudge to pass.

Her sister hopped around after Hooyip chattering about home, asking bizarre questions, and preparing for the night.

Why did the water disappear, and why did it return? Winkle looked at her shadow. She was the one who made it happen, wasn't she? She closed her eyes, then tried to think. The stinging had something to do with it—but what then? Winkle concentrated on the water. She tried to will it to disappear. Nothing happened.

She heard Aster laugh and make monster sounds, then pretend to swallow Hooyip up like some great fish.

She's so annoying sometimes. Winkle spread her hands toward the water. Last time it dripped upwards maybe, and there was the dark. What else was there?

"What, my sword?" Winkle heard Hooyip talking to Aster, and she watched the two rest against a tree. The alakdan drew the sword and sliced it through the air. "It's bone. It is the jawbone of a monster from the flames."

No. Winkle shook her head. She needed to concentrate. She wasn't anything special. Why could she do something like this now? Winkle rubbed her eyes and then her forehead. That wasn't true either. If she's learned anything from all the schools she attended and all the different classes and students or tests that have compared or categorized her, she's always come out near the top. She knew how to figure things out. She knew how to problem-solve. Winkle watched the ripples in the water. What did she think of before the water disappeared? Everything here was so surreal. Maybe it was hunger. She did feel hungry. What was the order when it happened? First, her stomach growled, and then the surface of the water started to evaporate. Then she felt a twang of pain up her spine and heard a tin-can echo of a whisper from her shadow. Winkle tried to listen.

"Hey, Periwinkle. You want to help us?" Hooyip asked. "We need to clear the ground if we want to sleep. Find a tree for shade, dig under them a little. It's safe here, but it's still best for us to hide."

Dig a place to sleep? Is this what survivalists do? Winkle cleared away sticks and brambles from the ground. Maybe they were lucky Hooyip found them. Near the pond, Hooyip showed Aster how to clean the fish. It did not smell as bad as she imagined, but the descaling and gutting looked nasty. Aster didn't seem to mind. Winkle watched her little sister slice into the fish's stomach and scoop out the innards with her index finger and wondered if mom would ever let Aster handle a knife like that. When Aster pulled out the innards, the intestines sounded like a zipper.

"Hey Periwinkle," Aster said. "I'm going to make our feeenger food. It's going to be raw! We should save some of the fish and carry it with us if we get hungry tomorrow."

"That's a great idea." Hooyip said while fileting the fish.

Winkle thought about potential differences in anatomy between humans and the alakdan. "No—Aster. Salmonella, we can't eat old food that's uncooked."

"You need to apologize before you talk to me!" Aster

said. "And I eat bananas all the time. Even after I've—"

"No. I mean—"

"Apologize."

"No, this is important. You can't eat rotten—"

"Apologize."

Winkle looked at Hooyip, who pretended not to hear the conversation. The alakdan cut and re-cut the same fish while refusing to look up. After a while, the knife wasn't even touching the fish anymore, and it was not cutting anything except open space as Hooyip made slicing motions across the fish's bones.

Winkle wanted to ask Hooyip about her anatomy to either confirm or deny the existence of salmonella in a species different from humans, but her dad always told her to respect people and their differences, no matter their race, color, or culture. Winkle decided it was best not to offend their new companion with explanations about infectious diseases. Maybe raw food was different here.

Periwinkle made three equal sized indentations under one of the thicker and shorter trees. Aster would appreciate having the same amount of space as her and Hooyip. With the sticks and dirt cleared away, the sleeping spots looked like little coffins. Winkle smoothed away the barrier between two of the ditches to make Aster's spot look more square and less like a coffin.

"Come eat with us, Periwinkle," Hooyip said.

Fish and snails were laid out on shaved wooden branches—all of it raw. When Winkle walked over, Aster pursed her lips, furrowed her eyebrows, then turned away.

"I'm waiting," Aster said.

"Fine, Aster. I'm sorry. I didn't mean to get you all wet like that. I didn't know what happened. I wouldn't ever hurt you. You know that."

Aster nodded. "I helped make everything, Winkle. I

made the snails. I made the fish. It's like we're camping. Eat with us."

The gray forest darkened. Aster was right, it was like camping. Stars twinkled through the sky, and Winkle sat next to her sister and tried to look for some normalcy in the woods.

"Who are the sylphs?" Periwinkle asked.

"Well, I haven't seen one since I was a child," Hooyip said. "The one I met was young. He had hair like the leaves. His eyes and hands were colored like the roots of a tree. He did not quite walk, but instead he drifted along with the wind. They can manipulate the things that grow in the forest and control the wind and the water. They arrived when the Ember Lands arrived. That's what I was taught anyway. Their history reaches to the beginning of time. They should know a lot more about the Abyssal Vine than my own people."

"And you know how to find them?" Winkle asked.

"No." Hooyip sighed. "I just know that the one I met from when I was young lived in this forest, but this forest is massive. I will find him or his friends because that's what I have to do." Hooyip looked down, and her tail traced lines in the dirt. "I might be the last alakdan left by now. This quest is all that I am." Hooyip looked at the ground.

They thought their private thoughts. Then Aster picked bones from the food, considered it, and popped it in her mouth.

"Anyway, I'm going to find those sylphs and figure out where the Abyssal Vine is and destroy it so that it can never grow again. Easy."

Winkle saw Hooyip's head droop and then the alakdan turned toward her and beamed. Winkle wondered how anyone could remain so positive after Hooyip's ordeal, and she understood why Hooyip called herself a hero.

Aster picked away at the food. "You have to try this, Winkle. It's raw. That makes us organic farmers. We could sell this at the grocery store. Slimy foods market. Eat, Winkle."

Winkle took a deep breath. At least Hooyip cut away the heads and tails of the fish before serving them as food. The fish felt flaky, more than slimy, but the snails did not feel the least bit flaky, and instead felt the precise way she imagined. She wiped the t from the snails against a rock and swallowed the creature up so she didn't have to think about the taste. Once they were done, Winkle watched her sister run over to the area that she cleared away for beds.

"We should go to sleep, Aster. I think it's getting late." Winkle stretched out on the ground next to her sister. Stars sparkled through the canopy of gray and seaweed colored trees. It looked like this sky had a lot more stars than the sky in her neighborhood. The light illuminated the sky more than it illuminated the ground, and blanketed by the night, and with the area above her aglow, Winkle felt as if she floated within a dark wave.

"This place has more stars than where we live," Aster said.

"Mmm hmm."

"Periwinkle, am I significant?"

"Hmm? It's hard to see out here, Aster. It makes it hard to concentrate, too. I couldn't hear."

"Oh."

"Hey Aster, the cluster of stars looks like a turtle." Winkle turned to look at her sister, but her sister may as well have vanished because of the dark.

"Nooo those stars look like a bug. That one above you looks like a potato bug."

She imagined her sister must be pointing at something.

"And that one might be where we live," Aster said.

Winkle thought. Was it that simple? Were they on a different planet or on a star somewhere? "I wish I knew more about astronomy," Winkle said. "Maybe then I could figure out where we are."

"Aaw-stonomee?" Aster said. Her speech impediment gave her trouble with the word, and she gave the vowels and consonants a few more tries.

"Astronomy. It's when you study the stars and the planets and outer space."

"I know the word." Aster tried the word again before giving up. "Aaasstow-nomy. I'm still not done with my aawwrs. The speech therapist is still working with me."

"I wonder if there are any speech therapists here," Winkle said. Her sister struggled with her speech impediment since she began talking. No one was perfect. Winkle did not even start talking until she was six. Her parents had her take singing lessons to help her catch up with the other kids. Singing was like her warm blanket, but she was never sure if people just told her she did it well because it took her so long to talk or if her voice held some intrinsic quality. With talking, she always felt she languished behind other kids, so even after she learned to speak, she preferred not to talk to people unless she had to.

Periwinkle felt something tug at her shirt. Aster held Winkle's arm and cuddled against her as she fell asleep. Periwinkle watched the sky. It occurred to her that no one knew her here. There was nothing to stop her from changing who she was, and she could even become a self-proclaimed hero like Hooyip. She could be confident, brave, and put things in order by taking her sister home. Taking her sister home would justify her worth, and she could pretend to be worthwhile and good until the confidence became real.

Chapter 4
Doors and Hills

Her back hurt. Her neck did not want to move, and Periwinkle felt like a rock weighed down her head on top of another rock, then broke it apart and buried her.

"I'm awake!" Aster sat up. One eye remained closed, and she looked around. Aster's hair formed a sort of white paste on her mouth and cheeks the way month-old birthday-cake frosting glues a cake together. "I'm ready! I'll go!" Aster said. Her eyes drooped closed.

"Ha! I knew it. It was safe here!" Hooyip chewed the last bits of snails from their dinner, crunching up the shells along with the creatures.

"You even eat the shells?" Winkle asked.

Hooyip tapped on the bone that grew around her forearms and elbows. "It's good for the body!"

"I want some." Aster yawned. "I'll eat the shells."

"All gone." Hooyip placed her hands on her hips and smiled. "We should go. The forest is large, and we have a lot of looking to do if we're going to find the sylphs."

"Come on Aster. Let's stay together." Winkle held her sister's hand and walked next to Hooyip.

"So Hooyip," Aster said. "How will we know how to find the sylphs? Will we have to make hand signals or something or look in the bushes? My sister and I have this bush we hide in. Maybe you can do that thing with your eyeball tails and trick them into coming out. Then we can see them when they think we're not looking."

"Well, we won't be able to see them," Hooyip said. "They hide better than I do. But there's a treaty between our people. We're supposed to help each other."

"The people here help each other?" Winkle asked. "Is there a treaty with all the people who live here?" What was it about Hooyip that she couldn't just accept?

The trees looked different in this part of the forest. They grew taller and their trunks and bark felt delicate. Periwinkle thought more about Hooyip. Was she jealous of the alakdan's poise or composure? No, jealousy had no part of it. She liked her, but maybe it wasn't distrust. Maybe she wanted to be like her.

"Well, like I said..." Hooyip swished a branch she carried to move away cobwebs that hung from a tree. The corner of her mouth crinkled up with worry. "It's been a long time since any of us have seen a sylph, and not everyone who lives in the Ember Lands is a friend." She threw the branch into the gray forest between the wisps of spider webs that cascaded from the branches of the trees. "Does everyone get along where you come from?"

Winkle heard the branch crack against something solid, and she tried to look further into the woods. Threads that trailed from one tree draped onto a stone, and then cascaded over a wooden structure that rested far below the base of a hill.

"Do you know this part of the woods?" Winkle asked.

Hooyip smiled. "I have never been here before! But I am a skilled survivor."

Winkle pointed toward the branch, where they saw a man-sized slab. Its corners crumbled into a pile of rubble.

"What is that?"

The trio stared at the structure.

"It's not natural," Hooyip said, shrugging her shoulders. "Let's look around. Maybe there's something useful."

"Stay with me," Winkle whispered to Aster.

Hooyip wiped leaves from the stone. Lines meandered in an intricate pattern that covered the face of the slab.

"It's like mom's knitting," Aster said. "Like a pattern she makes when she knits at home."

"It looks destroyed." Hooyip pushed against the stone which stood taller than her, and it rocked to the side before creating a divot in the dirt from which it did not budge. Hooyip patted the stone. "Stuck."

"It's a door," Winkle said.

Aster touched the stone and ran her fingers along the carvings and its edge. "I bet I could fit past it."

Long threads from the tree billowed and brushed against Winkle's cheek. The air felt dry.

Aster tried to look inside the stone door.

"Do you hear buzzing?" Winkle asked. She heard the air crackle, and black fires smoldered across the leaves and grass atop the hill. A perfect line of flame rose higher and pulled apart as if split open by a hammer and wedge. "Something's coming through it!"

Red eyes peered through the dark flames at Winkle and her companions. The eyes rose off the ground, swayed for a moment, and floated downward.

Periwinkle felt Aster huddle behind her. The head of a wolf appeared through the fire. It pulled itself out with two massive paws, but the rest of its scaled and legless body slithered behind it and seemed to stretch forever back into the fire. It beat down the hill toward Winkle and her sister.

Hooyip shoved Winkle toward a boulder, and Winkle tumbled to the ground. The alakdan deflected the creature with her sword. Up close, the creature's head equaled the size of Hooyip's entire body. Burned and broken wood fell through the portal and rained down the hill.

Periwinkle heard a yelp. She looked for Aster, but her sister was gone. The monster slipped past Hooyip. The back of its body still trailed at least twenty yards up the hill and into the portal.

"Aster!" Winkle called. The monster skirted the hill and lunged toward the door in the hill.

Hooyip swiped at the creature with her sword. "Find your sister! These are the type of monsters that usually come through the portals." The creature's snakelike body slammed Hooyip into the stone door, and a crack formed where Hooyip's back banged against its surface.

Winkle's legs would not move. She balled up her fists. More debris fell through the portal, and Winkle saw the rest of the monster's body silhouetted in the flames. Beside the wolfen head, three more necks writhed from a slug-like foot out of the portal. Two vaguely human heads writhed atop two of the twisting necks, and the third head remained looped inside the portal.

Winkle mumbled. "It's ok, Winkle. It's ok to pretend you're brave." She took a breath, then darted around the burning debris that spewed from the portal and slipped into the dark doorway. Behind her, she heard Hooyip's bone-bladed sword strike the creature.

Winkle smelled the dampness of water. Light from outside pierced the gargantuan ceiling, and Winkle realized the doorway concealed a passage deep into the hill. The light provided scant illumination for her surroundings. "Aster!" Winkle called, but Winkle heard nothing.

She stepped forward. Her shoes lost footing on the slick ground, and when she braced herself with her arm, her wrist and fingers rubbed across the slime that covered the stone floor. Winkle's arm sliced open where it struck the jagged ground. Her head spun.

She looked at the blood and remembered when her parents took her and Aster to the Valugan Boulder Beach. They attended a funeral for one of her father's relatives. It was the first time she ever met her family in the Philippines. The beach had more rocks than sand, even though it had sand, too. She remembered the first time she walked out into the ocean. The water felt colder than she expected, despite news reports that said it was at least ninety degrees that summer. When she entered the water, parts of the ocean hurt the arch of her feet where rocks ladened the bottom. She slipped and cut open her shin that day because algae grew anywhere the stones found enough light from the sun. The blood spilled out so fast that it clouded the water and sunk in a trail to the corals.

This place must be old. The algae spread and grew even into parts of the cave beyond the light. Its slickness turned to grit as she rubbed it from her fingers, and the blood from her arm mingled with the algae on the ground. Winkle looked, but she saw no sign of her sister. She listened, and she heard fighting outside the cave. The trickle and flow of water inside the hidden entrance sounded softer. The sound continued deeper beneath the hill, and Periwinkle followed, hoping that her sister wandered off in the same direction. "Aster! It's me. It's Periwinkle. You can come out now. Aster, stop hiding. Please."

She followed the pool of water into the caves. Its surface sparkled from the bit of light that filtered down from the ceiling and made the ripples in the water look like crystals.

Winkle heard a crash from the entrance of the cave. She saw the flicker of a fire and spun around to see the contours of the alakdan tumble inside the entrance. Hooyip sheathed her sword. She must have won. Hooyip was a genuine hero.

"Hooyip!" Winkle said. "It's me! I can't find my sister." Winkle planted her foot to run toward the alakdan and felt as if something tugged her shoulders toward the water. Her right leg slipped, and she fell into the pool. The current grabbed her and swept her into the cave.

Once in the water and into the dark of the cave, a voice whispered to her. "This is where we belong," it said. "I shall rest here and grow."

The edge of the pool grew further and further away. Winkle tried to swim, but the current sucked her into the dark.

"Are you strong?" the voice whispered. "Are you like me? I have more to offer in the water."

The water splashed into Periwinkle's nose. She felt her body twist and fall through various spillways and tributaries, but never felt as though she might sink. "Calm down, Winkle. You can figure this out," she told herself.

"It is colder down here," the voice whispered. "Wait until I have rested."

She shook her head. Who spoke to her? She reached out and felt the slick walls scrape across her fingers. She tried to look for a figure or a shape of someone in the water. "Not now, Winkle," she told herself. "You can't think of that now. Concentrate."

The wall felt like rock. There must be a crevice, or a finger hold, or some jagged or imperfect edge. The current felt constant, but not too swift. Winkle grabbed for any handhold on the wall. Her injured arm banged into a divot, then she forced her other arm into the rocks and wedged herself between a crevice in the rockwork.

She pulled herself out of the water. Her eyes adjusted. This room was darker than the entryway. "A…Aster? Are you in here?" Water dripped from Winkle's clothes. She tried smoothing and wringing out her pants and shirt. If she wanted a chance to be brave, she thought. This was it.

Periwinkle waved her arms out in front of her and found the wall. The largeness of the area made her feel exposed. Along the walls, she felt something cold and metal. It held something—a torch. She found a striker mechanism attached to the sconce with a container of oil. Whoever made this place needed light as well.

Periwinkle dipped the torch into the oil and chipped the rough striker material against the metal. Sparks flew from the mechanism and after a few tries, the torch lit. Winkle's eyes widened. Wild green plants trailed from the tributary of water and covered the ground. The cave reached on much further than the light from her torch, but to her right, she saw a gray wooden door. It was busted and, likewise, overgrown with plants.

Hand tools, some broken, but many still usable, littered the ground. Winkle used her foot to roll over a large shovel, then kicked aside what must have been some sort of rake.

"Follow the water back the way I came? Or search for my sister right here?" Aster might have panicked and ran off. In the dark, she would have gotten lost. Would Aster have stayed in one place? No, not with what happened outside. Periwinkle knew her sister. She would have tried to hide.

Winkle needed to be systematic. She was here now and did not know where the water led. "Ok, let's start, Winkle," she said to herself. "We'll go room by room. Hooyip is fine—she's fine. The one thing that matters is finding Aster. You can do this, Periwinkle."

***

Winkle yawned and stretched. She walked out of another room, then looked and stamped her feet to stretch her legs from sneaking around for so long. The first three rooms both held supplies and bags of dirt—not even a rat or a bug. In another room that smelled of soot, she found a small knife with dried dirt encrusted on its blade. Carvings in its wood handle had worn down from use, and she made out what looked like an arm, or maybe a leg, or quite possibly a stick, but what would be the use of carving a stick into a handle?

"Door number four, Winkle," she said. Periwinkle took a breath. "Please be here, Aster." The door teetered on its hinges. She kicked in the door like some cowboy from the old spaghetti-westerns her dad made her watch, and it crashed against the wall and splintered apart. At least there were no more tools. This was more like it.

Books filled shelves along the walls, and an archway led into another room that looked to contain large drawings and more books. Winkle ran to the shelves and grabbed a book. It smelled old. Those were some of her favorite types. She flipped through the pages and saw that many of the pages contained drawings of trees, flowers, and shrubs. Details about each one either preceded or followed the pictures.

More drawings depicting specific parts of each plant accompanied what must have been information about their cultivation and care. Periwinkle traced the drawing of a bush that had delicate purple flowers. They were all drawn by hand. The information looked hand written as well. She wondered what the creator used for colors. Did the pigments come from the plant itself? She held the pages to her nose. Besides old paper, she smelled pollen, oils, and flowers. Periwinkle smiled.

The torch revealed a mecca of hand-written materials. She leafed through a second book as she walked through the archway to the next room—hills, dales, rivers, all with foliage and flora. On one hill, a hill covered by brambles and green bushes, the author drew two humanoid creatures floating amongst the plants. Just like Hooyip said: hair and skin like the forest, eyes the color of flowers. Those must be the sylphs. She needed to show Hooyip and ask her if she knew this location.

"Do you like it here?" asked a voice that sounded much like the creak of an unsettled door.

Periwinkle stumbled and dropped the book. Her stomach turned.

"I don't think this place is for me," the creaking door voice said.

Winkle spun around. The creature rose from the floor. Periwinkle backed away into another bookshelf, and she realized the creature did not quite break through the floor but melted through it. The thing was all neck and stretched at least eight feet up and curved down like an inverted fish hook. The neck terminated into the head of an old man full of wrinkles and stringy white hair.

"I am The Not," the creature said. "I do not think I like it here, but I cannot find a way out."

Winkle fumbled for a thought. She thought of dark places and school. "Are you a librarian?" Winkle asked.

The Not's head twisted around to look at the surroundings before it moved closer to her.

Winkle stumbled back against the shelf and saw nowhere behind her to run. "Uhm. Do you live here?" Winkle asked.

"No-o-o, I do not live here," The Not said. "I came through the fire, and now we are stuck. We are part of a part, and we were separated by an onslaught of heat. I think I would like to return. We saw you outside. Do you live here?"

Winkle shook her head and looked at the cavern floor.

"How did you get in? Have you seen anyone else?"

"I can only arrive from below unless I am pulled back, but I am often left alone. No-o I have seen no one else. Not since we were trapped inside. It is too dark here. I grow with the light, and I am trying to find a way out. The others also look for a way out."

Winkle thought about the creature she saw outside. It looked similar. The body looked the same, but its head was different.

"Who are the others?" Winkle asked.

"You already met one of us, but he was removed by that one with the sword. He was The Sweeping, and he only comes out at night. He still remembered how to change his appearance. Do you remember how to do something like that? Long ago, I forgot what I could become."

Winkle felt for the knife, but her hands sweat. She shook her head and moved to the side around the bookshelf. "I am just me. I can't transform into anything. You said there were more of you?"

"There were four of us, but now three remain. The No arrives from above. She is looking for food, so if you see her, you should go somewhere else. She is the youngest and still has a lot to prove to the first, but I am old, too old for that. I want to get out or to find some light, and you have a light."

"You won't try to eat me, then?" Winkle asked.

"I do not do that sort of thing, but if you are afraid of being eaten, stay away from the other one as well. She is our beginning and is much older than even me. She appears from the side. I think she might like it here, and if she does, she will want to grow more of us. To do that, she will need to eat. She is faster than even The Sweeping. She ignores me unless I find something interesting." The Not stretched, and he followed Winkle and her torch as she moved.

Winkle saw no way of making it to the entrance without first trying to move past The Not. She had to find Aster and leave these caves before The Not or the other two remaining parts found her sister. "No! I am not interesting at all, and I can show you where there is more light. It's like the one I have. If I take you to it, will you pretend we've never met?"

"Whether I pretend or not, we have already met, and we are all part of the same thing anyway. That is just how things are." The Not remained transfixed on her, then coiled over the book that Winkle dropped. A small growth budded from its neck, which displayed eight feather-like fingers that plucked the book from the ground. It shook the book, then tossed it aside. "The light you can make is not enough for me to live, but maybe if you help me with something else. I shall pretend we are apart."

The Not produced a second feathery bud holding a large hexagonal nut about the size of a fist. With its red paint, Winkle recognized it as some sort of hold-down nut fastened to the fire hydrants near her home. She saw one removed when a technician serviced the fire hydrant in her neighborhood.

"This came through with us from the fire that separated us from our whole, but it is not from where we live." The Not's neck and head craned around the nut to look at it. His eyes squinted and looked through the hole. "It is so exact, and I think it is something that I like very much, but I do not know what purpose it serves. Can you explain such a thing to me?" The Not's eyebrows arched. "If you do, I can leave you alone, but you must tell me soon because I can feel the original moving nearer."

"Fine." Winkle said. "I have seen that thing before, and I can explain what it does, but you need to do more than ignore me for that. What can I do if the one who forgot her name finds me—the original one? I need to find someone before I leave, and neither of us can be eaten."

The Not looked at Winkle and pursed his lips. The wrinkles in his forehead and around his eyes pressed together. "She likes to watch the snow. We live upside down to most, and we live in a place where it is unhealthy to move, and when she looks up, sometimes it is hard to see the snow unless it falls on the exact spot where we live. Sometimes she ignores her food when she watches the snow." The Not held the nut in front of Periwinkle. "Now tell. What could be the purpose of a thing like this? I think it is a lot like me."

"It is a nut," Winkle said. "It keeps things together so they cannot move or fall apart."

"Does it help keep things connected, or is it separate?"

"I guess it can be both. It is missing the part that it connects to, but it is also separate and it is strong on its own. I stepped on one once and I remember it hurt. I suppose it has its use even when separated because of what it might accomplish."

"What is your name?" asked The Not. "Where are your other parts of your part?"

"My name is Periwinkle, and I am by myself right now but looking for my sister. Are you sure you haven't seen her? She's tiny, but looks a little like me."

"No, I have not seen her, but I think I like that I have met you, even if you are not what I needed to find. Because of that, Periwinkle, you must go right now, because our first one has almost arrived. Remember, she can only enter from the side, and The No can enter from above. If you see either of them, you should try to leave. The first will pull me back soon, and I can do nothing to stop her."

Winkle moved past The Not. She saw it unwind and retract into the floor as it tried to stretch its neck and coil

around a shelf, but its length continued to lessen. She heard
crashing beyond the walls.

Chapter 5
Below the Root

Hooyip twirled her sword and returned it to the belt strap against her waist. She looked at the high ceiling of the cave and the furnished ledges with broken stone banisters and old shelves and other odds and ends ready to tip from their precipice.

Why was something always ready to fall on her head or crash through the walls, or swamps and sinking. How she despised swamps.

Nobody was here. Where could the two little ones have gone? Was it even up to her to find them? The littlest one was nice, but the older one, well, she was a little frightening. Hooyip felt certain that the occurrence with the water had something to do with Periwinkle, and an ability like that felt dangerous. It sure was nice having someone else around, though. Starting this quest was the first time she ever had to be alone, and it all felt like it was too much for her. Was she really the last alakdan?

Hooyip saw a stream of water sparkle in the cavern, and she saw dust prints that swept through the dirt. *Periwinkle!*

But Aster was younger and much frailer. Which of the two would a hero look for first? It had to be the youngest. Aster's youth allowed her to act brave. Her size, though, dictated her actions. Hooyip thought for a moment. Aster might have crept into smaller spaces.

The alakdan scanned the area and spied a tunnel. Some sort of service tunnel maybe, or a space used to shuttle around small carts of goods or tools or agriculture or any other items that needed transport in what looked to be some labyrinthine cavern. That had to be the spot. A broken cart that smelled of dead bugs and soil, slumbered near the passageway. It squeaked as Hooyip rolled it away from the crevice, and the sound echoed through the cavern.

When she crawled into the opening, Hooyip heard a click, then a snap. A metal rod sprung from the ground and ricocheted off her chitinous shoulder. A broken chain from the ground snapped up and whipped against Hooyip's ribs, and she felt the impact of the chain even through the bony growths that protected her skin. Something like that would have been fatal to Aster, she thought. Hooyip smirked at the idea that tiny Aster probably weighed too little to set off the broken mechanism. The alakdan righted herself and saw a metal plate on the bottom of the broken cart. The rod and chain must have been used to propel carts through the tunnels—it looks like it would still work—if they weren't all overturned.

Once she entered the tunnel, the walls quivered and the sounds of crumbled stone trickled in from the entrance. Hooyip subdued the wolfen, worm-like creature that entered through the flames, but hidden in the fire was something much larger, and she felt certain the wolf was just some sort of scout used to clear the way for whatever followed behind. Better to find her two companions and sneak out before meeting the new creature from the fires.

The tunnel curved in long sweeping turns, and she passed rod-and-chain mechanisms like the one that raked her ribs, embedded into the ground. As she continued through the tunnels, the rods made their audible click, and this time Hooyip knew to roll to the side, at least as much as she could in the cramped tunnel to avoid the smack of the rod or a slash from the metal chain.

Come on Aster, how can I be a great alakdan hero if I can't even find a little girl in certain peril before a monstrous beast devours her?

The maze of service tunnels emptied into a second cave. The air tasted like roots and dirt. Dust-covered jars remained dormant on shelves. A withered root larger than a full grown alakdan encompassed the entirety of the lone table in the room. The root was fat, and it retained its shape and avoided decay for however long it held residence on the table. An even larger root leaned against the wall, and it looked like someone must have harvested a portion of its bottom most roots. Hooyip ran her hand along the surface of the root on the table. Its outer skin felt solid, but some of the fibrous veins snapped away.

There was moisture in the dust. An imprint of a small line snaked and curled beside the root. Something else used to be here. Hooyip looked around and found two more service tunnels as well as an archway that led into a larger hall.

An overturned cart blocked her passage through the first tunnel, and Hooyip saw no signs of anyone, even someone as little as Aster squeezing past the rubble or the transport. Hooyip needed to try something else, so she left the tunnels and explored the hall. The rocky ceiling of the hallway reached much lower than the ceiling in the entryway. Maybe Aster ran through these same hallways.

Hooyip wondered what type of creatures used to live beneath these hills, and she wondered why were the hills abandoned. She entered one of the smaller rooms and saw red and gold tapestries that covered the walls. Each tapestry appeared to show a memory for the family that must have lived in each collection of rooms. Sewn-in silhouettes depicted people among the forest and the hills as shadows on the land. One tapestry showed two of the silhouettes toiling to gather fruits into baskets from strange silver bushes. Another tapestry depicted a gathering of people bringing gifts to the birth of two children—twins from the included details, and the next tapestry showed the two twins, this time taller, at work by a burning red forge. The woven fabrics looked melancholic somehow, despite their vibrant colors. Hooyip wondered which family member viewed them last, and she remembered home. Was this what happens once everyone disappears?

The rocks on the floor shook and rumbled, so Hooyip sped to the hall. A tendril broke through the ceiling ahead of her.

Hooyip pivoted through an archway to her right. She found herself on one of the strange balconies that she saw when she first entered the caverns. The service tunnels from earlier must have led her through a gradual ascent through the hill. She looked over the balcony and saw piles of collapsed stone where the entryway had once stood.

"It keeps coming from the ceiling," a tiny voice called. "You should stay up there. It doesn't like to look for me on these ledges. Maybe I can come up to you."

"Aster? What—no. There's a balcony under this one? Like the one I'm on?" Hooyip wasn't able to see any ledges underneath her, but she figured Aster must have been close because her voice was too little to carry from much further down.

"Yes, but this one is broken," Aster said.

The room rumbled again. Hooyip heard the walls behind her begin to collapse in the hallway. She maneuvered her tail around the corner and waited. If there was movement, she would feel the palpitations and changes in the air, but there was nothing. She peered out around the corner. A serpentine body, similar to the one from the fires, hung motionless from the ceiling. It bore the face of a young girl with sun kissed hair like that of a lifelong seafarer.

The creature's opaline eyes scanned the cavern system. She hissed, "I feel that you are here, little morsel, and I am one who must eat. Even though you would make a small meal, I have had nothing since our arrival, and it is in my nature to grow."

Hooyip crouched, then reached for the hilt of her sword. *Strike first.* She had it ingrained. The first to attack has a better chance of winning. Surprise is the biggest advantage. Hooyip had to stay quiet. She had to stay hidden.

"I'm gonna come up to you!" Aster yelled. "I know how to get there!"

The creature smiled and reared back, ready to plunge toward the ground and toward the sounds of Aster's call.

Hooyip dashed from the corner, and the creature's eyes locked on her before it sunk under the floor.

"What—are you?" The creature asked. "Who would try to attack me without my looking? Is that a noble thing to do?"

Hooyip sprung toward the creature and swiped at it with her sword, but the monster careened to its side.

The creature bared her teeth. It snapped toward her, punctured Hooyip's shoulder, and threw the alakdan backwards.

Hooyip tumbled against the wall. She heard footsteps patter through the hallway. "No Aster!" Hooyip scrambled for her sword. "Stay where you are."

She was lucky in the forest. She only won because the debris that spilled through the portal smashed into the first creature and pinned it against a boulder. Hooyip survived this long on her own by hiding and running away. If she did that now, then Aster would be all alone. Hooyip's stomach turned. In her training, when she did not run away, a lot of her sparring sessions ended with her beaten and on the ground.

"Why do you want to eat some little girl?" Hooyip asked. "Maybe we can talk about all this like civilized individuals. We can help each other."

The creature smiled and recoiled to prepare for another strike. "I am The No, and it is my nature to consume. If I can do what is expected of me, then the one who made me will grow and keep me beside her. Do you hear the creature running toward us? I hear it. She does not even know that I am here."

Hooyip felt the vibrations in the air. Aster must be getting closer. If she keeps going, she'll run right into The No. The footsteps moved quicker and tramped along to a regular beat.

"She will arrive soon," The No said. "Once I consume her, it will make all of us stronger. What can you do, then? I shall eat you as well, then more of us can grow, and I shall have proven my worth."

Aster's footsteps echoed through a hallway behind The No. Hooyip hated races, but she couldn't leave Aster alone, either. She lunged at the creature. Even in the collapsed hallway, the monster avoided Hooyip's sword.

She saw Aster behind The No, running through the hall, and Hooyip panicked. *The No would get to her first.*

Hooyip squirmed from between the wall and The No's body and climbed atop the monster. She ran along the length of the creature's back. Aster froze and huddled on the ground. Hooyip felt the creature whip its body around.

Only one way. Hooyip pounced from The No's back and tried to shield Aster with her arm. The No bit down hard, and Hooyip heard a crack.

She scooped Aster against her chest with her other arm and forced her way back to her feet with The No clamped to her forearm.

"You said there was a balcony below the one I was on?" Hooyip asked. The pain made her dizzy and numb. She wondered how long she could stay conscious.

"I'm sorry Hooyip! I didn't know she was here."

"The other balcony?"

"Below yours. I was able to see you."

Hooyip twisted her arm and jutted her elbow into the roof of The No's mouth. She yanked her arm free. The plates on her forearm shattered, and teeth tore through her skin. She felt her arm throb as it hung limp at her side. "Hold on to my back, Aster. You can't let go." Hooyip ran toward the balcony, and The No followed.

"I can see it, Hooyip," Aster said. "They're everywhere."

Hooyip wasn't sure what Aster saw. "I know, Aster. She's right behind us. I'll hurry, but you have to hold on."

"It's like a string. I can see it," Aster said.

Hooyip saw the balcony. *They would make it!* She sprung toward the ledge of the balcony's stone banister and swung from its edge with her good arm.

"You cannot win," The No hissed.

The balcony crumbled, and Hooyip lost her grip. Darkness obscured the ground far below her. She saw The No crash through what remained of the balcony. Hooyip saw the second balcony below them, but it, too, began to crumble. There was just the cavern floor somewhere in the darkness rushing toward her, maybe 70 lengths down, maybe more. If she could shield Aster, then maybe at least the little one could survive.

Hooyip felt Aster loosen her grip. She saw the girl's little arm reach toward The No and brush through the air as if brushing away webs between low slung trees, and The No's head jerked downward when Aster motioned with her hand. Instead of biting into Aster or herself, the sudden spasm from The No knocked them onto the ledge.

"How did you…ugh no time to wait for you to explain," Hooyip said. "I know where we have to go." She led Aster from what remained of the balcony back into the hallway toward one of the small service tunnels embedded into the rooms.

"You cannot escape like this," The No said.

"She's right," Aster said. "She always appears from above me."

Hooyip needed to stay ahead just long enough to get to the tunnels. If they made it there, she could rest. Her strength dwindled, but she saw the tunnel. Hooyip no longer heard the pursuit of The No.

"I'm scared," Aster said.

Hooyip pushed Aster into the tunnels in front of her. As they crawled, The No snapped at them from above. Rows of needle-like teeth gnashed at their haunches as the monster struck even quicker than before. Hooyip and Aster crawled as fast as they could.

"We need to keep going," Hooyip said. Her arms and legs felt weak, and then Hooyip heard a click.

"Aster!" Hooyip yelled. She grabbed the little girl and rolled to the side. A metal rod sprung from the floor and cut into the fiend. Its body descended into the tunnel. Hooyip heard a second click, then a third. She heard chains lacerate The No's body.

Hooyip's vision blurred. She felt herself being pulled along by two little arms as she slipped in and out of consciousness. Wrapped around one of the delicate wrists was a woven rope band with a strange metal crest.

"This is where I hid before she found me," Aster said.

"It's like our hideout back home. I know it's small, but we can both fit. Then we'll find my sister."

Before she passed out, Hooyip smelled old roots and soil as Aster pushed her into a hollow that felt like the rough trunk of a tree.

Chapter 6
Nuts and Bolts

She had no business being here. Her arms resembled noodles and her legs were as strong as potato chips. She failed to have a nervous breakdown while hiding against the wall because she felt too afraid to breathe. She hoped that this would all end soon, and once an array of books fell and banged against her head, burying her on the dusty floor, once an old wooden shelf fell and broke atop the books, the other sounds stopped.

"Only rubble here." Periwinkle heard from a woman's voice. "Oh, The Not, I had thought you found something while searching up above. You even resisted being pulled back, but there is nothing here but books and rubble, and if we do not eat soon, then even you might disappear, what with your requirements and all."

"I would like to leave here," The Not droned. "There is nothing for me here, and it is so dark, so dark."

"Well, I will find the one who killed our Sweeps, and I will eat her all up, and once The No finishes the smaller one, we should have enough to sustain us."

"I do not think this is a place for us," The Not said. "If we stay here, I shall starve. If I starve, I will not be needed. I will keep searching for the better light."

"Do not worry if you fail with your endeavor. Before you disappear, you can be reabsorbed, and I can replace you with something more suitable for our new habitat. You will still be a part of us, even though you will no longer be a you."

"I would rather remain The Not."

"Then you must find better light before I decide this is a place that we like."

Periwinkle heard the creature slither away. Her legs shook from fear which made the toppled books rattle. It took a few moments to regain any strength before Winkle could crawl out from under the capsized shelf. She backtracked to the room where she first met The Not. The book she found with the picture of the sylph remained on the floor, and she riffled through the pages until she found the illustration with the hill in the dale with the brambly green bushes. The book felt too heavy to carry, so Periwinkle ripped out a few of the pages, folded them, and placed them in her pocket.

Her spill through the current from earlier would have pulled her far from the entrance. Everyone says to stay in one place when lost, but there was no one out here looking for her, and it was up to her to find Aster, so she had to keep moving. Winkle found the torch that she dropped when she hid from The Not, but it extinguished when it fell to the ground. Periwinkle dug through her other pockets, nothing but the pages from the book. She didn't have her bag and her dad's gifted lighter anymore, so she fumbled along the walls to try and find another mechanism for lighting the torch.

What was that creature, exactly? Was it like her—displaced from its home? Winkle's fingers ran across a holder for another sconce, and upon finding a striker mechanism, Periwinkle clicked the apparatus. Sparks settled into the torch and rekindled the light. Somehow, she felt accomplished. Somehow lighting the torch brought her confidence.

Even with the light, Winkle still had to squint to see ahead of her in the stone hallways, and the dark and the silence frightened her. She trusted that The Not would leave her alone because he already said that the glow from her torch was useless to him, and she did answer his question about his treasure.

As she searched the system of tunnels for her sister, Winkle murmured a song from back home by the Red Hot Chili Peppers. "I walk through her hills…" Winkle forgot some of the lyrics but continued the song with a part that she did know. "I never worry…" She continued to sing the song in the dark and it did make her feel a little better.

Periwinkle entered a room with several heavy wooden tables. She did not want to call for Aster, so she crept around to check in any nook or cranny she could find. Magnifying lenses of different magnifications were strewn across tables, and she grabbed a small one thinking it might come in handy. Like many kids, she learned how to focus and refract light through a lens to create heat, and she had a microscope that her mother bought her on her tenth birthday. The magnified world fascinated her, but what she liked most about it was the strange consistency. No matter how close or how far away someone looked, a magnified rock or a magnified piece of sand remained similar to an unmagnified specimen, and neither one looked too far removed from a rock encrusted mountain. The system just repeated itself at a different scale. She wondered if that was how all things worked.

Like the other rooms under the hill, this one displayed an ever-present layer of dust. Unlike the other rooms however, she thought that a spelunker or a jeweler would have marveled over this room. Periwinkle opened a wooden door behind one of the tables. She discovered a closet no bigger than her coat closet back home that a few puffy jackets might fill, but this closet hid bits of polished glass and polished stones. No Aster—but tucked in the closet were also crystals and small cuts of gems that shone in a myriad of pinks, emeralds, and crimsons when she opened the little drawers of a cabinet. If she ever made it back home and brought these to a jeweler, then she was sure that she'd find some pieces had to have value.

She rummaged through the shelves in the closet. Periwinkle found bags of colorful pulverized rocks that stained her fingers. One bag held stones with a pale green-gray pigment that she had never seen in any type of paint, chalk, or pencil. It reminded her of the place in the forest where she and Aster first arrived, and she thought she could use it to draw or paint if she ever found time to rest in this strange place.

Each bag held crushed stones of a different color. The crushed stones felt like chalk but retained a gem-like translucence. She took three small pouches, each one no longer than her index finger, and she tied their drawstrings shut, then strung them around her wrists since she did not have a bag or a purse. Periwinkle found the other stones too unwieldy to carry and had no way to transport anything so awkward, regardless of their value.

"Ok Periwinkle," she told herself. "Time to focus. Your little sister is lost. You need to do better. She needs your help. You can do this." Periwinkle sighed, "Keep looking no matter how tired or scared you are or how dark this weird place is. Even if you are trapped and alone. Alone."

Periwinkle felt useless and worried she may never see Aster again. She heard a scratching noise as she continued her search, and the more she tried to focus on its origins, the more unsettled she felt. Periwinkle looked to the darkest places in each room. She searched in the shadows underneath errant chairs, tables, and shelves. She checked behind barrels, expecting to find this place's version of a mouse or a cricket, but she found nothing.

The scraping persisted. She eased open a door. Perhaps some creature walked ahead of her and hid as she drew closer. She crouched and peeked through the bottom of the door. The room was dark, like all the others. The scratching continued. She expected to see an elusive creature to attach to the sound, but there was not even a shadow, and the noise was neither closer nor further. She let the door close and sat with her back against the wall. The sound continued with no increase or decrease in din or volume. Winkle covered her ears, hoping to see something scurry through the hall or cruise along on the opposite wall but still nothing, and she closed her eyes as she felt throbbing in her ribs and head.

The scratching turned to the muffled sounds of hands and knees crawling, tapping, and clicking across a laminate or tiled floor.

"You were wrong because you are not alone," spoke a voice from the dark.

Winkle's jaw tensed. She knew the origins of the sound.

"You have not been alone for a long time now."

Winkle wanted to talk. But her throat felt parched.

"I was with you in the water." The voice felt like pressure or like drowning. "Let me stay. Please let me stay, and you will never fear the water because I am the Berberoka."

The pressure continued in her temples. It spread through the veins in her neck. She felt cold over her shoulders and felt a rising liquid beneath the surface of her skin. The cold traced down her arms and flowed under her wrists.

Periwinkle held her head in her hands. "Why are you... I

need to find my sister. I'm supposed to be the one to protect her. I can't do this. I'm not anything great. I'm just an imposter."

"I can help you protect her."

Stupid, stupid girl, thought Periwinkle. Is this a mistake? "Can you help me find her?"

"Good now, of course, but we must be careful to keep others out because you are warm to us, and this place is so cold. The heat you radiate is like a beacon and it reminds us of home. Please allow yourself to listen when I try to speak, and know that you have already helped me once. You were my escape from the Abyss."

Periwinkle opened her eyes. The pressure of drowning passed, but the coldness in her blood remained.

"I am still very weak, but something is coming to find you. Its goal is my goal, and its nature is my nature. I think it is looking for you. It has found a way out of here, I think. Make sure you find where that is."

"What if I can't do it?"

"You are resourceful. You are smart. But if you ever want to make it home, then do not dwell with despair. If you want to help your sister, then I shall try to reawaken once you find the creature who has learned a way out."

The clawing sensation receded, and the last words the Berberoka spoke were that neither one of them were imposters.

Ok Winkle, what now? If something is looking for me, then I should be ready. Periwinkle tried to prepare for whatever was about to visit her next. Winkle gave herself three exits: two pathways through the wild hallway depending from which direction the visitor arrived, and another escape was back into one of the smaller rooms that emptied into a series of connected rooms before it filtered back into this same hall.

Periwinkle shifted the small knife she found to an accessible position in her pocket. Not that she would ever try to fight someone. She was quite content and determined to choose the flight part of fight or flight, but maybe the knife might work to pry away a rock, or cut through a rope bridge and swing to freedom, or some other rescue-pets thing to do. No, that wasn't her. She had to use what she knew and asked herself what would Bob Ross do at a time like this?

"Ok Winkle," she said to herself. "Look for happy little mistakes." She paced and waited, and then waited and paced. Maybe the Berberoka was not very perceptive at all. Maybe it just tricked her away from finding Aster.

Cracks formed on the hallway floor, then it started to crumble in front of her. A balding head pushed through the stone, followed by two wrinkled eyes. The eyes darted left and right. Winkle recognized the creature's creased and mopey expression right away; The Not blinked.

"You're my pursuer?" Periwinkle asked.

The Not poked the rest of his head through the floor and stopped his ascent just after his chin emerged. "Aah, I am The Not, and I can only enter from bel—"

"Yes, I remember. You only enter from below," Periwinkle did not like to interrupt people when they spoke, but she remembered that sometimes The Not took his time with his oration, and she was in a rush and a little nervous about what her sister might be going through now. "Why are you following me? You said that you would leave me alone so that I would not get eaten by the rest of you."

"Well," The Not said, and then he paused. "I have found you, and that is because I have looked for you." The Not waited again. "I have found you because I have looked for you."

"Yes. You have found me," Periwinkle said, thinking that

maybe he needed a response.

"Oh good. We are now having a conversation. A discourse. I have fou—"

"Yes, you found me." Periwinkle wondered if this is how she might talk after a certain age.

"Well, I have a question for you. It is about my treasure." The Not scooted up through the floor and popped out the strange pink feathery appendage from his neck. The feathers unfurled, and he produced the same large fire-hydrant nut from before. "I would like to know more about the nature of this treasure, and since you have shown expertise and acumen about its use before, I have decided that you, Girl-Periwinkle, are the most knowledgeable source that I am acquainted with in this world." The Not paused just like earlier and watched Periwinkle for her response.

"I have decided tha—"

"Yes," Periwinkle said, hoping to quicken the conversation.

The Not smiled and displayed seven large flat teeth, but mostly gums. "I do not have the opportunity for such conversation. The No, quite often talks about growth and sustenance. There was The Sweeping, but he only came out at night, and he is no longer with us, and I have always found our originator quite intimidating even though I am almost as old as she. She often told me that I was not the first, and that I was a copy of the copy of the first and that she could make a copy of me or even a copy of a copy of—"

"Wai—stop," Periwinkle said. "What was it about the treasure?"

"Yes, expert Periwinkle. I need you to answer a question for me. Do you think the treasure reaches its fullest potential the way it is now or when it is connected? This has become crucial to me, and I have not seen it connected, so I cannot decide. You have seen it connected, so you can help me decide."

Periwinkle thought about this and knew that the Berberoka told her that The Not must have figured a way out already. "Well, I know the answer, and I know the answer with no ambiguity, but so far, your one promise is that I get to live. That is not sufficient or fair. You need to give me something better for my information."

The Not's snakelike body curled upwards through the floor. "Is this something that is required by your people—to be treated fair? If that is part of who you are, then I suppose I must give you a favor as well."

Of course it wasn't something required by her people, Periwinkle thought. No one in her family and no one that she's ever called friend or almost friend had ever been treated fairly. The few people who ever received fair treatment were the type of people who never needed it in the first place, but she needed The Not to tell her the way out from under this hill. Periwinkle did not like when people promised things they knew weren't true, but she needed to find a way out as fast as possible so she could try to find her sister and they could both escape. She was not sure what to do.

"No," Periwinkle said. "My people aren't very fair at all, nor do they treat other people with any sort of fairness or honesty. Mostly, the people I know use each other to get what they want." Periwinkle slid down to the floor with her back against the wall. "I don't even know an absolute answer to your question about your treasure, but I can help you figure it out for yourself, and I would like to find a way out of here so I can try to return home. I miss my sister."

"I am old," said The Not. The lines and wrinkles on his face looked even more dry and gaunt. "I have learned that honesty is not worthwhile, but conversation and time can be their own treasures. You are a very abnormal individual, Girl-Periwinkle. I have found a way out from underneath this hill, but I did not give it much attention because it does not work for me other than to let in a trickle of light. Maybe it will work for you because you are small and abnormal."

"Can you tell me where it is?" Periwinkle asked. "I can tell you more about the treasure if you like, but I can't promise that what I know will help you."

The Not swooped closer to Periwinkle and wavered in front of her. She felt his breath against her cheek, then he backed away.

"It is where we have started to take root and grow into the rocks. Real light spills through a tunnel, but it is much too small for us to fit. Maybe the amount can sustain me, I suppose I shall see. You would have to figure out a way to follow me down if you want to find it." The Not peered through the hole of his treasure. "It has lines on its inside, and they are not as uniform as the outside. I did not see these lines before."

"May I see your treasure?" Periwinkle asked.

The Not dropped the nut and let it roll across the stone ground. Periwinkle picked it up and pulled the small knife from her pocket. She slid the nut over her knife blade, and it rested flat against the handle. "When it is connected, it works a little like this," she said. "And this handle here connects to something even larger." Periwinkle held the handle against the door and swung the door open and closed. "When your treasure does its job, it keeps the parts from falling off so they can perform the functions of their job even better. It helps hold everything together once it is connected."

"Oh," The Not curled his body around Periwinkle and moved his head closer to her makeshift nut and bolt. His head equaled the size of Periwinkle's torso. He continued to shift all around the knife.

"You asked about potential, though." Periwinkle tipped the knife on its side and let the nut slide to the ground. "I think it might have the most potential when it's like that. It's kind of like the light you're always looking for before it's made anything grow and before anyone's decided what it should do."

"Oh," The Not said. "Thank you, Girl-Periwinkle. Just like I thought, this has become a valuable and important treasure, but I think you should hurry now. Our originator stirs and she is upset with The No because The No has not accomplished what she was made to do, so the originator went out on her own. She found us something to eat. I shall ask her to pull me back because I can only enter from below. If you can find your way down, you should see the place where I found real light."

Periwinkle nodded. "You are a very proficient and exceptional conversationalist, and I am glad that I met you."

The Not's face turned downward into his characteristic mopey disposition, and he looked even more melancholic. "That is nice of you, expert-Periwinkle." His body retracted through the floor. The rubble flicked aside.

Winkle looked through the hole. It continued three or maybe four levels down, close to where they entered the hill.

"Ok Winkle, you can do this," she told herself. "You have to move fast." The hole was maybe an eight-foot drop to the next level. Easy-peasy for a hero in an old spaghetti western or a detective from a film noir. She stepped her legs through the hole to see if they would fit. No problems there, and no problems for the rest of her. It's just a quick jot through, and in a few minutes, she'd find the exit.

"Nope, not doing it." Periwinkle crawled her legs back through the hole. What good to Aster would I be with a broken arm or leg, or if I pass out from hitting my head?

Then how long would it take me to find her? The fastest racer is always a competitor who completes the race. That's how I'll do this.

Winkle thought. The hex nut rolled toward her when The Not dropped it. He didn't give it a push or anything, so toward her must be a slope downwards. Periwinkle stood up and started running. "Come on Winkle. Gotta keep the brush moving if I ever want to finish the painting."

Now that she moved quicker, the hallway seemed to spiral around and down. She passed the first hole and continued her descent to look for the second hole and the third—no stopping to see the sights, no stopping to find some entryway to the forest, and no stopping in hopes of finding something, anything, that might return her home.

Periwinkle's chest tightened as she ran. She ran past another hole and continued onward. She heard water down below, then stopped to look through the crushed and broken floor, and there she saw The Not as well as his two attached companions. They took up residence in a much larger cave, and Periwinkle wondered what sort of craftsmen must have lived in these halls to build such intricate pathways and chambers in the rockwork beneath the hill. Seeing the entire creature's body, it looked less like a snake than a willow tree made of flesh and cartilage rather than wood and bark. Winkle shivered at the sight. Each of the three limbs and heads branched out from a central undulating mass. The longest must have stretched at least 30 feet. Its base disappeared into a pool of water that reflected bits of light.

Winkle looked down at the stream. It was the same that washed her away when she first entered through the cracked stone door that led into the hill, and then she saw it—the source of light that The Not had found. From above, it looked like little more than a night-light at the bottom of a wall, and its glow looked scant enough to just light the small stream of water that flowed around the creature.

A tendril from the central body pulled something along the ground. Winkle's throat felt dry as she recognized the contour of the body and the two tails trailing from the figure. Periwinkle could not tell if Hooyip still lived. She had to get closer. As she crept down the slope toward the larger cavern, she saw a flicker in the shadows dash behind a stone sculpture. Periwinkle shivered and felt both hope and dread; it had to be Aster. She needed to do something. Aster always had her own sense of morals. Periwinkle knew her little sister would try something to help Hooyip, but her sister was still so small, Winkle could not let Aster put herself in danger.

"Come on, Periwinkle, you have to think before Aster gets herself hurt." Winkle balled up her fists and pounded on her legs to try and force them to stop shaking. She saw the little shadow move again. This time even closer to the giant creature that encircled Hooyip. How could her sister feel so brave? No Aster, Winkle thought.

"Ok, you need to stop," Winkle whispered to herself.

One of the beast's heads crawled closer to where Aster hid. The skin along its long neck was shredded. Periwinkle had not seen this one before. Its face looked human, female, and young, which made the sight even more gruesome. The mangled limb and face drug itself near Aster's hiding spot.

Winkle grabbed a rock and threw it at the beast, and the rock rattled to the ground before touching the creature. "Y-you need to let her go," Periwinkle said. Winkle tried to pick up another pebble, but her arms and hands trembled. Winkle felt angry at herself. Oh, come on, Winkle, think! What can you do?

"Ah, you are the thing found by The Not," said the head from the center.

Her features were sharp, and the creature's silver hair crested her neck like the waves against the piers that rest atop beaches along the ocean.

"Have you come to feed us as well? The No, for all her zeal, failed to find us a meal, and we will need quite a large amount of food to help her recover. I am not sure if this one will be enough." She squeezed Hooyip and lifted her off the ground, and Winkle saw the alakdan's chest move and arms strain against the tendrils.

She thought of the advice from The Not, but needed to stall long enough to get closer to Aster and long enough to figure out a way to revive Hooyip. Winkle's hands continued to shake, and she felt sick to her stomach.

Come on, Periwinkle, remember what mom used to tell you. Understand who you are, then look around. If you're the odd one out and you want something to go your way, then you have two options: be cleverer than anyone else or prepare ahead of time because the only way someone who looks like me gets what they want is if everything is perfect.

"And even then, Winkle?" Periwinkle mumbled to herself. "You're still too weak and still too brown." *No. Wrong answer.* "You have two choices, Periwinkle."

"Could you please tell me your name?" Winkle asked. "I was told that you had forgotten it a long time ago, but our names are important to us. They help give us purpose. I was named after the color of a flower when it blooms in the spring. My parents said they had many names to choose from, but that color felt like it fit me the best. I do not think I could ever forget my name. Is it the same for you? Do you remember your name?"

"My name?" the creature asked. "When something's purpose is just to survive, what use is there for a name? I have not forgotten my name, and it does not matter if you know it. Although I do not know who first attached it to me.

"I think you might be wrong," Periwinkle said. "Your name does matter. Just like mine. They tell us who we are."

"And whether you learn it or not, your time here, like this one who has attacked us, is short."

"I would still like to know your name then, before I am eaten."

"My name is Nephthea. It is ancient, and it is greater than the small part of me you see now. My name will outlast these caverns. It does not matter what memory you create of my name. Nor does it matter if you speak your own name again because it will be forgotten like the names of all the others that I have consumed."

Periwinkle continued to move closer to the creature and between The No and the spot where her sister hid. "I do not want my name to be forgotten," Periwinkle said. "I am lost in this world, and I want to go home. The person you have has promised that she will help me get home, but I'm afraid that even with her, I'll never find a way back. I know that without her help, this world is too much for me on my own. Please let her go."

The No crept closer to Periwinkle. Then Nephthea retracted the weakened body of The No into herself. "The No is our youngest one," Nephthea said. "And I do not know if she will survive here even if she finds something to eat. Oh, little girl, whether it is me who consumes you or something else, at your best you are just a piece of rubble holding on to your debris." She squeezed Hooyip tighter until the alakdan's body fell limp.

"Our body has already started to grow into this cave, and without sufficient current to remove us, this is where we will remain. For us to survive, we need sustenance. It is our nature. I will not eat you out of spite. It is what I must do for us to survive, and trapped in this place as you are, your end is inevitable."

Periwinkle saw the trickle of light beyond the tunnel, and even though the small tunnel was too narrow for Nephthea, the passageway was large enough for Winkle and her companions.

"Please stop!" Winkle said. "I have something. I have something I can show you." Winkle inhaled. She felt a stab of pain in her ribs, and a rush of cold ran from her neck into her chest and arms. She opened the pouches of the colored minerals tied to her wrists.

"You need a favor from me, then?" the Berberoka asked from somewhere hidden inside of Periwinkle. "Of course, I will help you, but you must allow me a little more freedom as well. Will you do that for me?"

"Yes, I will do whatever you want. Please, just help me save my sister and my friend."

"Very well, then."

Pain from Periwinkle's ribs spread into her back as the water in the pool sprayed upwards into a mist, carrying with it the translucent and powdered gems from the bags. The room flushed with an array of whites, grays, and greens that refracted through the stones and illuminated the cave.

Nephthea stared at the display. "I… haven't seen a sky like this in a long time." She uncoiled her tendrils from Hooyip and strained her body upwards as the flicker of lights shone against her face. The alakdan slid to the ground.

"I forgot something like this existed," Nephthea said. "Where I come from, we live underneath a cliff in the littoral zone—at least when we are not washed around like flotsam with the current. Sometimes we are below water, but when the water recedes, we can see the unfiltered sky. However, the cliffs and the clouds always loom above. We never see all the way to the top. Other than The Not, if we were to look at the sky directly, it'd be too much and we'd shrivel away, so our goal is to always expand as much as we can under the cliff side before we're washed away or before the water disappears forever. It is always a race with no rest."

"We are always racing to stay just below the surface of the water so we do not burn from the sky. But I do really enjoy its apricity. It always looks best when it snows, and it gives us the opportunity of rest from the heat, but ultimately, unless we continue to expand, all of us just wash away like rubble and we fight to hold on to our own bits of debris."

Winkle saw Aster sneak from behind the rocks and try to revive Hooyip. The Not curled forward and raised its neck to cover the girls from Nephthea's view.

Winkle ran to her sister. She jostled Hooyip and helped pull the alakdan to her feet. Under the shade of The Not, the three companions snuck toward the dim light of the tunnel, knowing that it was too narrow for Nephthea to follow. Winkle saw the kaleidoscope of light reflect on the rocks behind her.

Chapter 7
Debris and Water

She was not sure why she felt so down, but Winkle wanted to cheer herself up. The whole mess with Nephthea made her feel sick, and she thought about what Nephthea told her: at her best, she was just rubble holding on to debris. It bothered her, so she tried to get Aster talking and patted her little sister on the shoulder.

"You were brave back there, Aster." Periwinkle tied her sister's hair into a bun and waited. She hoped the compliment would be enough to get Aster chatting for the next three hours while they walked.

Aster shuffled her shoes through the gray leaves. "I guess so."

"You were, and you were so good at hiding. It's amazing Nephthea never found you." Winkle had to be careful, sometimes she forgot Aster wasn't five or six anymore, and she didn't like being talked to like she was a little kid, even though she wasn't much taller than a first grader.

"Thanks, Periwinkle, but I was afraid the whole time, and I didn't know what to do. I think Hooyip was caught because o—"

"You did great!" Hooyip said. "You saved me! Some hero I am. Without the help of my two younger companions, I never would have made it out of there. But I suppose neither of you are ordinary girls from what I have seen. I was a goner for sure, but Aster put me in some tree or something."

"I tried to hide you because you were tired!" Aster said. "You were so fast, like bbrrrm brrrm brrrm brrrm!" Aster narrowed her eyes and performed her full body run that sent her arms and torso swinging. "You grabbed me and we jumped straight down. My stomach whooshed, but then I tried to find water and it got you, so I followed you. I didn't know. I was gonna wait." Aster took Periwinkle's hand and continued to ramble on with her story, and Periwinkle felt better because sometimes she just liked being around her sister.

She wondered what Hooyip meant about Aster not being ordinary and thought about her own bargain with the Berberoka. Maybe she should keep her new companion a secret for now, until she knew more about it herself. Was the Berberoka a part of her? Was it stuck inside of her? She looked for the light to break through the trees above her, felt perplexed that even the light looked dark and gray, and almost forgot about the picture she found of the bushes and the hills and the sylph. Winkle unfolded it from her pocket as they continued through the forest. She showed the illustration to Hooyip.

"I know about this place," Hooyip said. "We have the same picture in some of our books. I've been told stories about it. No, I've never been there myself, but it has to be the same place. They taught me that those thorny bushes don't grow anywhere else. But it is so far away. We will have to leave the forest to get there, and the fastest way out that I know of is across the Broken World Chasm. It would take months to go around, maybe even longer."

"The Broken World Chasm?" Periwinkle asked.

"I've been near it once, and I never entered the bridge, but I think it'll be north from where we are now. Like most heroes, I'm good with directions. I can get us there."

Not that north, south, east, or west mattered much to Periwinkle in a place like this; everything looked the same. The entire world just had the strange colorless tinge, and she never was good with directions. Periwinkle watched Aster hop across some fallen logs, then kneel to dust something away with her hands.

"I've discovered a hidden pathway," Aster said. "Like we're explowrwers."

Periwinkle had just about had enough of hidden passages and doorways. Aster's hands looked filthy. "Come back, Aster, we can't wash your hands out here. What if you have to eat with those things?"

"But I found something! It has colllllor. Come see."

At least her sister felt happy again. Periwinkle scuttled over the logs. Aster was right. She saw the brown pathway, which was overgrown with moss. Back home, people would ignore the dullness and sheer normalcy of the color, but here the moss-covered stones looked almost radiant. She saw more of the brown color peek from under the leaves, and it formed a definite road leading somewhere.

"Well, it is a pathway," Hooyip said. "And it does head north. I'd guess it must have been well used since it's so worn and someone took the time to put it here, but maybe we should take a different route. One that isn't quite so traveled. Maybe it'd be safer if we stayed away from this pathway, even if it does look a little older."

"Why?" Aster asked. "We know where we're going, and this is going where we're going. What's wrong with taking a path to where we're going if it's already been used and it's going where we're going?"

Hooyip touched Aster on the nose.

"I guess you're right," Periwinkle said. Winkle had another reason for wanting to follow the path as well; the colors of the road and the colors of the stones do kind of blend and fade in to one another. The ineffable Bob Ross might wonder what hidden little creations might live along this path and then maybe approve of the idea of observing how creation and nature mix. The path itself looked like something out of one of his landscapes. "Hooyip, maybe my sister is right. Couldn't we just follow this path if it's already heading north? We should try to find someone that could help us get home as fast as possible."

"Ok!" Hooyip strode to the stone.

Except for occasional interjections by Aster about the flora or some other random topic, Periwinkle felt like they walked without conversation for what must have been hours in the forest. They dusted leaves from the moss-covered pathway as they walked to make sure that they held the correct heading.

Up ahead, the trees looked larger, and the forest seemed to drop away. Periwinkle noticed Aster getting tired and took her sister's hand and began humming the "Black Parade." She sang just above a whisper for only Aster and herself. Winkle wasn't sure if she had the lyrics right, so she switched to the "Kuduro" instead, something that always made her sister happy.

Aster giggled, shook, and put her hands up. "Oi oi oi!"

Periwinkle felt Aster tumble into her knee. She heard a crack and saw tar colored smoke at the edge of the forest. She coughed from the smell of burned hair.

Hooyip steadied the two girls, and then all three crouched and watched the black fire ahead of them spread, engulf the trees, then dissipate into smoke. They covered their noses and mouths once the smell turned rank. After the fire burned out, one of the tallest trees rattled. They saw a large shadowy figure, half the size of the tree, smash something that looked like a smaller tree, and then toss it downward. The ground shook. Then the figure disappeared as if it were some hallucination.

Periwinkle heard a whisper. Aster and Hooyip did not seem to notice. "My, my, my," said a voice. The voice sounded feminine and almost like a teacher scolding a student. "We have a predicament now. What is a strange child to do?"

Veins in Periwinkle's spine, neck, and arms flushed with cold. She avoided eye-contact with Aster and Hooyip. The Berberoka returned. "Maybe I shall stay around for a while to keep you safe. It is better for the both of us if I stay awake right now."

Still, no one else seemed to hear the Berberoka's voice. It almost felt like a door opened just a crack and just out of reach, and when the Berberoka awoke, it remained at the entrance sending waves to swirl and crash into her. She felt it watching her, and she was not quite sure if it was terrifying or exciting. Was there even a difference, anyway?

"It's gone now," Hooyip said. "That tear was smaller than the one you girls came through. Do you see where the forest ends? That's the chasm. There is an old bridge we need to cross. I don't remember this road at all, but there should be a bridge that spans the chasm."

Periwinkle walked with her sister to the burned part of the woods. Steam permeated the air, and she smelled the scorched wood smolder in the forest.

"Do we keep going, Hooyip?" Winkle asked. "This is a little dangerous."

Hooyip stopped. "We have to. The bridge is there. I don't know of any sensible way around or through the chasm."

Embers crackled on the ground, and Periwinkle held

Aster's hand and followed toward the tall trees that marked the edge of the forest. There she saw the Broken World Chasm, a split so large that it threatened to tear the world in half. The stone pathway wrapped along its edge and terminated near two magnificent trees used as posts for a bridge. Threads of silvery rope enveloped the trunk and supported the railing of the bridge, which hung broken and limp and spilled itself over the edge of the chasm.

The giant bridge flapped over the side. Periwinkle felt Aster grab on to her waist, afraid to stand too near the edge of the chasm.

The larger of the two trees shook. "Hawww, haw, haw! You will not be crossin here!" A voice thundered from the tree.

Periwinkle saw the ground tremble, and a red light burned from the center of the tree. Humongous hands and arms covered in wiry black hairs pushed their way out of the limbs.

Hooyip jumped in front of Periwinkle and Aster as a ten-foot giant stepped down from the limbs of the tree.

"I say you won't be crossin here." The giant pulled a large cigar from between its lips and puffed the smoke into a noxious cloud above the three girls. His eyes gleamed white and the ember from his cigar shed a light that dappled the earth.

Hooyip unsheathed her white bone sword from her side.

"Haww, haww, haw! What you thinking to do with that? I would have smashed you and thrown you over the sides already if there was a bridge to cross, but now you've nowhere to go."

"We have to make it across," Aster said. We followed the road and need to follow it more to get to where we want to go."

"The bridge is destroyed. Burned and broken in the fire,

it did. I smashed the creature that came through the rift and threw it over the side! Can't see its corpse, it's so far down. I have thrown so many over the side, you'd think there'd be enough to rise up the sides, but this pit is so deep. I'll throw more over the side and they'll never pile this high. If the bridge were here, I'd throw you over the side too, and throw all who arrive over the side! I'd throw them all over this side. Right here by my tree."

Hooyip returned her sword to her belt and whispered to the two girls. "He is a Kapre, a tree spirit. I am not sure I could do much except run if he decides to attack us."

"Can you fix the bridge?" Periwinkle asked the Kapre. "We need to cross because we are looking for a grove that's across this chasm."

"Hawww hawww! I can fix it if I wanted, if I had what I needed to fix it. But if you'd try to cross, I would have to stop you! It is my tree that holds up this bridge, and if too many try to cross, then little by little the ropes pull into my tree and it becomes weak. It is my purpose to protect this tree and keep it strong."

Smoke continued to billow out of the Kapre's mouth and smoke wafted from the tip of his cigar, which never seemed to dwindle despite how long it burned. "But I do have a dilemma," the Kapre said. "Its roots dig down, down, down through the chasm, and I must keep the dirt fertile, but I have no reason to throw creatures down to its roots."

"How exactly can you fix it?" Winkle asked. "I'm not sure anyone could fix something as broken as this."

"Be careful," whispered the voice of the Berberoka. "I think you might make him feel annoyed."

"What I meant was," Periwinkle corrected herself. "Is there something we could do to help you keep the ground fertile or fix the bridge?"

"Hmm fix the bridge? If the bridge were fixed, then

more would try to cross it, and I would have more to throw over the side." The Kapre petted the bark of the tree. "I would have my purpose back in protecting my tree." He inhaled large gusts from his cigar. "I cannot fix it without more thread from a duende, but I cannot leave my tree to get it. Ahhhhhgh, I should just throw you three over the side!"

"No! Please," Periwinkle said. "Maybe we can get the thread for you."

"Then I would have my purpose back."

"If you tell us where the duendes are, we will get the thread for you, and you can repair the bridge."

"Haww haw haw, I shall tell you, but I do not think you will succeed. The duendes are ancient and maintain the pillar that holds up the world. I shall tell you, but when you fail, promise to return here so that I can throw—"

"Throw us over the side! Of course," Winkle said. "I promise all three of us will let you throw us over the side if we cannot return the thread to you. Will you need a lot of it?"

"I will need enough of it! Bring me the amount of enough, and I shall repair the bridge for you, and you can try to cross it and I shall try to protect the bridge."

"Very well," Winkle said.

"The duendes live east of me, but you can only see their village if you look for them. If you are not looking for duendes on purpose, you will never see them because that is how they keep hidden."

Periwinkle felt irked with his directions and had no idea which way was east, much less what he meant by knowingly looking for them or even what a duende might look like. "It's a deal then," Periwinkle said. Before she could ask anything else, The Kapre climbed back into the tree and faded away. The red light from his cigar continued to ascend into the branches until that, too, wafted out.

"That was pretty quick thinking," Hooyip said. "I've never tried to fight a tree spirit before. I'm not sure it would have gone too well."

"Do you know anything about duendes?" Periwinkle asked.

"I do! I have never seen one, and I know that none of my people have ever seen one! But we have never known how to find them before or known where they live. Now I know that they're to the east and we have to look for them. This should be easy. We look for them, sneak in, take some of the thread, which must be more of the silver stuff tied around his tree, and sneak away! We're all so good at hiding. This will be easy."

Chapter 8
This Will Be Easy

She wasn't sure if they were doing this right. She thought they followed the directions. If the Kapre gave them a map, then this search would have been easier. They walked weeks to the east and saw no end to the chasm. Thanks to Hooyip, they found the river, and Winkle felt positive that she looked for the duende the entire time. Aster even checked under rocks and behind the trees in case the duendes turned out to be miniscule. Periwinkle thought her sister enjoyed the looking more than the finding, but it sure would have been nice to have found something duende or duende related. Maybe she was not doing this right at all.

Winkle hid and waited with her sister. Under Hooyip's tutelage, they both developed a penchant for hiding and a talent for survival. Periwinkle listened for the crackling noises which preceded the fires that heralded the rifts into whatever abyss spilled into this world.

Hooyip taught her and her sister how to move like a predator. They both learned fast, but Aster had a knack for it. Her sister always knew the right way to move, the right place to step, the right way to do just about anything in what became an increasingly unstable forest. Winkle felt proud of her little sister, whom she trusted to make the right decisions, so she did not mind waiting for Aster to decide when it was safe to move on while Hooyip hunted by the river.

Aster nodded to her, and they crept closer to where they saw the flames. Often, they found nothing. Sometimes they found wires, strange splintered wood, or other debris that looked somehow familiar. One time, they found a crowbar that Winkle now carried tied to her side, much like Hooyip's sword. At first, she was not sure what she would do with a crowbar. It did come in handy to crack apart some nuts that they gathered from the trees. It had a surprising use as a shovel when digging out places to sleep, but Winkle found its best use was in grinding down flowers, leaves, or some rocks to use as drawing material. The problem was that everything had either the same sort of gray or pickle hue, but it gave her and Aster a way to pass the time. She even named it "Mister" because it was helpful like her father used to be, so it reminded her of home.

Winkle watched her sister for a signal. She knew Aster missed their mom as much as she did, even though they did not talk about it too much, because it just made them both feel a little morose. Instead, they concentrated on learning everything Hooyip tried to teach them—that and looking for any signs of the duendes.

Periwinkle and Aster moved fast, just the way they were taught. Winkle never thought she would enjoy this type of physical activity, but the physicality provided her a chance to turn down her mind and just react. They stayed close to each other, sped through the ash and cinders, and scoured the forest. Winkle kept watch to see if anything alive lingered from the portal. Aster grabbed anything of use. This time, she returned with a backpack. They trekked to the safety of the river bank to wait for Hooyip.

"This will help us," Aster said. "And it's blue." She

unzipped the backpack and searched through its pockets. Aster pulled out a pencil box, some paper, a stapler, and a notebook. "It's school supplies. Why would this make it through the flames?"

Winkle rinsed her hands and arms in the pale gray water. She had slight outlines of muscles in her forearms. She's never had muscles like this before. "I remember the color blue," Winkle said.

The water washed over her hands, and she listened. Her inner doorway to the uncanny passenger was shut. She thought about something the Berberoka told her; she was a beacon of warmth. Periwinkle saw splashes in the water. Hooyip taught her when to run. This was the right time.

Winkle grabbed Aster as her sister tried on the backpack, and they ran. Something large from behind her swept onto shore. She heard it fold into the earth. Winkle's heart pounded. She never turned to look and hoped Aster didn't either.

After their escape, they met with Hooyip, and they ate and dug holes for their beds. "It didn't feel safe," Hooyip told them. "This might be a rough night." The alakdan's two tails twitched in the wind. She couldn't tell if they were alone or not.

Nights like this, Periwinkle sung Aster to sleep because she knew her sister wanted to help keep watch and wanted to stay awake. "You're still growing," Winkle told her. "You need to sleep all through the night." Winkle tied up her sister's hair, which grew longer and bedraggled.

"You're still growing too," Aster said, trying to rub her eyes awake.

"We have Hooyip with us. She'll always keep us safe."

Hooyip smiled at the sentiment and curled her knees into her arms, then watched the black fires at the ends of the world die down.

"I know that. I know these things," Aster said.

Winkle continued to whisper her song. The melody remained soft enough so just Aster could hear. It was a song for her sister and no one else to remind them both of home.

"I know all these things, but I hope we can find the threads from the duende soon because I'd like to go home," Aster said as she dozed away to sleep.

The night air felt cold. Periwinkle stayed awake in the dark because it was her turn to keep watch. She learned to listen and heed the wind since her eyes were useless in the dark. She heard her sister's breath beside her. Winkle felt the warmth on her cheek, stroked her sister's hair, and made the promise that she's made every night since traversing the edge of the chasm.

"I will get you home, Aster, because maybe this is my fault. I wanted something extraordinary to happen. I wanted to put the world in order."

Periwinkle's palms perspired despite the cold. She knew the strange visitors were arriving again. Her body froze. She wished the Berberoka would awake, and she tried to whisper for her to open her door, but she did not.

There were two this time. They turned toward her and watched, just as she watched them. They spoke to her, but she could not quite hear their voices. The first time she saw ghosts like these, she called for Hooyip, but the alakdan saw nothing and felt nothing. That time, Hooyip stayed awake with her and assured her that nothing was there. Neither of them told Aster.

She tried to suppress her fear and counted each outward breath as she slowed her breathing. The Berberoka told her they would find her. Most of them were harmless. "Something about you," her uncanny companion had said. "You are warm to us." But the Berberoka agreed to keep her safe.

The two spirits continued to talk. Winkle shook her head. She still could not make out their words, and she closed her eyes, but it made no difference, and she still saw the two figures in the dark. Periwinkle shuddered; did she fall asleep? Both spirits almost stood over her now. Night remained. Now that the two spirits stood closer, she almost understood their words. Were they asking for help?

Periwinkle reached her hand out to touch the spirit that reached for her, but a black mist formed between Winkle and the spirits, then pushed them away. The two ghosts flickered, then disappeared. They were further in the forest again, watching her.

Winkle felt the Berberoka awaken inside of her. "No, not either of those two. They want to remain in this place. If you were to let them in, then maybe you would want to remain in this forest, too."

Her chest felt cold, and the ghosts remained until morning. Periwinkle kept it to herself.

***

When they found the homes of the duendes, Periwinkle rubbed her eyes. "Is that them?" she asked. "All we had to do was look."

"I see them too," Aster said. "They have stars in their eyes."

The duendes stood taller than Aster but much shorter than Periwinkle. They had long spidery arms, rather human-like faces with bulbous honkers of noses that tapered into sewing needle points, and most had pot shaped bellies which made them look a little like mascots at a theme park. Periwinkle saw the males wore hats with red, green, or yellow brims, which made even more of a spectacle in the gray-white drabness of the forest.

She watched the bustle from the forest. "How could such a place stay hidden?" Mud encrusted homes held back the forest. Four longer buildings, placed parallel to one another, resided in a center clearing.

"I have a hypothesis!" Aster said. She closed her eyes tight. "Eeeeeeeeee." Aster tapped both sides of her head with her hands. Her eyes popped open, and she perked her head up. "Yep! It works." Aster held her arms out in front of her and spread her hands.

"I made them disappear. Hypothesis's correct!" Aster wandered in circles. "I'm pretending I'm an adult taking a walk. I'm just an adult out for a stroll. I'm not lookin for anything but yard appeal and money on the ground." Aster ambled with an imaginary cane and continued to circle her sister. "Try it Winkle! I'm just doing older people things and lookin for funny shaped birds with strange beaks so I could write about it in my handy dandy notebook."

"Aster, that's not very nice," Winkle said. It was difficult to pretend the duendes with their star-filled eyes were not there when Periwinkle saw them walking through their village, but she covered her eyes, and she stopped looking for anything. Instead, she imagined the forest and the chasm beyond it. She imagined staring over the side and staring across its insurmountable distance. Periwinkle opened her eyes. "They all vanished," she said.

Hooyip watched. "I don't think they know we're here. Or maybe they're ignoring us and hoping we just walk through."

"Orr maybeeeee, they have to look for us, too," Aster said. "That's my second hypothesis."

"Hmm," Periwinkle pushed her hair from her face. "We need to find that thread."

Hooyip shrugged. "Well, I hope they're friendly." The alakdan picked up a small branch and tossed it in front of one of the duende. It landed with a thud in the path of the diminutive being and stopped her where she stood. All the duendes in the village turned and looked. "Hi!" Hooyip said, waving.

Aster hid behind Periwinkle and waved.

"Hypothesis correct," Aster whispered.

One of the duendes dropped his rake, removed his yellow hat, and scratched his head. "It has been a time. You may as well come in."

Another duende scrubbed her hands in her dress and ran toward Periwinkle and the group while even more duendes gathered behind the male with the yellow hat.

"Ohl whoal whoal whoal whoal whoal," the female duende said. "Visitors! We have not had visitors! Of course, you may as well come in. Of course, come in!" She ran with her spidery arms flapping, and she stopped in front of Periwinkle. "Did you come for lunch? Or did you come for stories and cakes? Oh, it's exciting!"

Hooyip extended her hand and nudged Winkle. "Don't be rude!"

Periwinkle shook hands with the male in the yellow hat who somehow made it over to her before the running duende, then shook hands with the running duende, and Hooyip did the opposite. Aster just put out both hands, but no one grabbed them because all the hands were occupied at the time, and Winkle pushed her sister back behind her.

"I would love some cakes," Hooyip said, who then introduced herself as Hooyip, the alakdan, and introduced Periwinkle Dalisay and Aster Dalisay as Periwinkle Dalisay and Aster Dalisay.

"See, friendly," Hooyip whispered to Periwinkle. "This will be easy."

Periwinkle felt like the duendes might break out into song at any moment. For not having visitors, the duende with the yellow hat seemed well prepared to usher in guests.

"It's rare rare rare we get guests!" said the duende with the yellow hat. "My name is Heus, and my wife's name is Salve!"

Heus and Salve walked the group to a cluster of large stone tables, which, for some reason, Periwinkle failed to see when they first entered the village. Other duendes occupied the tables, and others congregated to wait for service.

"Once in a while someone will find us," Salve said. "But I do not think we have seen humans like you this far east. You are humans, right? You look a little different for humans."

"You know humans?" Aster asked.

"Oh, we have the most important job in the Ember Lands. We know everything about everything." Salve's face beamed, and her mouth stretched into a smile. "Without us, the Ember Lands would not be the Ember Lands."

"Ahem," Heus interrupted. "They probably do not know. Yes, of course we know all about you humans from the north, though you know little about us. We maintain the Consequential Pillar. Our pillar bends the world up and supports the entirety of the Ember Lands. We are very important, very important indeed, you know."

"You can stay with us for a time, if you like," Salve said. "It has been dangerous outside as of late. Here, you will be safe."

Winkle felt a tug on her arm. Aster looked up at her, and she knew what her little sister wanted, but despite the hospitality, she felt it was too soon to trust the duendes. Winkle shook her arm loose from her sister's grasp.

Aster tried again. Winkle felt her little sister grab at her arm and saw Aster squint her eyes and purse her lips.

Winkle snatched her arm away a second time and shook her head. This, she felt, was one of the rare times her little sister had misread the situation. Asking for or about the silvery thread was a mistake, and even though sometimes little kids think they have all the answers, at times they need to follow the lead of their elders.

A pang of pain darted through Winkle's foot as Aster's heel stomped into her toe as they continued to walk.

"The Consequential Pillar?" Hooyip asked. "I've never heard of such a thing before." Hooyip scoured the village. "Where is it exactly? My parents have told me much of the history of the Ember Lan—"

"Oh no, you wouldn't have heard of it," Salve interrupted. "It is—"

"Salve! That is not polite, not polite at all. The alakdan was talking and you just interrupted her," Heus said.

"Oh I… I supposed I did. I do apologize!" Salve wrenched her hands into her dress. "Well, I am sorry for that."

"She is sorry for that," Heus said. "Like I have said, it has been a time since we have had visitors. Never mind her, but you are quite lucky to have found us when you did. You are just in time for lunch."

Periwinkle wondered about the pillar as well but was unsure if Heus changed the subject on purpose or if the duende was just a little scatterbrained and distracted.

"Food would be great, but we're looking for something," Hooyip said. We need a length of silver-colored thread to help repair a bridge. We were wondering if you could give us some because we've walked so far to find you."

"Ah, have you now?" Heus replied. "Be polite. Sit down first and eat. Then we could talk about trade."

"We could really use it now," Hooyip said. "We're kind of in a rush and on a very important quest."

"See," Aster said to Winkle. "Told you we should just ask."

"Here we are." Heus and Salve moved a bench aside and motioned for the trio to sit, and then they backed away and disappeared into the crowd of duendes.

"What now, Hooyip?" Aster asked.

"I guess we should eat. It has been a while since we've had someone else find food for us, but we should be careful. They're strangers to us, just as we're strangers to them."

Periwinkle sighed and sat down next to her sister. Her stomach rumbled from nervousness rather than hunger. What a different life to live in the forest and to walk on leaves and soil instead of carpet. Winkle considered the forest and wondered what threats existed for the duendes, and she wondered how they learned to compensate for those threats. Is hiding always sufficient, and how mundane is it for them to be asked about their silver thread or entertain visitors? Periwinkle looked for Salve and Heus, but she no longer saw either duende. She spied other duendes with yellow hats, but none looked like Heus. Her breathing quickened and everywhere she looked, she saw more and more duendes.

"How are you?" another duende asked without waiting for a response.

"You are well, I hope," another said. Each one who passed her by directed some pleasantry toward her or Aster.

Periwinkle smiled at each one. It made her cheeks tired. This could not be it; the duendes couldn't be this polite and hospitable. No one is polite to strangers unless they want something first.

Once they settled and the greetings subsided, Periwinkle smelled a familiar scent of freshly baked cakes and what had to have been a pungent, rooty sort of tea. Several duendes, who wore buttoned white shirts and plain brown vests, brought food for all those seated.

One of the male duendes, who carried one of the largest trays, moved toward Winkle and her group.

If the other duendes had eyes that were stars, his eyes looked like they housed an entire nebula. His tray never teetered or shook when he served the seated duendes, and he retained a smile as he conversed with everyone. By the time he finished serving others at their table, and by the time he reached Aster, they were so accustomed to his manners that his smile set Aster and Hooyip at ease. He poured a drink for Hooyip, then for Periwinkle, and then for Aster. The tea stopped below the same spot of each brim.

"My name is Servus," the duende said. "When I first saw you enter, I knew I had to meet you. For the missus," he said as he left a tiny pink cake in front of Periwinkle.

"And for the second missus," he said again and left a violet cake in front of Aster.

"And for the esteemed," he said with a smile to Hooyip, leaving her a small pink cake as well.

"Look Winkle," Aster said. "Mine is different. You think it tastes different? I wonder if it's the same under the frosting. I wonder if it's ube. Maybe it's an eggplant and olive flavor but a good eggplant and olive flavor, not like the normal olives or eggplants, but they found a way to make eggplant cake that tastes like a treat. Do you think it's tres leches?"

Periwinkle watched Aster tap her cake. Her little sister looked unsure of whether she should take the first bite or wait for someone to tell her what to do.

"That's an interesting piece of jewelry, young one," the duende said, nodding at Aster's bracelet.

"I found it," Aster said. "It's not mine, but it felt so warm and it made me feel safe, like I was home. If I knew who it belonged to, I'd give it back. Have you seen something like it before?"

"Ah, I think I have," Servus said. "The one you have is very old. You said it feels warm, little one?"

"Yes, it feels warm even now. I don't know. It doesn't look warm."

"Well, maybe it found the right person after all." Servus straightened a cloth in front of Aster for her to use as a napkin. "It was very nice meeting you. Maybe we will meet again."

"We can meet now, if you like. I don't think I'm going anywhere now. Hooyip told them we needed silver thread even though my sister shook her head at me, but I knew it would be ok."

Servus's eyebrows furrowed, and for half a second his eyes darted to the other duendes. His smile returned. "Maybe your older sister's advice was correct. My time here is up, and there are more cakes for me to deliver."

"Thank you for the food," Periwinkle said.

"Yes! Thank you," Aster said. "I bet my sister and I can make something for you sometime. We'll find some way to pay you back for the food. Our father taught us we shouldn't take anything without giving something in return."

"Well, when you get older, maybe. But just know, you always owe something to someone." As he left, Servus took the hand of a smaller duende and led him into one of the longer centralized homes.

Hooyip tapped Periwinkle on her shoulder. "These duendes are so difficult, I can't find anyone that'll tell me how to get the thread that the Kapre told us about. Maybe he was lying."

DING! DING! DING! Periwinkle saw one of the female duendes at her table tapping the side of her cup. The tapping continued louder and louder until all in attendance quieted.

The duende stood and raised her thin arms. Her bones poked through a blue vest that hung about her shoulders, and it was adorned with a brooch made from a bright cluster of purple berries tied together with reflective thread. The same thread Periwinkle saw that fastened the bridge to the Kapre's tree. "Because our guests have found us, we should tell them the story of our work and how vital our existence is to the Ember Lands."

The duende's fingers entwined as if matriculating through the threads and scenery of some imagined tapestry. A fine mist arose from baskets of fruit at the center of the table.

Aster turned to her sister. "Can you see them, Winkle? I think it's all connected somehow." She held her hand over her cake and gazed as if following a trail that wound over the table and upwards to the duende.

"Something above the table? I think I see something," Periwinkle said.

"No, it's more."

A vision of a giant iron pillar, as if pulled along by a chord, appeared above the table and in front of the duende and started to rotate. She explained that the Consequential Pillar bore through the darkness and broke the Ember Lands away from the Abyss.

The vision shifted to show a landmass bent in its center, and, at the bend, it rested atop the giant spike. Black fires surrounded the edges of the Ember Lands as remnants of the dark.

"The Pillar itself birthed the duendes as caretakers," she said. "And without us, the Consequential Pillar would seize, the black fires that warm the land would extinguish, and the Ember Lands would then crumble and return into the Abyss. We are the wardens of the Pillar." The Consequential Pillar continued to rotate as the duende spun her hand. "We are the bringers of existence in the Ember Lands."

Servus, with his nebula eyes, returned to collect the plates and cups from Periwinkle, Hooyip, and Aster.

"Good story?" he asked. His professional smile remained on his face, and his eyes shone even brighter now that night crept in and the black fires at the edge of the world dwindled downward.

"I—I think so," Periwinkle said. "Thank you for the cakes."

"You must all be very important!" Aster said.

Servus looked toward the fruit on the center of the table. He collected it so the girls could see it before he placed it with the assortment of bowls and trays. All the fruit had rotted. "Well, it is quite a story, isn't it little ones. We've told it for a long time."

Chapter 9
Periwinkle and the Garden

After a few days of staying with the duendes and the continued stories of their role in the Ember Lands, Aster felt a little perturbed. Her sister and Hooyip were no closer to finding any of the silver thread, and the more Hooyip asked and insisted, the less any duende wanted to talk about anything, let alone some magical thread strong enough to hold up an entire bridge. All the duendes ever did was talk about the Consequential Pillar, even though no one would ever let her see it.

Aster grew comfortable with the layout of the village, and for the most part, they all treated her well—much better than they treated her older sister and Hooyip. One of the duendes even gave Aster and Winkle haircuts so their hair didn't droop in their faces so much. She figured they were nicer to her because she was little.

In the mornings, Aster liked to visit the cheese monger because, well, the cheese monger gave her cheese and it tasted about as good as any she has had before. Aster had a triangle type cheese this time. She peeled it apart like the string cheese at home, but this triangle type tasted much stronger and maybe more like cream than cheese, but it somehow still peeled and didn't smash or break.

Today, Aster wanted to visit the fishmonger to sniff out what he had available. The fishmonger lived the furthest from the village. Periwinkle didn't like it when she walked that far out, but Aster knew her sister was busy helping some of the duendes build a new garden for the purple berries they liked to eat so much. It was Periwinkle's way of repaying the hospitality, and it made it easier for Aster to explore further from the village.

Aster ran to the fishmonger's home. He lived beside the river, and sometimes Aster had trouble finding him because she didn't always look in the right place. Also, she liked that the walls of his home were covered in mud, and Aster scraped her initials into a different part of the outer walls every time before knocking on his door.

When the fishmonger answered, Aster showed him the cheese. "I got triangle type. You have any of the snails today?"

The fishmonger's hat was green, and all the duende men in the village liked to wear hats, which was how Aster figured somebody could tell they're men and not women. Aster enjoyed talking to him because he kind of had a limp. He walked in a circle when he tried to think about something, even though she imagined the fishmonger thought he was walking back and forth.

Aster looked at the circle worn into the dirt and stopped peeling her cheese. "I'll give you the whole thing if you have four big snails that are still fresh."

The fishmonger scratched his head. "That's not the whole thing! You're eating some right now."

"It is the whole thing. You can see it in my hand, can't you. This is the whole thing, and this is the part I'm eating!" Aster divided the cheese into two parts. "You get the whole thing if I can have some snails. You have to cook them too, because Periwinkle says I can't use fire."

"Oh. I guess that would be the whole thing then." The fishmonger paced in a circle. "Fine, but wait out here, and I get the bigger part."

Aster ate a bit more of the cheese from the triangle and walked to the side of the wall so she could watch the fishmonger work behind his house. He pulled up a basket from the river, which he used to keep the fish and snails cold and fresh. Aster savored the smell of the cooked snails over the fire.

She drew in the dirt while she waited and was trying to work out why some duendes seemed to disappear. She felt she was on the verge of another hypothesis when the fishmonger returned with her snails.

"These make good amino acids," Aster announced.

The fishmonger looked at his sack of snails. "No, they're snails. Amino?"

"These can give me amino acid strains to form my proteins. Then I'll get stronger like my sister and my friend. And I can build my antibodies, which is good because we've been out in the wilderness for so long."

"You owe me the rest of the cheese. If you're trying to trick me."

"But I'm not tricking you. I'm just explaining that I wanted these to get stronger. That duende at dinner gives me carbohydrates, and that gives me sugars so I can think, but I need more proteins too."

"Oh. Ahh." The fishmonger nodded. He scratched his chin. "The ones that bring the cakes at dinner? Carbo? Servus brings carbodraits?" He rubbed his head and peered at Aster.

"Do you know Servus?" Aster asked. "I see him at supper, but that's it. I wanted to talk to him about something."

"Servus? The one who works the tables? With those bad

eyes, hmm."

Aster felt that the fishmonger was being rude. His own eyes had plenty of stars—not as many as Servus's, but plenty more than anyone she's met back home. Aster nodded, "That's him. Where does he live? Like you're a fishmonger and you live in the fishmonger's house. The cheese monger lives in the cheese monger's house. Where does he go when no one's eating?"

The fishmonger paced and bumped against his door twice. "Longhouse. Last one. House number four. Last chance. No one in four makes it. Shouldn't mess with him, though. He does his work too well. Ignore him."

Aster traded what she had left of the cheese for the sack of snails and smiled at the fishmonger. "Thank you! Maybe he likes these snails too."

"Enjoy the snails."

She shoved one snail in her backpack to save for later, and on her way back, Aster crept around the perimeter of the town's new garden to look for her sister. Periwinkle tilled the soil and planted seedlings for the new berry bushes. Hooyip was questioning a duende, probably asking where to find the thread they needed for the Kapre, but more and more the duendes looked like they were frustrated with Hooyip. Aster didn't think Hooyip noticed.

Periwinkle's approach was too soft, and Hooyip acted too forward. Neither, Aster thought, had come any closer to finding what they needed; they both looked in the wrong places.

The longhouses were such an oddity in the village, and most of the duendes that disappeared, disappeared near the longhouses. At first Aster wondered what the fishmonger meant by the fourth one and the last longhouse because a house resided at either end, so either one could have been number four, but once she looked at them, maybe the fourth house was obvious. The roof of the fourth one had holes. Its run-down walls were a little frightening and out of place compared to the other homes. It looked older and tired.

Aster watched the fourth house. None of the duendes ever invited her, Hooyip, or her sister inside any of the homes. They set up camp inside the village, and no one had told them to leave, and every day they were invited to eat with the duendes in the village, but they never entered any of the homes. She remembered Servus's green hat, but many of the duendes wore green hats, so that didn't help. It was time to act like Hooyip.

Aster knocked on the fourth door, and a female duende who stood even shorter than her answered. Her head jerked from side to side, and she had trouble looking up from the ground when she talked.

"Eee-eello," the duende said and continued to look down.

"Is Servus here?" Aster asked. "The fishmonger told me that this is where he lives. I very much would like to see him. He served me a purple cake once, and it tasted like sweet beans. The other day, he served me a yellow cake, but I preferred the purple one. Usually I don't like—"

"I can find him," the duende said, and she walked away.

"I like your dress," Aster called after her. She seemed nice. Aster wondered if she had a speech impediment like her.

Aster grabbed two of the cooked snails and held them in front of the door when she saw Servus. "It is snails."

Servus folded his sleeves. Aster decided she needed to learn to fold her sleeves like him. Her sleeves always unfurled, and they never looked so neat and as organized as Servus' did just now. She would have to ask him about how he makes his clothes look so nice.

Servus smiled. "It is you. I knew we would talk eventually." Servus thanked the female duende who answered the door, and then he directed Aster to the fields. "That was Silva. She is very intelligent. She's the one who devised a new method of planting and gathering for us, and she figured out a better way to arrange and build our garden beds. Thanks to her, the duendes now gather vegetation from the forest for supplement or ceremony and not out of necessity. She is one of the smartest duendes in our village."

"She sounds very knowledgeable," Aster said. "Is she a genius? Maybe she can sit with us sometime at supper. I've always wanted to meet a genius. I've read about some before."

"Genius?" Servus asked. "Well, maybe it's more obsession. Just her obsession put to an acceptable task. Maybe she's that. Which reminds me, I must see my man about the oubliettes." Servus looked back into the longhouse. "Right my man? My man. But I doubt she would join us. She is a little shy."

"My sister is like that," Aster said. "My sister is very smart as well, and she also prefers to be alone."

Servus nodded. "I think that's how a lot of the smarter folk act. There's the shadow of the thing and the thing itself. Sometimes people get them confused, but it's tougher on those who find an answer, and I think it's difficult to be around those who can't understand the world in… well, it's difficult." He pointed again to the fields. "Walk with me and act very nonchalant. Can you remain nonchalant? Because I'm afraid your friend will be removed soon."

"Of course. I know what nonchalant is. It means like nothing has happened. Has something happened, Servus?"

"Your sister is safe because she is polite. They all say that. But your friend Hooyip is very insistent, and she asks for information that is not volunteered to her. She did not understand the warnings."

"Do you mean the way all the duendes ignore her now? They ignore my sister, in a way. Even if they're nice to her."

Servus nodded and led Aster past the new berry field. "Did you know you are uniquely perceptive? It is likely why you took that bracelet and likely why the bracelet decided it belongs to you."

Aster fiddled with the bracelet around her wrist. It still felt warm whenever she touched its threads and its metal crest. Servus pointed toward the fields, and Aster saw her sister continued to toil with plants and work, but she did not see Hooyip no matter where they walked or where she looked.

"Everyone likes your sister. She is very proper, and she is safe," Servus said. "But Hooyip continued to ask about what we did not want to tell her. She did not respect the importance of the duendes." Servus sat on a rotted log deep beneath the shade of a tree. "I think you are a sartor—a tailor."

Aster scrunched her eyebrows together. "I know what a tailor is. I even know about haberdashers because Winkle reads to me. I'm no tailor. You're just changing the topic because you don't want to tell me where Hooyip is." Aster felt a little frightened for the first time during her stay with the duendes.

Servus sighed, removed his hat, and rubbed his head. His eyes sparkled and cast a radiant light across the log.

Shadows from the trees pulled toward Aster as her fear and anger rose, and Servus shook his head.

"I shall help you because you are indeed a sartor. Right now, Hooyip is safe. She wanted to find the thread and soon they will show it to her, but she will never be allowed to leave. Instead, she will work to create more of our thread, which we use to maintain the pillar."

Aster relaxed. "What is a sartor?"

"It's that bracelet you wear. It's old magic in the Ember Lands. We are all threads warped and wefted through a loom and pulled into a visible tapestry—or connected and woven. I think that's how it goes for the sartors. I'm not one myself, but for now, my job as a duende is to serve, and I have served many visitors who have found our village. On occasion, a sartor finds us during their travels."

"Old magic?" Aster asked. "We don't have that where I'm from. Not the way you mean. I've seen a magic act before, but they just hide things from us when no one's looking."

"No, this is real. Try to look. Slow down your breathing. Relax your limbs one limb at a time. Start with your head, then your shoulders and arms, hands, all the way. Then look again at the slow world. Do you see anything between the light and the shadows?"

Aster tried to understand what Servus meant. She looked for a while at the shadows and the light. The light that glistened from his eyes shone brighter than the bits of light that broke through the trees, but she was sure that was not what he meant. "I can see the dust falling through the light, but I don't think that's it, is it?"

"Try to watch the dust, then. That always worked for me. It's a memory. The Ember Lands are just a memory of fire from the Abyss. It is just like the dust—a remnant from the thing of the threads. Maybe you can see them there."

Aster concentrated again as the dust wafted between the pale yellow of light and dim grays of shadows and the almost shadows. Some of the specks jumped in odd patterns as she continued to watch, as if string yanked the dust along invisible paths. Then she saw what he must have meant. A faint line, at first slighter than spider's silk, but then spates of color trailed from the particles of dust and connected to the thickening line. Pink threads dawdled from the specks that floated upwards, yellow threads from the specks which dropped straight down. They entwined and unwound, and threads from Servus entwined into the yellow-brown threads of the rotted stump. She had seen something like it before in the cave and when they first learned the story of the Consequential Pillar.

"In time, I have been told, sartors can see the threads of everything. That's what sartors do. They can manipulate the threads as tailors and recreate the fabric as they see fit. I did not believe it at first or understand it, but a visitor taught me enough so that I could see some of the threads. Since then, the world has looked different." Servus returned his green hat to his gray head, and he rubbed his neck, then adjusted his boot. "I'd imagine in time and with help, you'd become a skilled sartor."

"It's pretty. But if Hooyip is in trouble, then I need to find her." Aster shook her head. She didn't have time to get distracted by sartors and tailors and dust and lights. She looked at Servus and her eyes widened. "My friend is a hero. She can't be lost here."

"This won't help for my recital, but let's go, then. I shall need to check on something first."

Aster followed Servus back to the longhouses, and they stopped by the second house.

"Please wait here. I'll be quick."

"Okay, I guess." The feeling of dread returned when Servus scampered inside and left Aster alone. She wished Hooyip and her sister were with them. The second longhouse looked to be in better condition than the fourth house. Its walls looked newer, but still somehow dreary compared to the smaller homes and even compared to the fishmonger's home, which seemed to have a sort of independence. What did Servus mean by his recital? Aster sighed and watched an acorn on the ground turn with the breeze.

She's given a recital before. Her dad used to take her to guitar lessons back home. Her first recital she was afraid, and the teachers set up a smoke machine because it was Halloween. Because she was so little, the smoke engulfed her while she played, and she had trouble seeing her fingers. The pictures her dad showed her afterwards just had the stage covered in smoke. Her shoes and one of her elbows poked out a bit in the fog.

A young duende exited the home. A round basket teetered between his hands, and Servus followed behind him to close the door. "This is Armiger, my younger brother," Servus said, tapping his hand on the younger duende's shoulder. "He's deaf in one ear, and his other ear is a little lame as well, so it helps to tap his shoulder to get his attention.

The smaller duende looked up at Servus, and Servus turned him toward a cluster of trees in the village. Armiger looked up at his brother in surprise, and Servus nodded. "We'll take you to your friend," Servus said.

"Thank you. Hey Servus, what is the recital you mentioned? You said this won't be good for the recital."

Armiger looked at Servus, who must have heard enough of the question to show concern.

"The recital is what duendes undertake to become principals of our community. We must recite the history of the Consequential Pillar to those who would become our peers, and they judge us on how well we recite the history. Once we complete and pass the recital, the principals accept us as full members of society. That is why my brother and I both live in the longhouses. Each house marks which attempt a duende is on. I live in the fourth house. My last attempt is in a few days. My brother will be on his second attempt."

"What happens after the fourth attempt?" Aster asked.

"If the other principals do not accept a duende after the fourth attempt, he or she is taken to join the Consequential Pillar, and in that way, they serve our infinite society and support the Ember Lands and keep the pillar turning."

"Join?"

"Yes, not your concern, little one," Servus said with a smile. "Let's head to supper. Your sister will be there and after dark, we will take you to your friend. We'll have to be careful, but I'm sure by now you have some curiosity about the Pillar. We do not allow visitors to view the Pillar and leave. The silver thread your friend searches for is made there as well. Once we obtain it, you and your friends must leave this place as fast as possible."

Aster nodded and walked with the duende to the supper tables. "Hey Servus, why didn't you pass the recital?"

Servus shrugged. "My last attempt, they said my pronunciation for some of the history sounded vague. The attempt before that, the others told me that my words sounded too precise. I will try again."

"But it's your last chance," Aster said.

"So, I must work hard to be accepted." Servus's eyes dimmed a little, but even so, the cluster of stars that made up his eyes continued to saturate the area with light. "You know, little one, there are other sartors in the Ember Lands. Watch for them. Look for them. Their magic is more sincere than ours. It is not like what they have shown you here. Instead, it is real."

Aster pursed her lips. "You're trying to change the subject. You should just leave this place. You're nicer than the other duendes. Maybe this isn't where you belong. It's not smart to try again, and you're really smart. Hooyip can survive in the forest. I think you can, too."

"Maybe I'm just afraid, then. Sometimes after working for something for so long, it's easier to stay on the path you know instead of trying something new. Even if you know it won't be successful."

"That's not a good reason to try again. The duendes above you are either too incompetent or too privileged to let you join them."

Servus stopped by one of the serving tables. He stopped his little brother and pointed to the cluster of trees. "After," he said. "After. After."

Armiger nodded. He was not much taller than Aster. Armiger patted Aster on the shoulders, much like Servus did to him. Then the smaller duende pointed toward the trees. He brought his forefinger to his lips. "Quiet," he said. Armiger filled his basket with rolls of bread, covered them with a cloth napkin, adjusted his vest and green hat, then started his job serving the other duendes.

"I need to stay and take care of my brother as long as possible," Servus said. "Maybe my recital won't be acceptable, but his might. And once he passes, he will have his own home and all the benefits of the other duendes."

"I still think you should both leave. You can even come with us if you want. You can teach me to be a tailor! Winkle won't mind and neither will Hooyip. Once you help us find her, we'll all leave together. We're going to save this world, you know."

"Well maybe that is something to think about. Sometimes, though, stories are most wonderful once they end. Besides, after we do this the principal duendes won't be too happy with me or my brother—my man. My man."

Aster mumbled. "It sounds like they'll never accept your recital if you show visitors their stupid pillar."

"It's time for you to find your sister, little one. What type of cake would you like this time? The purple, the pink, or the yellow?"

"I guess purple. It's almost like ube."

"Good, then. You and your sister come find me after supper. The way to the pillar is difficult for strangers. We have to find our lamb."

That didn't make any sense to Aster. She hasn't seen any lambs since they've stayed with the duendes. Not a one, but there were a lot of things that didn't make much sense about the duendes. She knew a different meaning of lamb. A meaning like fugitives who were hiding from the law, and she wondered if she was somehow on the lam.

"Aster! I haven't seen you all day." Periwinkle grabbed Aster by the hand and turned to Servus. "I'm sorry if she's trouble. My sister likes to talk a lot and if she doesn't have someone to talk to, she has a way of finding someone and tricking them into listening."

Aster thought her sister looked a lot like her mom when she tried to be stern.

"I can't find Hooyip anywhere, and I'm getting worried," Periwinkle said to Aster.

"Your sister is never any trouble," Servus said. "She has a lot to tell you. Please make sure you listen."

"We have to act nohmal," Aster said. "Nooohhrrrmal," Aster felt frustrated that she still sometimes had trouble pronouncing her R's. "I'll tell you all about it when we eat."

Servus's smile returned. "I must go, and I shall meet with you two later."

Aster recounted Hooyip's capture to her sister, and she talked about their plan to find the thread and rescue the alakdan. As they ate, none of the duendes spoke to Aster and Periwinkle except to mutter pleasantries. Aster was disappointed because she had learned to enjoy the conversations she started with the duendes during supper. Before today, she learned how they built their homes, and she heard stories of other travelers, but this time it was almost as if she and Periwinkle were not even there and most of the duendes she tried to greet looked right past her as if she were a ghost.

Aster had no appetite for the cakes and tea, even though Servus did manage to bring her the purple cake. She crumbled it apart on her plate and lined the crumbs up like army soldiers marching to the edge of the platter. Even Servus didn't speak to her during supper, and she started to feel a little crummy. She felt her sister's arm around her shoulder.

"It's ok, Aster. I trust your plan. We'll get out of here, find the thread for the Kapre, find the sylphs and get back home. You and I will both be Hooyips this time. I'll make sure everything turns out fine."

Sometimes her sister knew exactly the right things to say to make her feel safe. Aster pushed some of the cake crumbs over the edge of her plate, and then she heard the panic and mutterings of the duendes. The duendes around her yelled warnings and pointed to the sky. A shadow blanketed the table. A second shadow covered Aster and her sister. She looked skyward and grabbed her sister's hand. Her stomach tumbled and her throat fell silent because she was too afraid to scream.

Chapter 10
Aster's Hypothesis

Periwinkle felt her little sister's fingers dig into her hand as the duendes gathered in a clearing. She felt the temperature rise. Then the heat made it difficult to breathe. The shadows of two beasts eclipsed the clouds as they hovered above the village, and their black wings made them look like ocean rays gathered in foul synchronicity across the sky.

Wisps of flame and cinder clung to the creatures. The flames fettered about their hands and chests like ivy. The creatures were difficult for Winkle to comprehend; neither had legs nor any lower half in view, and shredded skin dangled from their torsos as if they ripped themselves apart at the waist.

A small duende tugged at Periwinkle's shirt and pointed to the center of the village.

"It's Armiger!" Aster said. "This is Servus's little brother. We're friends."

Armiger pulled at Winkle's shirt. "What, ok, yes," Periwinkle said. She followed Armiger through the crowd. The duendes assembled in a clump, and Armiger tried to push their way beyond the edges of the group, but he was too weak and too little to make any progress.

A hand broke through the crowd and grabbed hold of

Periwinkle and the smaller duende.

"Don't let them go," Servus said from within the assemblage of duendes. With his help, Armiger, Periwinkle, and Aster joined the crowd and forced their way toward to the center.

"This is good," Servus said. "Not in the center, and not at the edges. The center and the edges are the most dangerous spots with the manananggals."

Manananggal? Periwinkle looked again at the creatures. These were two of the same monsters that destroyed Hooyip's home, but there should be a third. The two figures were scrapes of crimson and smoke above them, and they descended toward the crowd.

Periwinkle saw other duendes head inside their homes. "Shouldn't we go inside?" she asked.

"No, it's not allowed," Servus said, trying to cover Armiger from the manananggals above. "This is how we survive. Sometimes enemies learn how to find us. The principal members of society must hide, and in this way, persist. Those of us who have not met the requirements of society stay outside to protect their legacy. Once the attackers take what they want, they will move on."

The heat wafted over Periwinkle and her sister as the duendes at the edges of the group burned. The manananggals carried duendes from the edges into the sky, then away from the village.

"Why aren't they fighting back?" Aster asked. "There are more of us!"

"No," Servus said. "It is our job to keep our enemies here. If we fight back, then they might try to attack those who hide in the houses. When they have their fill, they will leave."

Periwinkle huddled over top of Aster. She heard buffets of air above her. The manananggals shrieked as they carried away more of the duendes.

"They've gone. We should look for her now," Servus said. "While the principals are hiding and there's still confusion."

Periwinkle rubbed her eyes. Her hands shook. Servus was right. She remembered what Hooyip told her about being brave. Bravery meant focusing on what needs to be done and then trying to do it. She needed to protect her sister, and she needed to find Hooyip. If they were to ever make it to the Vine, she had to triage her fear until the end of the journey.

"Remember that, Periwinkle," she whispered to herself. "Put your world in order."

"The lambs," Servus whispered to Periwinkle. "Look for the lambs."

"There aren't any lambs!" Aster said.

Periwinkle looked through the village. She saw duendes trying to take care of the injured. She smelled smoke from fire smolder atop the young bushes in the field. "We have to find the lambs?" She hasn't seen a single one since their arrival. Armiger grabbed the sides of her head and turned her toward an untouched copse of scrubby trees. The trees did not grow as high as those in the deeper forest. Why had she missed them before?

Armiger pointed. "The lambs," he mouthed in a near silent voice. "There the lambs."

She saw them appear beneath the trees. Perhaps the lambs had been there always.

"Ahh, I see!" Aster said. "We've never looked for them before, so we never found them before."

Servus nodded and pointed. One of the lambs started to graze. "They eat the grass, but they also eat the pine seeds that fall from those trees. We need to take three seeds that they find appetizing, but we need them before they are eaten. The seeds left on the ground are too old. The seeds in the trees are too young. We need the ones aged to their liking, the newly fallen. Those will open the way down."

A lamb rummaged on the ground.

"See. There. It just ate one. We need three before there are no more for the day. If there are none suitable, then we cannot enter."

Periwinkle understood why the duendes didn't need guards or weapons to defend their most sacred treasure. They watched the lambs, then Servus darted toward the lamb that continued to graze, but the other lambs head-butted him down as he tried to grab for the seeds. Aster tried to follow him, but a lamb knocked her over as well, and she tumbled away from the lambs and their seeds.

Aster stood back up and kicked the ground. "This is difficult."

Periwinkle waited. She saw Servus try again. This time, when the lamb knocked him over, Servus raked his spidery fingers across the ground to scatter the seeds away from the lamb's mouth, so at least they were not eaten.

Aster and Armiger tried to go in together, but both ended up on their backsides because of the ferocious head-butts from the lambs. Periwinkle closed her eyes and tried to listen for the Berberoka, but she heard nothing. "Still sleeping," she sighed.

Periwinkle looked but did not even see the seeds that the lambs tried to eat. Servus and Armiger must have better eyes than her and her sister. Aster had always been athletic—even more so now because of the time they spent with Hooyip, so Aster committed to a plan of instinct and speed. Servus was the biggest; Periwinkle decided to follow him.

Periwinkle waited for Servus to try again, and she sped behind him. Three of the lambs knocked him away, but they did not see her following the duende. She looked on the ground—cream-colored cylindrical seeds. Winkle seized two of the seeds away from a lamb's finger-like lips and gripped them in her fist as the other lambs trampled her.

She crawled away from the animals and opened her hand.

"Ewww," Aster said. "Your hand's covered in spit." Aster stared at her and repeated again. "Ewwww, you're covered in spit. Get it Periwinkle? Ewwww, and they can be Ewwwwes."

Periwinkle smiled. "But I only have two, and Servus said we need three."

Armiger kneeled beside them and smiled. Then he opened his hand to show one more seed.

"Good then," Servus said. "Give them to Armiger and he'll open the way down to the pillar. Hooyip will be there."

Armiger took the three seeds, moved away from the lambs, and kneeled on the ground. He bent close to the ground, cupped his hands around the corners of his mouth, and spoke a strange word, "Aawaa."

He spoke the same word again to each of the seeds "Aawaa, aawaa, aawaa." Armiger stood next to Periwinkle and smiled, then he pulverized the three seeds on the ground and said it one last time "Aawaa."

Periwinkle almost expected the seeds to burst or explode like the paper and powder Fourth of July bang-snaps that kids throw at each other's shoes. Instead, the ground stretched apart into pastels and opened a kaleidoscopic chasm of pinks and teals, lemons, and beiges. The seeds continued to stretch the ground, and the subdued colors raced through the gashed soil.

"The only way is down," Servus said. "Please hurry. Few things have color in our world. The others will notice this."

Periwinkle entered the slope. The residue from the myriad of pastel colors tingled across her skin when she entered the opening. She kept her sister close to her side.

They descended, and she saw the passage behind them slurp itself closed. The ground had a strange epidermal feel, and Winkle's shoes sloshed on its surface. The further they walked, the colder the temperature dropped until her sister's breath coalesced into fog with every outward huff. The ground felt more solid as well, the more they trekked from the opening.

Servus watched behind them, as if expecting someone to follow. "We need to hurry. If any of the others find out you've entered, then they will never let you leave."

"Why are you helping us?" Aster asked.

"The duendes live long lives compared to humans, and I have never met a human with a sartor's band. It's almost inexplicable that any human could even see the threads and arrays that join this world together."

Aster's entire body shrugged. "I'm not that special."

"Then the real answer, I think, is that I've known myself too much, and I've experienced everything the world can offer."

"That doesn't make any sense."

Periwinkle squeezed her sister's hand. Servus wasn't such a bad guy. She knew what he meant, even though she didn't think she could explain it to Aster. Sometimes what someone is expected to become just isn't enough; they tire of who they are.

When they turned the corner, Periwinkle saw the structure that gave purpose to the duendes and directed their society.

The Consequential Pillar towered above an endless darkness. The sound it made reverberated in Winkle's chest. Its apex skirted the ceiling just as the duendes described. Its surface was that of a pore-less obelisk, and it spun like a gray barber's pole or a perpetual mill that ground meal into dust.

Periwinkle heard something yawn from within her, and

she felt dampness and cold stream through her arms and into her wrists, which froze her fingers. She felt the Berberoka open her thoughts. "So, this is the one that broke away. Her size is what I imagined, but seeing her up close is even more fantastic."

"You talk about the pillar like it's alive," thought Periwinkle.

"Oh, she is alive, and if you were to follow her down to her origins, I do not think that you would be happy. I'm sure even I could not hold you together if you tried such a thing."

Servus pointed. "Your friend will be by the bridge."

The decline toward the bridge remained empty, but Periwinkle saw duendes walking to and from the pillar. They labored to pull the silvery thread from the obelisk and harvested the material by force. Every heave and yank moved the pillar through a herniated turn to yield more thread to the duendes.

It looks like taking more than collecting. "Is she in pain?"

The Berberoka stirred inside of her. "Yes, she is in pain, but she is also free. Maybe she could bring about her comfort on her own, maybe she could leave this place on her own, but doing so means returning that freedom and falling back to the kingdom in the Abyss."

The thoughts of the Berberoka and the spectacle of the duendes made Periwinkle uneasy. Was this the only way to cross the chasm and find their way home?

They stopped at the end of the slope. "I see her," Aster said.

"Yeah, Aster. I see her too."

Hooyip stood in front of the duendes and stood closest to the pillar. Shackles locked to metal anchors in the bridge held Hooyip, where the alakdan took part in the arduous cultivation. Periwinkle saw Servus's hands tremble, and

Armiger patted his shoulder to try to calm the older sibling.

"Are you ok?" Aster asked.

Armiger looked up at his brother.

"I'll be fine," Servus said. "That bridge into the void is where they send the duendes to join the Circumstantial Pillar after failing their last attempt with the recital."

"Come with us," Periwinkle said. "Help us free our friend, then leave with us. It isn't right what's happening here. Aster told me all about it. Go with us."

Armiger pulled on his brother's sleeve and nodded.

"Yes. Flee with us," Aster repeated. "We're on such a heroic adventure! We're helping Hooyip avenge her people and we're going to save the entire world. We're going to do great things."

"Well, maybe we can find the sartors together, little one. Perhaps they can teach my little brother some of their magic. Maybe even I can learn some of it, too."

Aster nodded.

"If we free her, how do we leave?" Periwinkle asked. "The way is closed."

Servus smiled at Winkle with his most professional smile. "The way out differs from the way in, and like all that has to do with my people, the exit will open if you look for it. But you do have to arrive at that conclusion on your own."

Armiger pointed to a cluster of barrels and a tool rack opposite the pillar.

"Yes, the key," Servus said. "We'll keep this simple. My brother and I will talk to those working. You'll have to move fast. The key to your friend's shackles should be on the rack."

Winkle and her sister watched as Servus and Armiger approached the duendes working by the pillar. Just as he said, Servus started up a conversation with the duendes who kept watch over Hooyip. Winkle pulled on Aster's hand, and they crept beside the wall toward the rack. It was similar to what Hooyip had taught them; keep a structure to one side of your body—it could be a tree, a wall, or anything to keep part of yourself covered, and then follow the shadows. Even though moving the distance took seconds, it felt as if the journey to the rack lasted hours. They crouched behind the barrels, and Aster reached for the keys which hung from a knob on the tool rack.

Periwinkle shook her head and grabbed her sister's hand. One of the duendes arrived and dipped a wooden ladle into a barrel. Water sloshed over its sides onto Winkle and her sister, and Winkle eased her hand over her sister's mouth, who was about to speak. They waited for the duende to finish his drink and prayed that he didn't look over the barrel. Winkle saw pebbles skid across the rock floor and heard another set of footprints shuffle to the barrels.

She heard the water plop as the duende returned the ladle. "Ok, ok, Armiger. I'll take a look," said the duende by the barrel, who then walked away.

Periwinkle snatched the keys. "Once she's out, I think we're going to have to run," she whispered to Aster.

Six duendes who worked to gather the thread spoke with Servus and his brother as Hooyip continued to force the thread from the pillar. Periwinkle didn't know how long Servus could keep them occupied.

Winkle's back and arms felt cold. "I know you prefer plans and subtlety, but sometimes, brute force is the answer," whispered the Berberoka. "Do not worry. If anyone touches you, I will keep you safe."

Periwinkle opened her thoughts. "I'm worried about my sister."

"Indeed, yes. She is little after all."

"We have to try it now," Aster whispered.

Periwinkle took a deep breath and inched to the side of

the barrel. She darted toward Hooyip and the edge of the bridge. A lock looped the chains into a hook that was embedded into the wall. The duendes saw her.

"Hurry up Winkle!" Aster Screamed.

Periwinkle saw Servus and Armiger tussle with the group to keep the other duendes away, but one of the duendes crashed into a water barrel. Aster tried to move, but the barrel knocked her aside. She careened toward the void at the end of the bridge.

Periwinkle dove.

"Aster!" The keys flew from Winkle's hand down into the dark as she grabbed the backpack strapped to her sister. Aster's legs dangled over the edge of the pit, and Hooyip held onto Winkle when she started to slide into the abyss.

"Hello you two," Hooyip said. "I think we should really find a way to leave right now."

Periwinkle frowned as Hooyip helped pull them back to the bridge. "The keys…"

"I saw."

The other duendes held Servus and Armiger to the ground. "This is a shame for you and your brother, Servus," said one of the workers. "I think at this point all of you will be joined to the Consequential Pillar."

"Hey," Hooyip said. "I won't blame you if you run. Maybe this is how—"

"No, not now. We can't leave you, Hooyip." Winkle grabbed the crowbar from her belt that she scavenged from one of the fiery portals in the forest. She tried to pry apart the chains. Links in the chain started to bend, but the crowbar snapped back in her hands, twisted her wrists, and then flew into the pit. Periwinkle grabbed and shook the chains that bound the alakdan. "Do something, you stupid spirit!" she yelled.

Water from the overturned barrel collected in Winkle's

palms.

"Yes," the Berberoka whispered.

The liquid coated the links of metal and squirmed into the keyhole of the lock. Water continued to force its way into the lock until the metal burst apart. The shackles remained around Hooyip's ankles, but the chains pulled free of the hook.

Hooyip darted to her feet, then sped into the crowd of duendes, knocking them aside to free Servus and Armiger. Hooyip and Servus pummeled the duendes against the wall and against the barrels of water. "We still need the rope for the Kapre!" Hooyip called.

Periwinkle saw strands of rope dangle from the pillar and trail into the abyss. She stepped to the edge of the bridge. It was there, she thought. She only needed to reach out for it. She pressed up on her toes and strained to touch the threads and felt them brush against her fingers. Periwinkle looked down, and the room spun. She moved one foot over the edge.

"What are you doing?" Aster yelled. "You'll fall in! Stop it, Winkle."

Armiger yanked Periwinkle from the brink of the bridge, and then the small duende shoved a length of the silvery rope into Aster's backpack.

"They have it," Winkle called to Hooyip and Servus. Her heart raced, and she felt Aster grab for her hand.

Periwinkle squeezed Aster's hand, and the entire group ran to the slope that headed toward the entryway. When they turned the corner, the familiar array of pastels split apart the doorway. On the other side, they saw a pantomime of shapes as duendes readied themselves to enter the room that housed the Consequential Pillar.

"Well, what now?" Hooyip asked.

Periwinkle thought about what Servus had told her. The

way out is different than the way in. She just had to remember to look for it. "Oh my gosh!" Periwinkle said.

She walked to the wall and put her hand against the dirt covered stone. "We can leave whenever we want."

Periwinkle heard the duendes from behind them running up the slope. She saw the duendes from above step through the portal. "It's like you said, Servus."

The colorful door of lemons and beiges, and pinks and teals opened in front of her, and she stepped through, pulling her sister with her.

When they left the underground cavern and stepped outside, it was as if the entire village stood and waited for their arrival. "Oh," Aster said. "I guess we were too loud."

Heus, the duende from days ago who first greeted them when they found the village, stepped forward. "Ohl whoal whoal whoal whoal whoal. Let's all slow down and stop."

Salve, the female duende who always seemed to accompany him, walked toward the group as well. She rubbed her hands on her dress and shook her head.

"We cannot let them leave," Salve said. "This happens once in a while. Very rare. Very rare, but sometimes this happens."

"I don't think we should give up," Servus whispered. "At best they'll chain us all in front of the pillar and put us to work gathering its thread. More likely it'll be worse."

Periwinkle stepped in front of her sister.

"We can run," Servus said. "We'll keep walking, and then we'll run when they come after us."

Periwinkle looked at her sister. Aster's eyes widened and her hands felt clammy. It took a lot to intimidate her—even if she was young, but the group of spidery armed, pot-bellied duendes in their colorful hats no longer looked like jovial mascots from a theme park. The group of duendes continued to gather around them.

Servus nudged Winkle forward, and they walked to where the crowd looked thinnest.

"Servus!" Heus said. "I am shocked. Your final recital day is coming soon." Heus removed his yellow hat. "This was your chance to become a principal of society. Think of your brother. What chances will he have, with his condition and all? I told you. You have a chance to be a part of something great."

"Well," Servus said, smiling. "Once I see these little visitors safely out of the village, I'll perform the recital. I'll even offer to recite the history of the pillar early if you like—or even backwards. How did it go? I remember last time they said I was vague. Before that too specific, but I've been working on the delivery this time. No vagueness at all, my man."

Servus pushed the girls forward and started reciting the long history of the duendes and the Consequential Pillar.

"Oh that won't do," Heus said. "Just hold them for us and turn them around right now."

"There's too many of them for me to fight," Hooyip said. "And they took my sword. I think I can outrun them, but I won't leave you."

"Well, this is quite a predicament," thought the Berberoka. "I have a trick or two, but I am so tired from that last bit with the lock. This won't be good for me—or for you at this point, my young accomplice."

Periwinkle's hand hurt from Aster's grip on her fingers.

"I have a hypothesis," Aster said. "It's like when we first found them. Remember, Periwinkle. They don't have to be here."

Heus and Salve led the crowd of duendes toward them.

"We can make it," Servus said. "Go. Now!"

They ran and did their best to avoid the duendes. Servus, Armiger, and Hooyip tried to push a path through the legion of scattered duendes for Winkle and her sister.

"Remember, Periwinkle, pretend we're just old men in the forest looking for old men things. They'll disappear."

Periwinkle tried. She saw Heus clench Servus's arm, and Armiger pry at Heus's fingers. She felt another duende pull at her waist, but she stopped believing the duendes chased after her. She stopped believing Heus and Salve followed from behind. Little by little the duendes in front of her disappeared and popped out of the path toward the forest. She heard the rustle of the chase. She felt the heat from surrounding and approaching bodies, but she continued to run and kept Aster in front of her—neither one looking back until they felt safe in the faraway forest where she saw a rock in a faded hand strike Servus in his temple.

"We made it!" Aster said. "I told you that place wasn't for you." Aster spun around, but Hooyip caught her and turned her head forward.

The alakdan gave Periwinkle a quick look and shook her head. "Hey Aster," Hooyip said. "Let's keep going. Servus told me he and his brother will find us in the forest. He said they'll be there waiting when we look for him."

"I ammm looking for him," Aster said. "I made sure I was always looking for him."

Periwinkle took her sister's hand. "Come on Aster, I'm sure he'll be up ahead."

The three walked deeper into the gray woods. When the silence grew too heavy for Aster, she pulled Periwinkle's arm around her shoulder and chest and buried her head into her sister's side as they walked.

"Hey Periwinkle, remember when dad painted the floor in our den? He made the concrete look like the stars and the clouds."

Periwinkle looked at the imprints of her sister's shoes beside her own. They were half the size of hers. "Yeah, it was all gray and white and more gray. I always thought it looked like stones. The bumps in the concrete made it look real even though it was just paint."

Aster rubbed her eyes on Periwinkle's sleeve. "Maybe you're right."

"He only used two colors of paint, but the floor must have had seven or eight different hues and they piled on each other, you know."

"I remember how long it took him," Aster said. "Was dad an artist? Sometimes it's hard to remember him. Was painting the floor some kind of art?"

"No, but it was really fun. I remember how he let me help even though I couldn't get the colors or the blending right," Periwinkle said. "I kept trying to make everything symmetrical, but that wasn't what was needed. Dad kind of made it work anyway."

"I remember," Aster said. "There was this part where the heel of his shoe left a mark in the paint. It was by the bookshelf. Sometimes he tried to cover it up with the shelves, but it never looked right. At the end, he left it alone."

"I remember."

They walked without any more conversation and let the silence consume their thoughts.

Aster pursed her lips. Her little eyebrows furrowed, and she shook her head. "It wasn't his shoe. It was one of his night slippers—the pair I picked out for him for Christmas. The indent. It was my favorite part."

Periwinkle felt useless. She wanted her sister to feel happy and safe, but she never knew how to make that happen. She pulled her sister against her as they walked.

"Aster, it'll be your birthday soon."

Chapter 11
Ten-Years-Old

"What day do you think it'd be?" Aster asked.

"I don't know for sure what day it is, but I think it must be December or January by now."

Periwinkle watched her sister try to count out the months and the days. Aster smiled.

They only talked about the village of the duendes when necessary, like when they needed to check if they still had the rope, or the one time when they smelled rotten food and tracked it down to a half-eaten snail in Aster's backpack and Hooyip wondered where Aster found it.

Periwinkle tried to categorize the trees as they walked to keep her mind busy. Few animals lived in this forest, and she wondered if that was normal for the Ember Lands. She felt safe with Hooyip, and she tried to learn what she could from the alakdan. Would she even recognize the Vine when they found it, and did the duendes know even they would be gifted as food for the manananggals, if the manananggals found the Abyssal Vine first?

"I guess I would be their gift, too," Periwinkle mumbled.

Aster ran to the brown stone road. The edges of the stones cracked and crumbled, and Aster wobbled when she jumped from stone to stone to avoid the moss that grew in the cracks. "We're almost there," she said. "We'll be able to cross that bridge soon. I remember how wide it was. You know. Do you think it got even wider? I bet it's wider than our state."

"Quiet, Aster," Periwinkle whispered. "Remember last time. He is pretty dangerous. What if he forgot about us?"

Aster wiggled the backpack on her back. "Oh, I guess you're right. Maybe Hooyip can just force him to fix the bridge."

Hooyip laughed. "I don't have my sword, you goof! Even with my sword, I don't think I could do much to him."

Periwinkle saw the Kapre's tree alongside the chasm. Its gnarled form still had a bit of the silver rope tied around its trunk. "I'm not sure if what we brought will be enough."

Hooyip nodded. "How is he even supposed to reach the other end? Although, he is a forest spirit, I guess. Just like you're a water spirit."

Water spirit? Is that what she was? Periwinkle looked at her hands. She rubbed her eyes and her head. How much will she change if she spends too much time here? Hooyip didn't seem to think it was so strange for people to use magic.

"Maybe I should go first," Hooyip said. She put her hand against the bark of the tree, and then knocked on its surface. Some of the bark fell from the trunk.

Aster mimicked Hooyip and tapped the tree. "Nothing? Maybe he doesn't know we're here."

"Hello," Hooyip called and knocked again.

They heard a long, drawn-out groan from the top of the tree. "Go away. I don't want to talk to anyone anymore."

Periwinkle cupped her hands around her mouth and called to the top of the tree. "We've brought the silver thread from the duendes. You said you would let us go across the bridge if we could get the thread."

"Oohhhhhhhhhh, just go away. That was a long time ago. I don't want to see anyone anymore. Come back in 100 years. Maybe I'll feel better by then."

"Hey!" Hooyip called. "We don't have 100 years. By then, the Ember Lands could be destroyed with all those beasts and monsters searching for the Abyssal Vine. I know you know what I'm talking about."

"Well, I'll be fine in 100 years. My trees will grow back by then. Everyone destroys everything anyway. I said, just go away!"

Aster picked up a rock and threw it at the top of the tree. It made it about as high as the second branch, which really wasn't that high, and it didn't quite hit the tree at all. "You said you'd help us. That's not nice to lie! We have your thread! You better help us! We have to save the world! I don't know why you'd say you'd help us if you were just going to lie. You're wasting our time, and when we save the world, we're also saving you, so you need to stop hiding up—"

Periwinkle put her hand on her sister's shoulder to try and calm her.

"Oohhhhhhhh fine then. See what has become of me— this great and wonderful Kapre."

A red light sparked from the top of the tree that trailed smoke upward as the red light seemed to float downwards. The giant Kapre materialized bit by bit. First his legs, then his belly, then his chest and arms, and at last his head and his gray and crackling cigar. The Kapre did not climb so much as pour himself out of the tree, and he slid between the branches like a dejected child. He dropped from the tree and landed on his backside, then remained on the ground with his back against the tree. His arms flopped to the ground, and the cigar continued to burn in his mouth. "Whoa is me," the Kapre said.

"What has happened to you, Kapre of the forest?" Hooyip asked.

"Can't you see? Are you tiny people so thick? They cut branches from my tree and its sister tree. OHHHHH They were horrible!"

"The Oni. Three of them. Horned headed, snaggletooth monstrosities. Looking for that Abyssal Vine. I was going to help them pass the chasm because they were big. Ohhh, not as big or as strong as me, but they were bigger than you, so I thought from one big person to another, I would help them. Then they took branches from my trees and tried to disappear. They said they needed it for food! Food! They violated my home and my purpose as a watcher of this bridge and a caretaker of these trees."

"Where are they now?" Periwinkle asked.

"I threw them over the side. Down, down, down, into the chasm where they belong. Where their bones could shatter on the rocks. The land will overtake them so the smallest denizens of the Ember Lands can gnaw on their flesh and on their organs and muscles until it becomes unrecognizable meat. The measly creatures that live underfoot and the rot and the mold will process the Oni in their bowels and excrete the idea of what used to be those who broke my branches. They will move through gut and into the soil and the dirt and the muck and the mud so my trees can find them again. This time as food. My trees will absorb everything left that was known as those Oni into itself and fix what they stole, and I shall live and sleep inside what used to be Oni."

Periwinkle winced.

"That's—" Aster muttered.

"—But we have the threads," Hooyip said. "We can help return your purpose."

The Kapre slouched. "No, no no. Not until my trees

regrow can my purpose be fixed. By my own generosity, I turned traitor to myself, and now I am ruined until the gifts of horticulture returns to my trees, these miraculous babies that house the Kapre." The Kapre's head remained still. His chin rested against his chest as the cigar burned away and its embers lit the dark.

"We could tie them," Aster said.

"No, he's being ridiculous," Periwinkle said. "Think what will happen if we fix your bridge. If we fix your bridge, then you will once again have it to guard, and you can return to being the monster that throws anyone over the side who tries to cross it. You can go back to being normal again."

"What, what?" The Kapre's left eye looked up.

"Don't you see? Once your bridge is repaired, your reason for being here returns."

"Thinking," the Kapre replied. The corners of his mouth drooped, and he slumped forward.

"Aster, please show him the thread so we can figure out if it's sufficient."

"Of course it's sufficient you twits, you numbskulls, you know nothings. What are you thick? It just needs to not be broken. Can't you see the rest of the thread is bro-ken. As long as it isn't broken then, IT. IS. SUFFICIENT."

Aster pulled the silvery material from her backpack and held it in front of the Kapre. "Suuuficient."

"Eh?" The Kapre touched the thread and ran it through his fingers. He snatched it from Aster. "That's the stuff." He closed one eye and held it close to the other, checking for quality and imperfections. "Eh then. Maybe, eh. Smallest one, go stand by the edge. I need perspective."

"No. She will not," Periwinkle said and directed Aster away from the Kapre before walking close to the edge of the chasm. "And don't you dare throw her over the side."

"Ehh, what would I do that for? There's no bridge yet."

The Kapre looked at Periwinkle and squinted. He held out his arm as if measuring the chasm and Periwinkle. "Ahhhhhh. It won't work!" He threw the rope to the ground, then slumped back down on his belly, lying with his face in the soil. "I have no purpose. All of it is… Whoa is me."

"Oh, I am tired of this!" Hooyip said, trying to roll the Kapre over. "I'll make you get up and fix this bridge if I have to."

"You can't lift me. I'm big."

Hooyip turned around and pushed at the Kapre with her back.

The Kapre flailed his arms in the dirt. "Look, you small brain, small head, know-nothings. The other end of the bridge is really far. Really, really, far. I would need a tailor, a sartor, to help me catch the thread. This is a TWO-sartor job. I warp but the other sartor needs to catch the threads so I can weft it together."

"I don't understand," Hooyip said. "Is it because your arms aren't long enough? Maybe we can find someone else who can sew so they could hel—"

"A tailor! T-AAY-LO-R! Someone who can see the threads of the threads. The filaments of everything. No one understands me!" The Kapre rolled his head to the side and wheezed out a grunt.

"I can see the threads," Aster said.

"Noooo," the Kapre said. "Yes, I dropped the thread on the ground. But the real threads. My threads. Your threads. The real ones."

"I can see them right now. Yours change color from blue to dark, dark brown. Is it because you're upset? The silver threads aren't silver at all. They're white like bone, and they connect to everything. Is it because it was removed? I bet it looked different before they took it from the pillar."

"Eh?"

Periwinkle stared at her little sister. "He's talking about something I can't see. Isn't he Aster?"

"I think so. It's like all of us, all of everything is just made up of these thin little threads that stretch and weave into one another. I can't see all of them, but if I try, I can see some of them."

"Hmmm," the Kapre said, sitting up. "Have you had training? Maybe we can fix the bridge? Who was your teacher?"

Periwinkle saw Aster open her mouth to reply, then she choked up before any words came out. It was not often she's ever seen her little sister cry. If she had to be honest with herself, she always thought Aster was stronger than her, even if Aster was only nine. "It's ok Aster. It sounds like you know what he's talking about. Do you think you can help him?"

Aster nodded.

"If my sister says she can help you, then she can help you. Please fix the bridge for us."

The Kapre crawled over to the girls. His face was larger than a tree stump. "How much can you do? Can you try to untangle some of them?"

Aster shook her head no and rubbed her eyes. "If you teach me what you want me to do, then I'll learn it."

"Ahh oohh, then this might be fun. A student. Ain't had one of those in ages. Since before the last and other last Abyssal Vine appeared. Since before that. This will be fun."

The Kapre ran to a tree catty corner from his own and patted the trunk. The branches spread open. He pointed to Periwinkle and then to Hooyip. "You two can live here." He patted the tree next to it, and again the branches spread apart. Then he pointed to Aster. "You, my student, will live here."

"But I want to stay with my sister and Hooyip," Aster said.

"Right then. You can live there also."

"We're going to live in trees?" Periwinkle asked.

"Yes. I need to show her how to help fix the bridge. She'll have to practice because right now she isn't smart. If she learns to become smart, then it will take less than a year. If not, then it will take longer. My last student took longer. He was an old, old person by then, but he learned."

"We don't have years," Hooyip said.

"Then we better get started," the Kapre said.

That night, they started their first lesson, and Periwinkle watched as the Kapre produced a small metronome. The Kapre explained he made it from someone's old broken battleax who he once threw into the chasm, but he said that the person's weapon swung with good timing. He then revealed thread woven from the grass in the forest and placed it all in front of Aster. He explained the items will be her tools and with practice, she will learn to work with the silver thread they found in the duendes' village.

Periwinkle climbed into the tree to explore the living conditions for the next, however long it would take her sister to learn the new craft. She heard a crackling sound from a nearby tree and tried to peer through the branches to see what made the noise and saw a cat sized creature with a black and brown striped tail. The cat made the crackling sound with its first few footsteps before it rested on the branch. Then Periwinkle, too, rested on her stomach and dangled her arms from the tree branches just like the creature and looked down at her sister. She imagined it must be how cats feel when they survey their kingdom beneath them.

The cat visited each day and always remained out of reach, but Periwinkle did not think anyone else noticed. "O cat," she told it upon every meeting. "How goes your hunt? Are you ready to watch the next lesson?"

She imagined this was what it was like to have a pet—just without having to clean up its mess.

While her sister worked with the Kapre, Periwinkle tried more and more to understand the Berberoka that resided inside her, but sometimes even small expenditures of power placed it into a slumber, and she still didn't understand what the Berberoka meant by finding her warm.

"Are you there, Berberoka?" Periwinkle asked. Periwinkle waited. It was as if a door inside her opened. Her arms felt cold. "What are you exactly?"

Periwinkle felt like she was being watched.

"Ok then, where do you come from?"

The cold spread to Winkle's back and then her neck, and in her mind, she saw a shadow move toward her. The tips of Periwinkle's fingers chittered together.

"Will you answer any of my questions?" Winkle asked.

"Yes."

"Well, what questions will you answer? How did you find me? How long have you been here? Are you an angel or a demon? Do you have a name?"

"Stay—I think my name is, Stay." The voice felt familial this time. "Please, Periwinkle. Do not make me leave. In time, we might grow closer, but you promised me freedom. For that gift, I will continue to help you."

Hooyip called to Periwinkle from the forest. "Come on Winkle. Those nasty little duendes took my sword, and I need a new weapon. Maybe we can find something in the forest."

They searched the nearby woods. "We should avoid using wood for anything," Periwinkle said, thinking about the Kapre.

Hooyip laughed. "He'd throw us over the side." She

stopped and held up a large rock. "Well, I guess. Maybe. Do you know how to turn this thing into a dagger or a knife?"

Periwinkle stared at it. "I've read about this, but I'm not sure it'll work." She placed the large rock on the ground and used a smaller rock as a chisel to flake the large rock into pieces. She sifted through some of the misshapen bits. "Not quite like what I've read."

Some of the random pieces of broken rock had sharp edges and points, but they looked like nothing suitable for a weapon on their own.

"Oh, I have an idea." Periwinkle collected the broken rocks. "But you'll have to do most of the work."

They spent the next two days tracking small game in the woods, and they looked for something at least the size of a boar. Before, most of their food came from the river, but Hooyip was skilled at tracking other animals in the forest as well.

The next day, a thunderstorm struck.

Hooyip didn't want to waste time. "Your sister really is something special. I can't tell what it is they're doing, but I've never seen a Kapre so excited. She must be picking up everything he teaches her."

"My sister is like that," Periwinkle said. "As long as she can concentrate, she'll figure things out. Learning anything comes easy to her." Periwinkle turned around. She shuddered when a bolt of lightning crackled nearby, and she almost lost her balance.

They both smelled it. Some creature must have been struck by the bolt, and they caught its scent when it burned in the rain. They crept closer to the flame created by the lightning, and they saw another creature rummaging around the fires.

"Oh," Periwinkle said. "Don't hurt it." Next to the fire, the cat-like creature that watched Aster learn her new craft, pawed at the fire. It saw the two girls, then darted off into the woods.

Hooyip grinned. "We couldn't hurt it if we wanted to."

They found the creature that was struck by the bolt of lightning, and they rolled it in the dirt to put out the fire. Its flesh burned off and crumbled into ash.

"This will work." Periwinkle said. "We can use the bones as handles. I've read about it before."

Hooyip scavenged the bones and fabricated three small handles from the burned creature's remains. Combined with the shards of rocks that Periwinkle flaked apart, they had tools suitable for cutting and jabbing.

"One for you, one for me, and one for your sister," Hooyip said. "Not as strong as my old sword, but it's what we have, and it's not made from the trees."

"Hey let's do one more thing." Periwinkle walked in circles. "Do you remember how to get back to the river? We need some water, but I wanted to find some shells or something. Anything we can polish."

Hooyip nodded, then led Periwinkle to the river before returning to the Kapre.

***

The Kapre's lessons, Periwinkle thought, looked a lot like weaving and dancing. One day, after a strenuous round of practice, Aster again asked what day it might be.

"Ok, you win," Periwinkle said. She fake pinched her sister's chubby cheeks. "Happy birthday, Aster."

"It's my birthday? Really? I'm ten years old?"

Periwinkle smiled. "You're getting so much bigger. Happy tenth birthday."

"Am I really getting bigger?"

Periwinkle lied and nodded.

"Ah'm gonna tell Hooyip and the Kapre!"

Periwinkle felt a little worried about what the Kapre might do at a birthday celebration, and once he found out that the day marked an important milestone for his student, he disappeared into the forest.

Hooyip taught the girls a song the alakdans used to celebrate the passage of time for their own people, and Aster and Periwinkle showed Hooyip how to play charades. It was then that Hooyip gave Aster the small dagger they made from bone and rock.

The Kapre returned almost two hours later. Periwinkle thought he might try to give Aster a cigar like the one with the endless embers that he kept in his mouth, but he produced something that resembled thin noodles with cooked eggs. He also offered the group a doughy and grainy red-bean cake, and out of sheer curiosity and politeness, they all finished the concoctions.

"For my student," the Kapre said. He held out both hands—one covering something that he held in the other. "You are much smarter and more capable than I thought. I did not believe you would pick up the skills of a sartor so well. I planned on being here a hundred years because you are too small to look capable or intelligent enough to learn the old magic." The Kapre slid his hand aside and held the metronome that they used for practice. "This will be yours to keep from now and forever."

Aster's cheeks turned red.

"I guess I have a present too," Periwinkle said. She pulled a string of polished shells from her pocket, each shell colored different shades of wispy grays, and she clasped it around her sister's neck.

Aster touched the smooth surface of the shells.

"Shells like the clouds," Periwinkle said.

Periwinkle stumbled backwards as Aster wrapped her arms around Winkle's sides. Aster squeezed until Periwinkle could hardly breathe, and she felt a little lightheaded. Under Hooyip's and the Kapre's tutelage, Aster really had developed some muscle in her little arms.

"This is the best birthday anyone could give me. Thank you, Periwinkle." Aster said, and she hugged each of her friends.

Not long after Aster's birthday party, the Kapre called everyone to a meeting by the destroyed bridge. "We are ready to make repairs," he announced.

Chapter 12
Warp and Weft

Aster and the Kapre stood at the edge of the chasm. Each positioned themselves beside one of the trees used as a post for the bridge. The Kapre held the silver thread in one hand and swayed his other in rhythm to some imagined beat. The thread wound itself around the bridge and then into the broken rope.

Periwinkle watched her sister purse her lips and concentrate. Aster matched the Kapre's movements and soon both the giant Kapre and little Aster swayed with identical and inherent timing. Each moment that the unbroken thread met with the broken ropes in the bridge, it melded itself together until it formed one sturdy strand.

Periwinkle could not discern what held the separate strands together or how they entwined. When the thread came to the edge of the rope where the bridge was severed, it meandered across the chasm with a snail-like momentum until it arrived at the other portion of the bridge. The process of joining and weaving continued for the rope, the Kapre, and Aster. Aster looked exhausted, and to Periwinkle, it almost looked like her sister resembled a flame the moment before it burned itself out. She wanted to stop them, but Aster showed no signs of quitting, so Periwinkle sat against a tree and watched and occasionally shouted encouragements to her little sister.

When the process ended, Aster wheezed and coughed, and Periwinkle saw blood run from Aster's nose

"Old magic, that was," whispered the Berberoka. "Dangerous stuff it is, too. Your sister can put broken things together just by seeing it in her head. Eventually, she can learn to take them apart. What will happen to her once she figures that part out?"

"She's made moving forward possible," Periwinkle whispered to the Berberoka. "The bridge. It looks like a spider web."

"Did you expect something else?" Stay whispered. "This is the bridge that spans the Broken World Chasm. It joins one part of the Ember Lands to the next. It can be a world in itself, and many of those who find their way to the bridge never find their way off."

"Have you ever been on this bridge?" Periwinkle thought.

"Maybe I have. I cannot remember if this is my first time in the Ember Lands. I know I've watched it and I've had my glimpses, but I have not explored it by myself. Some of my brethren might say that I have not even been successful entering the Ember Lands because of what I have done."

Periwinkle sighed.

"It's done," Hooyip said, helping Aster keep her balance. "We can finally cross."

"Eh what?" the Kapre said hastily. "I keep this bridge. I can't let you cross."

"But we helped fix the bridge," Hooyip said. "We were the ones who found the material, and we were the ones who brought you the material to make it a bridge again."

"But my purpose is to make sure people don't enter the bridge from this side and to throw people into the chasm."

"Well, what if you just let us through this one time?" Periwinkle asked.

"Ahhhh, that's no good. Someone might watch. There's always someone or something watching. If they just saw me letting you tiny things cross the bridge without a fight, I might lose my purpose again, so if you try to cross this bridge, I'll throw you into the chasm. Unless…"

"Unless you just pretend to attack us!" Aster said.

"Hey, not so loud, not so loud," the Kapre said.

"Well, yeah," Aster whispered. "We can pretend to come across the bridge. We'll start in the forest, and we'll try to cross, and you can pretend to chase us, but we'll safely make it onto the bridge because of the heroic efforts of Hooyip the adventurer!"

"Ehh, that is a plan." The Kapre sucked on his cigar and scratched his head. The smoke billowed over his face. "That is a very good plan. Maybe even the best plan we've had."

"I suppose it is a good plan," Periwinkle said.

"It is the best plan,' the Kapre said. "But you have to make sure you look afraid. You must look terrified. You should look like you're in horror at the thought of being smashed and thrown into the chasm where no one will ever remember who you were for all time." The Kapre thought for a bit, and then he turned to Aster. "You have to make me a promise, my student. Make me the promise."

"What am I promising?" Aster asked.

"Promise first. Then I shall tell you."

"That's a little silly, but I can promise."

Periwinkle wondered what it was with these spirits who always wanted people to make promises before letting them know what it was they promised.

"There's a monster that stalks that bridge. He is much worse than I'll ever be. He has the head of a powerful bull. If you're lucky, you'll see his foul countenance before he gets close. When you see the Minotaur of the Broken World Chasm, promise me you'll turn and run. No matter which way you think you're heading or which way you need to go. You have to run. He destroys anything that tries to cross the bridge. You are my student now and forever. I do not want destruction to happen to you."

"Ok, I promise," Aster said.

"You will turn and run. This is your promise as my student."

Aster furrowed her forehead.

"Let's start then," Hooyip said. "We'll go to the forest, and you chase us."

"Aiii, right," the Kapre said. "I've already started." The Kapre faded away into his tree until the last sight that remained was his faintly red cigar flame. "Start in the forest."

The girls moved into the forest like they were asked, and they fixated on the Kapre's tree and the entryway to the bridge.

"I guess he made a decent teacher after all," Hooyip said. The alakdan stepped out from the forest and they saw a blur of motion fly toward them, striking Hooyip in the chest. She flew backwards, deep into the woods. The Kapre stood smiling at the group and dusted off his hands.

"That wasn't the plan," Periwinkle said.

"Ehh, you were all moving too slow. You made it too easy to catch you."

"Can we try again, please?" Periwinkle asked.

They waited for Hooyip to return for a second chance, and again the Kapre disappeared.

"Fine," Hooyip said. "We'll show him what it means to move faster."

Periwinkle dug her shoes into the ground at the edge of the forest and waited for Hooyip's signal. Hooyip nodded, and all three dashed toward the entry to the bridge.

"Goodbye!" Aster yelled to the Kapre. "Thank you for—"

Periwinkle felt a rush of air, and Hooyip went flying a second time back to the forest. Then the Kapre's club whiffed across Winkle's nose.

"YOU WILL NOT ENTER MY BRIDGE!" the Kapre roared. "I WILL KILL YOU!"

Periwinkle and Aster stood shaking, and the Kapre smiled down at them. "I wouldn't hurt you, my little student. I'm just making sure it looks real!"

Hooyip returned, stomping on the ground. She kicked dirt onto the Kapre. "What are you doing?"

"I was doing like you asked!"

"Nooo," Aster said. "We are supposed to make it to the bridge."

"Ehh, maybe you can just stay here. I've never had a student as smart as you, and once you leave, it'll just be me again. You already have a home in the tree." The Kapre's cigar dimmed as he spoke. "I made it for you. We can keep learning the old magic. And more birthdays. Then there's the Minotaur. The great destroyer-bull is too dangerous."

"Well, we need to make it across!" Hooyip said. "That's where the sylphs are. That's where we need to go to learn about the Abyssal Vine! That's where we need—"

"Ok, ok, ok." The Kapre shouldered his club and disappeared. "Try it again."

"Are you ok, Hooyip?" Periwinkle asked.

"I'm fine. This time for sure!" Hooyip ran toward the bridge and again the Kapre sent her flying into the sky.

"Start from the forest!"

On the tenth try as Periwinkle and Aster followed Hooyip, who now limped toward the bridge, they heard a tremendous roar from behind them.

"Raaaaa, I'm gonna get all of you! Don't you cross my bridge!"

Periwinkle saw the Kapre moving his arms back and forth as if running, and he stomped his feet up and down, but ultimately, with all his work, he remained in place.

"Here I come," the Kapre yelled. "I'm gonna to eat all your bones! Raaaa!"

The three hobbled their way to the bridge.

"You are terrified because I will get you. TEAR-I-FIIIIIDDDDEEEE!"

"Are you kidding?" Hooyip asked.

Periwinkle let loose an "Eep!"

"Oh no!" Periwinkle said quickly. "He's after us. It is terrifying."

"I'm gonna pee my pants!" Aster yelled.

"Right right! Raawwrr. ALL of you are afraid because I will get you!" The Kapre jumped behind them and the ground shook. He continued to pump his arms and legs while remaining in place.

"Oh, come on!" Hooyip said.

Periwinkle jabbed her elbow into Hooyip's side.

"Aiiieeee! A great and terrifying Kapre is behind us!" Hooyip said.

"Ohh you are all too fast for me!" the Kapre yelled in response and swung his club over Winkle's head.

The three passed the Kapre's tree and hobbled onto the bridge that Aster and the Kapre repaired. It held their weight without any problems, and they continued to walk until the red ember from the tree faded from view.

Chapter 13
Bridges

The silver rope bridge swayed over the Broken World Chasm. Once on the bridge, Periwinkle realized it connected to a convoluted maze of bridges that spanned from one edge of the chasm to the other, and the path in front of her reached so far that she could not yet see the exit.

"Which way should we go?" Aster asked. "This place is confusing."

They walked until they arrived at the first fork. No signs marked any direction.

"We might be the first creatures to walk this bridge in over 100 years." Hooyip said. She shaded her eyes and tried to look ahead of their walking path.

Periwinkle sighed. "We need a system. We have two choices now, but what's going to happen up there or up there?" Winkle pointed to the next set of splits in their path. "We might walk in circles. If we're not careful, we could spend a lifetime here."

"I hope we have enough food for this," Hooyip said.

The three girls stood quietly for a moment, considering Hooyip's words.

"I think we'll be ok," Aster said. "Whoever made this bridge must have made it so people could eventually get across. How many places could it lead? There's this side and the other side and that's it!"

Periwinkle pressed her palms to her temples. She wasn't sure that had to be true. "Ok. I think I see what you mean, Aster. I guess we have two choices. If it is a maze, we can just pick the right or the left rope and keep following that, but it might take a very long time. Our other choice is to do what Hooyip taught us. Find a landmark or object or star or something in front of us, and find one behind us and try to move from marker to marker."

"I really hope this isn't a maze," Hooyip said.

"Periwinkle, what do you think?" Aster asked.

Periwinkle sighed again. "I don't want it to be a maze either, and we are just trying to get to the other side, so we do know where we have to go. Let's just call it a bridge forest and do it the way we've been doing it."

"Oh, I can help!" Aster said. "The Kapre taught me this." She grabbed hold of the rope and whispered. Her hand pulsated, and the rope under her hand glowed yellow. Once she finished, Aster left a bright red mark on the rope. "I can do that! And I can see it even when I'm not looking at it. It's like I can look for it and find its color within the string."

Periwinkle wasn't entirely sure what her sister was talking about, but her mark helped them know where they started. "Ok, and I guess we can head to one of the splits way ahead of us." The girls agreed and started with the left path.

"Do you know who first built this bridge?" Periwinkle asked Hooyip. "The Kapre said he's been there a long time, but I don't think he was the one who built this entire thing."

"I'm not sure," Hooyip said. "Maybe the sylphs built it. They move like feathers in the wind. The few I've met do anyway, so they could probably make it across the chasm without the bridge. Maybe it's like the pillar with the duendes, and it's been here always."

Upon approaching the next waypoint, Aster skipped ahead of Periwinkle and grabbed the rope railing. She enchanted it once again to mark their progress. "I see our next destination!" Aster pointed north in a relatively straight line and squinted one eye. "That one! Four-way intersection."

Periwinkle looked ahead. "Ooh, this might get complicated." She considered their current location, where they already had a choice of four paths. "At night, I guess we'll have to use the stars."

Aster looked up at the sky. "We're astronomers. I'll keep a lookout and let everyone know when the stars appear." She squinted. "It's four, then three, then three. That should take us until the night wakes up because of how fast we're going." Aster continued to skip ahead on the swaying bridge, with her left pant leg somehow stuck just under her knee and the other almost concealing her shoe.

Hooyip looked at Periwinkle and smiled. "Your sister makes this kind of fun. I've learned to hunt and navigate in the forests ever since I was smaller than her. Usually, it involves a lot of looking and thinking and considering and not too much talking. There is instruction, but it isn't made to be fun at all. I guess things are different with Aster."

Periwinkle nodded. "She's always like this. I think her brain just works faster and that she always gets everything out before everyone even understands what's happening. Sometimes she says things, and it's not until a few minutes later or hours later or days later when everyone else catches up. I think other people think she's being erratic, and it looks like a game, but really it's just Aster thinking a little faster than most."

"Ahhhh ok, I think I get it. She was talking about the pathways. So, after we make it to the next path that has a choice of four directions, the one she thinks we should head to after that has a choice of three directions, and she thinks we should take the path that leads to three choices again. By then, it will be night."

"Yeah," Periwinkle said. "I think the world would be better if there were more people who could figure things out like her." She held the bridge railing. "Everything would be better if we had more Asters."

Winkle made sure to always keep one hand on the ropes as she walked. Aster looked fearless, and Hooyip probably was fearless, but it was all she could do to keep from dropping to her knees and crawling—or worse—freezing solid and having Hooyip carry her the rest of the way. Her palms sweat every time she looked over the edge of the bridge. The bridge spanned so high over the chasm that she did not even see the ground.

"I wonder how many people get stuck out here," Periwinkle said. "There have already been two chances for us to have gotten off track." Her arm shook, but she tried to concentrate and hide it from Hooyip. "Steady breaths," she whispered to herself. "You can do this, Periwinkle."

"What? You ok?" Hooyip asked.

"Uhh, I'm fine. It's fine. Can you watch Aster and make sure she doesn't get too far ahead? Everything looks wide open, but we don't know that it really is. We can't even see to the other side. I don't want her to get separated from us." Periwinkle took a deep breath and grasped the left-side rope rail with both hands and stepped to the side to let Hooyip pass. Most of the bridges had enough room for two or even three or four people to walk side by side, but when they traveled by twos, the bridges twisted and swayed more than if they walked single file.

Hooyip strode past Winkle and caught up with Aster.

Periwinkle watched them both continue the path ahead

of her and toward their next waypoint.

"Ok, Periwinkle. You can do this," she told herself once she knew no one else was close enough to hear. "One foot, then one foot. You're not gonna die. Always keep the brush moving. We're not gonna die. It's fun."

"You don't like this," Stay whispered.

"Oh, you're back. Yes, this is a little tough," Winkle said.

"We can be out here for days. If the wind picks up, these bridges might blow all over," Stay whispered.

Winkle imagined the silhouette of the Berberoka waiting in the dark doorway in her thoughts. She had an idea to let her take over completely so she could curl up and hide in its door and lock herself up until this was all over.

"Maybe one day I'll take you with me and we can see where this door leads together," The Berberoka whispered. "I think the destination might be different for all of us."

Winkle heard chirping, but she could not discern its direction. She looked around and saw nothing, but she did not feel confident enough to let go of the ropes to make a thorough search of the sky or the path. If she looked downward too long, everything spun and turned blurry, almost to the point of losing her sight.

"Ok," Winkle said to herself. "Whatever you are chirping noise, just don't attack us. What is it that you see in me again?" Winkle asked Stay.

"It's all like I said," Stay whispered. "You are warm to us. A beacon."

Winkle felt the black doorway in her mind close, and she was alone again.

That night, having nowhere else to sleep, they camped on the bridge and hoped to remain safe. Hooyip finished tying Aster to the floorboards of the bridge and used a simple knot in case Aster needed it undone.

"You're next." The alakdan said.

Hooyip's voice was the last Periwinkle remembered before drifting off to sleep.

Once she awoke, billows of mist puffed across her face. Periwinkle gasped. No matter how quickly she gulped in air, she still could not catch her breath. She breathed faster and faster. Her throat closed up, and her eyes burned and watered.

"Winkle! Winkle."

Someone smacked her back. She felt the thumps echo in her chest. Sounds of the rhythmic thumps on her back grew louder. Something tugged and released from her chest like the removal of a hundred bandages from a wound. Her throat cleared, and she felt the air rush through her lungs.

She saw Aster kneeling beside her. "You twisted around, Periwinkle. You rolled right to the edge and were almost hanging over. Without the rope, you would have fallen."

Periwinkle regained her composure and untied herself. "I think I had a panic attack, Aster. It looked like fog beneath us. I felt like I was falling."

Aster nodded. "The clouds started out much lower, but it's been rising. We'll be in the clouds if it keeps doing that. I've never walked in the clouds before."

"Neither have I." Periwinkle looked for Hooyip and saw the alakdan far ahead waving at the two girls. "I guess we should try to catch up."

"Let's not split up too much today," Aster said.

Once they journeyed closer to the alakdan, Periwinkle saw why Hooyip wanted them to hurry. "They're brambles." Winkle touched one of the dry bushes in front of her, and its small branch snapped apart before crumbling into the wind.

"They're all sharp," Aster said. "They're sticking in my sleeve." Aster shook her arm, and then she picked the barbs from the plants out of her clothes.

"It doesn't matter which path we choose," Periwinkle said. "The entire bridge is covered." The plants grew between the boards of the bridge and wrapped around the silver rope that held the entire structure together. Four pathways wound together, but as far as she saw, each one was covered by the gray brambles. The largest ones grew as tall as Hooyip.

"I've been cutting at them," Hooyip said, pointing at the plants with the small stone and bone dagger fabricated by her and Periwinkle. "They look dried up and dead, but I'm pretty sure they're still alive. Even after I cut some branches away, they grow back in a few minutes."

"Hey, maybe we can eat these!" Aster crawled to the bottom of one of the bushes and returned with a handful of bluish-black shriveled berries. "There was a slug or something underneath the bush eating these."

"We might be better off eating the slug," Hooyip said.

Periwinkle's face twisted.

"Can I see them, please?" Hooyip asked. Hooyip split open a berry and its black juices spilled over her hand. "Well, so far, so good. In the forest, we're taught that if the inside colors are black, blue, or gray, then they're probably safe. If they're white, then we shouldn't eat them." She rubbed it into her skin and onto the chitin carapace that covered her hand, then tasted a bit of the juices. "It's sweet! I think they might be ok. If I don't retch or pass out in a few hours, then we're safe."

Aster grabbed hold of the rope bridge and changed a portion of its silvery threads to red.

"I don't know how useful that's going to be, Aster," Hooyip said.

"I think I might still be able to find it, even with all the mess."

Periwinkle and Hooyip cut a path into the foliage while

Aster collected the fruit. Within an hour, the pathway that they cleared in front of them nearly closed in from behind, and the three girls found themselves almost surrounded by the sharp gray vines. Periwinkle's ankles disappeared into the mist that steadily rose through the bridge.

"Aster, can you still see your mark?" Periwinkle asked.

Her little sister turned around and sighed. "Everything is all jumbled up when I look. The threads of these plants swallow everything. I'm sorry."

"It's ok, Aster. Keep collecting the fruits. Maybe we can eat them when we rest." Periwinkle did not want to say it, but she wondered how they were to rest or sleep in a place like this. If all of them slept, they'd be covered by morning and, with any attempt to move, the thorns would lacerate their skin. If someone stayed awake to cut back the regrowth, then they'd be too exhausted to help when they traveled. It's best to hurry and put the brambles far behind them, Periwinkle thought.

They arrived at another intersection on the bridge. By the time they decided on a direction, the path behind them disappeared in the regrowth.

"If I turn around, it all looks the same," Aster said. "If I turn around again, then it still looks the same."

"Aster..." Winkle said. Perhaps because of her concentration with clearing a path, she failed to notice just how quickly the fog continued to rise. Now that they stopped, the threat of losing their sight in the mist loomed in front of her. "Make sure you stay close to us. Close enough to touch." The mist blanketed her little sister from her feet up to the chest.

Aster pulled her arms up through the fog, and mist rolled off her hands and left a powdery residue. She rubbed it between her fingers.

"Strange," Hooyip said, who also caught the vapors in

her hand, then rubbed them between her fingers.

"I don't think this is a cloud," Aster said. "It's like our garden at home. I think these are seeds."

"She's right," Hooyip said. "This must be how this thing spreads. It's some sort of pollen or seed. We have to get to the end."

Periwinkle and Hooyip redoubled their efforts to cut through the brambles in a race to find their way out before the seed cloud covered them. Periwinkle felt Hooyip's hand on her shoulder, and they both tried to look for an end to the brambles.

"I can't see anything," Aster said.

The race was lost. Winkle reached out and pulled her sister close because she could no longer see Aster or Hooyip within the gloom of airborne seeds. She heard Hooyip pant and huff. Then Winkle felt the tension in the bridge sink as Hooyip sat down.

Periwinkle did the same and pulled her knees to her chest. Hooyip did more to cut a path than any of them. The alakdan must feel exhausted, Periwinkle thought. She felt Aster lean against her back as the seeds overtook them and their surroundings disappeared.

"Are you two ok?" Hooyip asked through her gasps for air.

"I can't see either of you," Aster said.

Periwinkle felt for Aster's backpack and rummaged for the length of woven grass rope given to them by the Kapre and tied it around Aster's waist. "I'm going to tie us together, Aster. I won't let you get lost out here."

"Th-thank you, Periwinkle."

Periwinkle felt Aster reaching for her hand.

"I'm kind of a little scared right now."

Periwinkle smoothed back Aster's hair. The truth was, she felt scared, too. "Hey Aster, we're ok. We're both doing fine." She tried to hum the "Antologia" that her mom sang to Aster when she was a baby.

"I-I like that song."

Periwinkle sang quietly first to try to remember the words, and once the words returned to her memory, she continued the song for her sister.

"Thank you, Winkle."

"We just have to wait it out," Hooyip said. "I haven't passed out yet and don't have any rashes, so at least I think we can eat the berries now."

Exhaustion doesn't matter when there's nowhere to go, Periwinkle thought. Sometime after the first day, they tried again to travel but stopped and agreed to sit and wait for fear of losing their way in the gloom. Maybe it was the third day, maybe the fourth, Periwinkle lost track of time. Rain kept them hydrated, but it did nothing to dissipate the seeds. It was all they could do to keep the brambles away and maintain a clearing. Periwinkle and Hooyip took turns removing the brambles when they grew too close and inundated their clothes or cut through their skin. They all slept in shifts while tied to each other and tied to the bridge.

Periwinkle placed her hand on Aster's back to make sure her sister was still breathing, then stood up and cut away some branches that grew near her sister's face. One of the thorns poked Winkle's index finger when she pulled away her hands, and the blood formed a red pinpoint at its tip. She tried to wave away the fog of seeds, wished they would disappear, then splayed her fingers in the rain to let the water wash off the blood. She closed her hand, stretched her fingers open, and tried to shake off the hint of pain. Her hand rubbed against the brambles and brushed against a thick fluid that felt like mucus.

"It burns," Periwinkle whispered, trying again to see her hand. She pressed her fingers together, and they blistered.

"Are you awake, Berberoka? We could sure use some help right now. There's plenty of water—"

"Stop. Please. I am exhausted," Stay said. "You are not like the alakdan. All your path clearing, you do not have a protective covering like her. I have been keeping your blood clean for days now. You are poisoned. This is all I can do. If you ever find solace from these things, then I can dilute the toxins inside of you until it's all expelled."

Something from the brambles chirped. She cut away more of the growth and this time felt the fluid flow from the branches onto her. It wasn't an accident, thought Periwinkle. *How long has this been inside of her?*

"Aster!" She couldn't let the liquid cover her sister or Hooyip while they slept. Periwinkle shook her sister. The chirps grew closer.

"Aster, Hooyip, you have to wake up!"

"Ow!" Aster said. "Something's burning me."

Winkle rubbed Aster's arms and hands with her shirt to try to remove the mucus. "I know. Don't touch the brambles. Something's in there."

"I can feel it too," Hooyip said. "I can even feel it through my carapace."

Aster screamed. "It's crawling on my shoes! I think it's coming out of the plants."

Periwinkle stumbled as Aster backed into her. She heard Hooyip stomping on the bridge, probably trying to abate the slime from coming closer.

"We need to go," Hooyip said. "I think it'll dissolve us if we stay here. We have to go wherever the slime isn't."

Periwinkle and Hooyip cut away the brambles in the only direction they did not hear the chirping. They worked their way across the myriad pathways of the bridge without knowing if they headed forwards or back. Only the rope which tethered Aster to her waist let her know her sister remained on the bridge. Periwinkle's arms felt tortured from the repeated cutting of the brambles. The sides of her stomach cramped, but the chirping multiplied, and Periwinkle knew within the brambles and clouds of seeds they had lost their way.

The rope around Periwinkle's waist tightened and yanked her forward. She crashed against the bony plates that lined Hooyip's back, then Aster banged into her and they all toppled over. The pathway opened up, bereft of the brambles and foliage, and the three rushed to regain balance. They crawled onward, and the chirps from behind them grew distant.

"It's done," Hooyip said. "Just a little further."

Periwinkle emerged from the cloud of seeds and welcomed the return of her vision. Her hands and arms burned and bore blisters from the spots where the slime had contacted her skin. Aster's legs and arms were covered with rashes. "Can you see your last mark, Aster? The last mark you left on the rope."

Aster shook her head and pulled thorns from her clothes. "Sorry Winkle. I can't see anything through the fog. It's still all tangled. Hey Periwinkle—"

"Oh, that's weird," Hooyip said. "There's something ahead of us."

Periwinkle squinted, and she made out small traces of smoke rising into the sky. "I think I see it."

"And there are tents," Hooyip said.

Aster rubbed her legs. "I didn't want to say anything because we were trying to escape, but this really hurts, Periwinkle. It feels like boiling water is moving up my leg."

Periwinkle poured some cold water from her flask over the burn marks left on Aster's leg by the slime.

Her sister's eyes teared up, her arms quivered, and her face turned pale. "It still burns really bad. It feels like I'm burning." Aster clenched her teeth, then passed out.

Periwinkle shook her sister and tried to wake her, but she did not move. She called to Hooyip for help, and the alakdan hoisted Aster into her arms. They saw little choice but to seek out the encampment for help. Periwinkle and Hooyip carried Aster and hobbled toward the smoke.

The bridges opened onto wooden platforms where Winkle saw six chalk-white tents which were marbled with sinuous brown veins. Three cloaked figures sat by a fire. They stood up as the bridges and platform flexed and swayed.

Periwinkle cupped her hands around her mouth. "We need help! Something in the brambles, it burned my sister."

One of the figures, whose cloak was the most tattered, removed its hood, which revealed the head of a giant bull.

Chapter 14
Minotaur

Periwinkle clenched her teeth and stared at the bull-headed being. She remembered the Kapre's warning. The fog of seeds remained behind her, and within the seed cloud slithered the creatures that burned and poisoned Aster. She looked to Hooyip. The alakdan cradled Aster in her arms. Periwinkle gripped the small dagger with its bone handle and chipped rock blade.

"I need help." Periwinkle called. "My sister is hurt."

The creature in front of her charged forward, and the two figures beside it followed like specters in flight. Hooyip turned to shield Aster. Periwinkle's body reacted without thinking, and she darted in front of the alakdan and her sister.

"She's hurt already!" Periwinkle yelled as she gripped the makeshift dagger. "Help her! Please." Periwinkle tried to force the Berberoka inside her to awaken.

The three figures stopped, and the bridge creaked in the rain.

The bull-headed creature and the two cloaked figures waited. Vapor wafted from their hoods.

"Please," Periwinkle repeated.

The creature in front extended its long arm across its

face. It pulled the bull-shaped head from its shoulders.

With the helmet removed, Periwinkle saw a woman with black hair pulled into a sharp ponytail that trellised between her shoulders. The woman's face was chalk pale. The fingers on her right hand bore the same strange colors as the white and brown tents. She nodded to the hooded figures beside her.

"We can help her," one of the hooded figures said as she approached. Her husky voice almost washed out in the rain. "I know these wounds. Follow me and take her to my tent. Your sister might recover."

No one else spoke. When they entered the camp, Winkle saw the tents were made of paper.

The girl led them into her tent. "Lie her down here," she said, and she motioned to some blankets stretched atop the wooden planks. The girl pulled back her hood. Her straw-colored hair fell across her face as she worked to apply an ointment over Aster's leg. She then soaked a length of cloth in a bowl and tied it around Aster's shin and calf and any other spot that looked red from rashes. "She's probably fainted from the pain. It's happened to all of us here, but she might recover once the ointment relieves the swelling and cools the burning."

"You're human?" Hooyip asked.

"Yes, we are all human here."

Periwinkle did not notice it at first because of the bustle and worry with her sister, but the other figure who escorted them to the tent remained in the entryway and held a dagger beneath the sleeve of her robes. She appeared much younger than the other two, maybe sixteen or eighteen at most, and her eyes and cheeks were nearly the same pale color as the woman with the bull-head helm.

"I think we're ok," Hooyip said to Periwinkle. "If the person at the door wanted to attack, she would have done so by now. I think she is just cautious."

The blonde-haired woman finished attending to Aster. "We have to be careful," she said. "In the last four years, everything we've come across has been hostile to us. Nine years ago, Tamar was only eight when we first entered the bridge. Fighting and surviving are all she's known. It's all any of us have known outside our own circle. It's gotten worse since the fires have opened in the Ember Lands."

"We were stuck in the brambles," Hooyip said.

"And likely in the seed clouds," the blonde said. "We've all been there one time or another. Not everyone makes it out." She sat on the floor in the tent's corner and ran her hands through her hair, then rubbed her neck. Cuts and calluses scored her hands. "My name is Miriam. The berries from those brambles are edible if you haven't figured it out yet. The seeds are too if you can gather them. They tend to migrate. Not much else grows out here, but it's how we've survived so long if you can avoid the worms."

Periwinkle heard the entryway cover flip aside. The lady from earlier, who directed the other two, stood in the entrance beside the younger Tamar. She watched Periwinkle and Hooyip.

"Miriam, that's enough," the black-haired woman said.

"Sorry, Deborah," Miriam answered. She stretched and shook out her hands. "The one that got burned is young. Probably younger than Tamar when we first arrived. They lived through the worms and slime long enough to make it out. They can't be useless. Two of them are just kids."

Deborah nodded. Her countenance was stern, and her cloud-pale skin sharpened her features. "I guess I should welcome you three to our camp. Miriam talks too much, but she's right. That slime digests anything that gets stuck in the brambles. Worms produce it. If the little one would have remained in it much longer, then it would have eaten away her legs. We have seen it before."

Standing closer, Periwinkle got a better look at Deborah's hands. The lady's right thumb, index, and middle fingers weren't just the same color as the tents, nor were they covered as if wrapped in gauze. They were the same material. Her fingers looked like they were fashioned from paper.

"Why are you here?" Deborah asked.

"We need to cross the chasm," Periwinkle said. "We're looking for the sylphs so we can put an end to the portals… and so my sister and I can go back home."

"You are just children," Deborah said. "I was a kid the last time I met an alakdan, and I've never heard of them traveling with humans. I'm not sure how you ended up on the chasm bridges."

"Where are you girls from?" Miriam interrupted. "How far north? Which town? The alakdans are from the south. So, you're heading south?"

Deborah waited for a response. Periwinkle didn't know what to say. She didn't want to tell them that she and Aster came from the fires. She didn't want to say that they're not from the Ember Lands.

"We're heading north," Hooyip said.

Periwinkle was glad Hooyip traveled with them.

"I found these two from a caravan," Hooyip said. "All wiped out. They were the only two left. They don't remember much. Only that they were with family. They would have been eaten by a nekroun. It's a scavenger that roams the forests to the south. I saw a portal open up, and when I made it to their caravan, they were the only two alive. I killed what killed their group."

"I didn't know humans made it that far south," Miriam said. We haven't seen any on the bridge, not in four years at least."

"And you?" Deborah asked, looking at Hooyip. "Why are you heading north, alakdan? Why were you alone when you found them?"

"It's like Periwinkle said, I'm going to find a way to close all the portals for good." Hooyip remained quiet as Deborah stared at her. "There's nothing left."

"I see," Deborah said. "You can stay as long as you work."

Deborah left the tent and walked by Periwinkle without another look. Even though Hooyip was an alakdan and Deborah was a human, Periwinkle thought their demeanor was somehow similar.

"You said the younger one is your sister?" Miriam looked over at Aster. "She'll recover. I'll look after her to make sure she doesn't fever. I've studied the plants here, all types of plants really. It's what I do. The salve will work. Tamar can show you around. There's only six of us, and it'll be dark soon. We can talk more then. Not many new people, alakdan, sylph, human, anything to talk to around here. We'll talk when it's dark. We'll get something to eat."

Periwinkle wanted to trust Miriam. Like Hooyip said, if the girls wanted to harm her or Aster, they've already had plenty of opportunities. Periwinkle moved the tent flap to follow Tamar outside. "Miriam, are the tents made of paper?" Periwinkle asked.

"Yes."

"Your name is Tamar?" Hooyip asked, trying to smile as they left. "You are the fifth human I've met! So far, all the humans I've come across have been agreeable. Thank you for helping us. It's nice to meet you."

"They're not all agreeable," Tamar said. She led them through the small encampment and toward two more tents a few paces from the ones inhabited by Deborah and Miriam.

Periwinkle wrenched her lips, and her stomach felt

uneasy. She wondered about the proper etiquette for meeting beings that looked human but lived in a different world. Was there a greeting or custom that all humans knew in the Ember Lands, and would they think of her as a savage born in the wild? Did it even matter anymore? Periwinkle looked over the edge of the bridge in the middle of nowhere and squeezed the rope railing to keep steady.

Tamar sat beside the two women in front of the next tent. She pulled a dagger from its sheath in her belt and handed it to the lady.

"My, my, you are young," said one of the seated women. "And an alakdan too. Well, this is a first. We are graced." The lady's weathered face mapped out years and experiences beyond those of Deborah's or Miriam's. Muscles in her gaunt arms surpassed even those of Hooyip's, and a hammer made from the same paper as the tents hung from her belt. Three necklaces with thin thread chains and oddly angled charms swayed about her neck. "I suppose it's a pleasure to meet you both. I'm Bethany and my friend and I are papersmiths for our collection of wayward women."

"You're starting to sound like Deborah," the other woman said. "I'm Lydia. We met Tamar and the others about six years ago when they rescued us from those brambles. Same as you, it seems. We've been stuck here ever since." Lydia set Tamar's dagger on a large flat stone and pulled out a tool with a rounded edge that she pressed and raked across the dagger.

"It's not so bad here," Bethany said. "A little more dangerous these days, but better than where we came from. Everyone in our town back home probably thinks we're long dead. It's what they've wanted anyway, and here we can practice in peace."

"What is a papersmith, exactly?" Hooyip asked. "Is that something common for humans?"

Bethany and Lydia laughed.

Lydia shook her head. "As far as I know, we are the only two papersmiths in the Ember Lands. It has to do with those brambles that like to surround people." She motioned to the dagger on her stone. "This was one of the first things we've made, so it's not as strong as subsequent tools or weapons, but Tamar here won't give it up."

"Just fix it," Tamar said.

Lydia proceeded to shape and flatten its blade. She wet the edge with a blackish concoction poured from a vial. "We've found that we can pound and shape those bushes into a paste. Miriam made a hardening fluid from the berries. I'm not quite sure how she's done it, but they're edible too, you know."

"Going to tell them everything?" Bethany's voice grated nearly as much as the brambles from the fog. "Once they learn everything of our—"

"Oh, excuse me, Captain Deborah," Lydia said. "Look at the girl's arms, brittle as sticks. She couldn't do it if she wanted."

"The alakdan's got arms," Bethany said.

"She's the first I've met, and I won't be impolite."

"Fine, but don't complain when they take all we have and cut our thr—"

"I'm sure you'll stay awake to watch them."

"That I shall! I'll watch them with both my eyes. They won't get anything over on me. Believe that."

Lydia shook her head and smirked. "Both your eyes, Bethany? One eye on each one? As if one could go somewhere... Oh, look then. What's your name, young one?" Lydia asked, pointing at Winkle.

"Both my eyes," Bethany said as she took the dagger from Lydia and continued to work its blade. "I'll watch with both."

Periwinkle wanted to laugh at their exchange. She knew that Aster would have trouble keeping from giggling at the argument between the two ladies. The two women must have known each other for a long time. Winkle wondered if people have stolen from their camp before.

"My name is Periwinkle Dalisay. My sister is Aster Dalisay." Periwinkle felt her hands clench up. "Sometimes people call me Winkle."

"See, now we're not strangers," Lydia said. "All friends."

"All friends, all friends, all friends. So easy then all friends," Bethany said, brushing away the conversation.

"Lydia, do you think you can make me a weapon?" Hooyip asked. "I can help gather some brambles. The slime isn't as effective on me. It has trouble burning through my plates, and maybe I can help in other ways, too."

"Oh, why not just make it easy for them to do us harm?" Bethany said while pacing in a circle.

Lydia smiled. "I can make something if you like. It will take a few days to get it right—after we have materials."

"Fine, fine, fine," Bethany interrupted. "I'll do it then. She'll just mess it up. Don't need to twist my arm. I'll make you what you need. A sword, I figure. Something larger than that fish knife you're carrying at your waist."

Lydia patted Bethany on the back and smiled. "We can use the help around here if it's from someone with arms like yours."

"We've been doing fine on our own!" Bethany said. "But yeah, I suppose we could use the help."

"Help for what?" Periwinkle asked.

Tamar took the repaired dagger from Lydia. "I hope the other one will be as useful."

"We'll have time to talk about it all later," Lydia said.

Periwinkle sat outside the tents and listened to Hooyip and Lydia exchanged stories.

Tamar sat for a time with them as well. The younger girl said nothing and kept her hood pulled over her head. She stood up once Lydia ended another yarn. "It's dark. It's time we eat," Tamar said. "Periwinkle Dalisay, come with me."

Periwinkle returned with Tamar to the two tents in front of the encampment, and Tamar retrieved some jars and a ladle from Deborah's tent.

"It's nice," Periwinkle said. "Your camp. It feels like a home. Thank you for helping us. Thank you for—"

"Check on your sister, then find Miriam and help me serve their food."

Periwinkle nodded. She saw Aster asleep on the blankets which Miriam made into a bed. She felt her sister's forehead.

"She has a slight fever," Miriam said. "But it's normal. She'll sleep it off. Wake up all better."

Periwinkle kneeled beside her sister, smoothed back Aster's hair, then tied it into a knot and sighed. "I just want her to be ok."

"Periwinkle," Tamar called. "Deborah said you can only stay as long as you work."

Miriam picked up some bowls and handed them to Periwinkle. "Don't mind her. She was my friend's daughter. Deborah and I have raised her since we escaped. She just wants us all to stay safe, the same as any of us. It isn't so easy out here, but it's better than across the bridge."

Periwinkle walked with Miriam to the clearing in front of their tents to meet up with Tamar and the other women. "Where are you from, Miriam, if I may ask? Everyone seems like family here. I'd like for my sister to meet you when she recovers. I think it might remind her of home." Periwinkle tried to balance the bowls without looking over the sides of the bridge. "I can't give that to her yet, but maybe if she saw all of you, it'd help her remember what that's like. She hasn't been home in a long time."

Tamar took the bowls from Winkle. "What's so good about home?" She ladled in servings of compote made from the berries in the brambles.

"It's where we feel comfortable. It's where my mother lives, and I miss her," Periwinkle said.

Miriam took a bowl, then left the younger girls to join the others. "Maybe another time, Periwinkle," Miriam said.

Tamar continued to fill five more bowls with the compote. "People don't make it off this bridge. Maybe you'll never return home." She pushed two bowls in front of Winkle. "Serve everyone else first. One bowl stays here. Don't touch it."

One short, thought Periwinkle. She found Hooyip chatting along with the two papersmiths. Tamar followed and served the others, then shoved the last bowl into Winkle's hands.

"Periwinkle, these two are amazing," Hooyip said. "Bethany and Lydia are extraordinary craftsmen. They don't just work in this medium, but they can create weapons out of almost anything. Bethany created these giant hooks made from paper. They're so light but rigid as well. They use the hooks to pull the bridges together to make this platform, and they use them to circumvent the brambles and the seed clouds."

"It's why we had to leave," Lydia said. "Our craftsmanship and metal work was superior to anyone's in our city."

"Any man's in our city," Bethany said. "We worked harder at it, and we were willing to learn skills they could not."

Lydia placed her hand on Bethany's shoulder. "They saw it as evil—an impossibility—and called us wayward from their beliefs. We left before they… well, before they carried out their will against us, and we made our way to the bridge, but we did not make it through the brambles." Lydia shrugged. "Deborah, Miriam, and Tamar rescued us. We've traveled with them since. It's been over six years."

"And you, Miriam?" Hooyip asked as they sat down for the meal.

Miriam shrugged. "Our story is similar. We had to leave and we left."

Deborah placed her skull shaped helmet on the ground next to her tent. "Miriam is one of the two cleverest people I've ever known," she said. "We grew up together. She practically learned to read since she was a baby. She read everything, learned everything."

Miriam pulled her cloak tighter around her shoulders and pulled its hood over her head. She traced a stick through the dust on the bridge.

Deborah curled her lip. "The only other person able to keep up with her was Esther, Tamar's mother."

"Oh," Hooyip said. "So she's here too? I was told there're six of you. I'd like to meet someone like that. Maybe she can help me figure out a way to destroy the Vine."

Darkness settled in, and Winkle thought it made Deborah look ghostlike and ethereal.

Deborah looked at the sky. "Esther built a cart that pulled itself using water pressure and different stages of heat. It didn't move very fast, but it pulled around whatever she needed. At first, the people in our city thought of it as a novelty—something exciting. But the more and more they saw a cart move itself through our streets, the more frightened and spiteful they became. They called it evil. They called Esther, evil. Just as they were frightened when Miriam brought some of our town's guards back from the dead."

"Not me," Miriam said. "It was the fungus. It grows on dead things. I just learned how to use it—distill it. Made it right for us. It fixed them, not me."

"The townsfolk became a mob," Deborah said. "Tamar was so little. She somehow wandered into my shop in the confusion, but they took her mother. Once they had her mother, the people gained confidence, and they wanted to go after Miriam next. Maybe they figured they'd destroy every wicked thing in our city all in one night."

"It's funny," Miriam said. "The way they acted, the things they thought. Esther would have thought they were funny, too. The people in our city wouldn't get the joke. I don't know what to call it when you have enough people who can't understand what they're doing, who can't understand their own joke or the way they act. The people from our city, that's what they are. They're funny. All of them."

The corners of Deborah's mouth turned downward and pressed together into a harsh thin line. "The mob formed fast. They feared the wickedness that possessed Tamar's mother—"

"Evil, Deborah," Miriam interrupted. "They used the word evil when they did what they did to Esther."

Deborah nodded, and her pale skin flushed with anger. "Esther created something they didn't understand. They thought it was the same evil that they said overtook Miriam when she healed the guards. I made it to Miriam first, and we fled with Tamar to a place everyone was afraid to follow—the Broken World Chasm. I'm sure the people in our city think we're dead."

"Us wayward women," Miriam said.

Lydia held up her bowl. "The wayward women."

"We are all bullheaded monsters of the worst kind," Tamar said.

Hooyip looked to the black fires at the edge of the world. "There are six of you…"

"Our princess," Bethany said.

"She's not a princess." Miriam said. "A Vizconde's

daughter. Our newest addition. She's not a princess. She's a Vizconde's daughter."

Periwinkle felt the bridge dip and rise. She saw a woman emerge from one of the tents, lit by the night's last glow of the black fires that surrounded the world. The girl's onyx hair was dark as the fires. Periwinkle watched the sixth member of the group take up her bowl and sit away from the others. Her right eye, cheek, and a portion of her mouth, shoulder and neck seemed constructed out of the same paper material as the tents and Deborah's fingers.

"We found Judith, our princess, with half her face and torso dissolved," Bethany said. "She was surrounded by soldiers in the fog. All of them digested. Their outsides and insides all partially eaten away from the slime. Best we could figure is that they were traveling south to start a new settlement. It was the only reason to send the nobles they did. Lydia and I fixed what we could."

"It's the materials," Miriam said. "I found a way. We bonded it to her. We bound it to her," Miriam corrected herself, drawing circles onto the bridge with a branch from the brambles. "They did most of it. I helped make it. They created new bones and ligaments from the paper and a new covering, too. I showed them where to connect the parts to make things work. It was something I read. We made her new insides out of the paper. She's still relearning to talk."

Periwinkle looked at the girl with the paper face. The replaced portions of Judith's eye, mouth, and neck maintained an eerie flatness as she ate.

"The girl doesn't speak much," said Bethany, who twirled a wooden spoon around her bowl. "But she is a beautiful girl."

"So, you are all from the north?" Hooyip asked. "You must know how to navigate by the stars from here. I've never been this far from my own lands. The sky is unfamiliar, and we lost our way within the seed cloud. If you can just show me which stars are to the north and which stars are to the south, maybe we can find our way through the chasm."

"You said those two with you don't remember a thing about where they're from?" Deborah asked.

Periwinkle nodded. She felt ashamed that she entered the world through the fires just like all the monsters that have ravaged this world, and even with the group's hospitality, she feared being honest with the women. "My sister and I don't remember."

"I don't remember either," Deborah said.

Hooyip looked at Lydia. "Lydia, you must remember."

"Sorry," Lydia said, looking down, then shaking her head. "Guess I'm not quite sure either."

"No more stories," Deborah said. "Tomorrow we'll harvest materials from the brambles for food and tools. We've had a lot of attacks recently. Portals open up every week now and there's limited space where we can move on these bridges."

Miriam threw her stick over the side of the bridge. "The brambles will migrate soon. I've watched their growth. It's time for them to die out and regrow. We'll have to leave here and follow them. Keep us surrounded on three sides."

"Tomorrow, Tamar and Miriam will show you how to grapple the bridges," Deborah said.

Periwinkle heard the women sing much of the night. They sang for entertainment and solidarity and to take their minds away from the past. When she finally joined them, everyone, even Tamar, felt comforted by Periwinkle's voice. It was the first time as a teenager that she sung for anyone other than Aster.

She started early the next day. Though it took her practice, Meriam and Tamar taught Periwinkle how to throw. The bridges creaked when the three girls pulled the rope rails with the hooks and tied them together. The release was easier; unhook upwards and the bridge shoots like a slingshot. Back home, Periwinkle avoided most things related to athletics. She enjoyed some of the games, and she enjoyed running around, but most of the sports and physical activities involved objects flying at someone's face. Usually she spent a lot of time just falling over. In the Ember Lands, necessity dictated physical activity.

Periwinkle turned around and saw one of the hooks flying toward her before it hit her in the stomach and bounced to the bridge, knocking the wind from her lungs.

"Wrap up the hooks," Tamar said while walking away. "It's time to gather materials from the brambles. You stay here with Miriam and Judith."

"Tamar is a little rude, but I can learn a lot from these women. They know how to survive." Periwinkle said to herself. "Are there cities where you're from?" Periwinkle whispered. She finished rolling up the bridge hook. "I know you're awake. My hands and arms are cold."

"Where I am from there is land, one castle, water, and the dark," Stay whispered back. "Where we are right now, there is only occasional rain. How long do we plan to remain here?"

"My sister is sick, and we're lost. I don't know which way is north or south or which way we have to go to find the other side of the chasm."

"So, once your sister is well and you regain your composure, we deceive them and rob them of their tools. Then we make our escape!"

"No," Winkle said. "We don't do that. If we're staying here for a while, then I want to learn what they know. They're able to make tools and weapons from paper that are as strong as steel. They have an incredible understanding of medicine. I can learn so much. These women are magnificent."

Periwinkle felt the Berberoka laughing inside of her. "Sometimes, you are not a very exciting person."

"Learning is exciting."

"Their lessons will not help you return your sister home. However, that is not why I'm awake right now. Something will be nearby soon, and I would like to protect my new home."

Periwinkle looked to the brambles where the seed cloud stretched to the limits of her sight. In an opposite direction, she saw the spider web of bridges continue its convoluted mass that stretched into the gray sky. Above the camp, she saw black fires.

Periwinkle ran to the tent that housed her sister. She heard crackling and saw a feathered, serpentine figure break through the portal of fire. It moved like some monstrous wave prepared to swallow up an entire shore of rock and sand.

"It has arrived for the competition which I have decided not to join, and it will search out the Abyssal Vine to try to win the gift of immortality," Stay said.

Once the creature emerged, Periwinkle saw two half-bodied shades speed overhead. The manananggals that fed on the duendes in the forest tore into the serpent. They pulled its green and red feathered wings apart before it emerged through the flames and sent the pieces of its body to crash into whatever end the bleak chasm provided.

The sky blurred as the heat rose, and the manananggals descended toward the encampment.

"Miriam!" Periwinkle called. "Help me with my sister!" She saw Miriam and Judith dart from their tents. Both women carried bows and tracked the manananggal in the skies. Periwinkle heard their arrows whip through the wind toward the monsters.

Judith ran toward Aster's tent and met Winkle at the entrance. Judith's placid face kept its eerie countenance, and she readied a spear while Miriam continued to fire the paper shafted arrows toward the creatures.

Adrenaline coursed through Periwinkle's body, and she saw Miriam, who guarded the furthest tents, manage two more shots before one of the monsters dropped down and raked her with its claws. The other descended upon Judith and Winkle.

Up close, Periwinkle saw the face of the creature. Its face and head looked almost human and almost feminine. Skin from its midsection dangled from what remained of a body.

Judith parried its first strike, and Periwinkle heard a rustle from inside the tent. Aster was still weak from the fevers and would make an easy target for the manananggal.

Periwinkle had to lead at least one of the creatures away from her sister, and then maybe Judith and Miriam could stall the other until the rest of the group returned.

Periwinkle lost sight of Miriam within the assault of the first manananggal. How long did she have?

The second monster circled Winkle to ready another attack against her and Judith.

Aster stood in the entryway to the tent and rubbed her eyes. "Periwinkle, what's going on? I think my head is still woozy." She looked peaked from the poison and fever.

"No Aster!" Winkle felt a rush of cold, and when the manananggal returned for its second strike, Periwinkle stepped in front of Aster and Judith, and she thrust her small dagger into the monster's chest. The handle splintered apart and lacerated Winkle's hand. The stone blade clanked on the bridge.

Periwinkle pounded her fists against the manananggal. It wasn't enough. Soon, the creature would tear her apart like it did the serpent from the portal. Winkle only thought about home and her colors and paintings and drawings. She thought about her favorite show. What would Bob Ross say about a situation like this? Beat the devil out of it, then whack its head with a brush and send the water and old paint flying. Winkle saw one of the bridge hooks entwined in the rails that latched the bridges together.

Before the manananggal's next strike, a strange black mist seeped from Winkle's arms and chest. The mist heralded the presence of the Berberoka, and the dark vapors shielded Winkle from the manananggal's claws.

It gave her time. She grabbed hold of the hook and pulled it upwards, releasing the bridge. The force sent her and the monster far from the tent and far from Aster.

Periwinkle had no weapons left. If the creature decided to return to the camp, it only needed to fly away and leave her behind. Winkle grabbed the manananggal's arm while it tried to right itself, and she felt the gusts from its massive wings.

"I told you," Stay said to Winkle. "I very much want to remain where I am."

Periwinkle felt drowned, like a swamp seeped out from her veins and skin. She saw an inky liquid bleed out of her arms and felt it spew from her spine to meet and absorb the creature's attacks. When the manananggal failed to cut into her, it carried Winkle upwards, then slammed her on the bridge, and again the black liquid shielded Winkle and kept her body from being smashed against the planks of the bridge.

Periwinkle saw Hooyip's tails flash behind the creature, then saw one of the creature's wings fall into the chasm.

"Periwinkle!" Tamar called.

Periwinkle felt herself being wrestled away from the monster as its other wing, and then the creature itself, plummeted to oblivion.

Winkle shook her head. "My sister."

"It's over," Tamar said.

Winkle looked across the separated bridge toward the encampment. The last manananggal returned to the sky, chased away by Deborah and her company. When Periwinkle, Hooyip, and Tamar rejoined the others, Periwinkle saw Aster was safe, but Miriam remained motionless on the ground with her right arm mangled and her right leg severed.

Deborah worked to stop the bleeding while Bethany and Lydia tried to cover Miriam in blankets to keep the body warm.

Chapter 15
Minotaur, Part Two

Periwinkle helped move Miriam into the papersmiths' tent, then returned to her sister.

"What's going on?" Aster asked.

"We're going to stay out of their way," Periwinkle said. "They have to fix her. She helped keep you alive. You were sick, Aster, and we were attacked. That lady helped you. All of them helped you."

"Oh. Was this my fault? Should I apologize?"

"No, Aster. It's just where we are right now. It's how things happen."

"Oh." Aster stared at the ground. "I'm a problem for everyone. Aren't I, Periwinkle?"

"No, Aster. That's not it."

"I'm always too small."

Hooyip arrived and ruffled Aster's hair. "Are you ok? You had a terrible fever for a while, Aster. There are worms that live in the brambles. Their slime got you pretty good. Then your sister fought off a monster to keep it away from you when you were sick. You should have seen her."

"I think I feel better now," Aster said. "Is that lady going to be all right?"

Hooyip sighed. "I think so. They stopped the bleeding.

Those women really know how to handle things. Bethany already started work. It looked like she was crafting an arm. She said if she can hurry, it'll grow into the muscles."

Hooyip looked at the morning clouds. "Those things… They were like the ones that destroyed my home. They attack so fast. If it wasn't distracted with you, then Tamar and I never could have finished it. This means a lot to me." Hooyip rubbed the back of her neck. "I have to figure out where the Vine will appear. If we can stop all of them from ever returning to the Ember Lands, this will be a safer place for everybody. Then maybe we can finally figure a way out to return you through one of those portals."

"That's how you could do the thing you did? You're from the portals, same as those monsters?" Deborah stood with her arms crossed, staring at Periwinkle from the entrance to the tent. "I suppose you are one of them—in your own way."

Periwinkle's stomach turned. Deborah looked like an executioner's ready to carry out her orders.

"I'm not one of them," Periwinkle tried to keep her voice steady. "But you're right. My sister and I came through the black fires just like the other monsters. We only want to try and return home. Hooyip's been trying to help us."

"Is there anything else?"

"I was afraid to tell you earlier, because my sister needed help."

Deborah sighed, sat down on the bridge, and shook her head. "If you told us you were from the portals when we first met, then I probably would have returned you to the brambles to let the slimes dissolve you. Nothing from those portals has been good for us. But I suppose people should try to understand those who are a little unique. If you weren't here to help, then Judith and Miriam probably wouldn't have made it."

"Is Miriam going to be ok?" Periwinkle asked.

"She'll be fine, eventually. Lydia and Bethany are good at what they do." Deborah held up her hand, then wiggled her three fingers constructed from the paper materials. "They work just as well as anything. Miriam's not just smart. She's tough, too. Knowing her, once she's realized what happened, she'll probably be fascinated by her new arm and leg." Deborah looked to Hooyip. "You really are a tremendous warrior."

"Tamar is as well," Hooyip said. "She's had great instructors."

"I suppose so. A girl as young as her when we first made it to the bridge shouldn't have had to live out here, but it is the lot. Yesterday, Miriam told me that the seed clouds and the brambles would dissipate soon. Every time she says that, they clear up in a few days." Deborah pointed slightly to the left of the brambles. "When that creature left, the direction it flew was north. We can give you one of our bridge hooks to help you navigate the bridges." Deborah paused. "Or, you can stay with us."

"Or you can come with us," Periwinkle said. "Maybe there's a way we can help each other."

Deborah chuckled. "You and your sister are so young. I hope you are not too polite to survive in a place like the Ember Lands. You're lucky the alakdan is with you." Deborah shrugged. "I don't think there's a place in the world for people like us wayward women. Lydia, Bethany, Miriam, even Judith now that she looks the way she looks— they are too far removed from the world, and people aren't ready for someone who can seemingly keep a person from death or turn paper into weapons. We have a place within these bridges, though. Where it's too complicated or too dangerous for other people to live. Stay with us a few more days until Miriam's health and her curiosity returns. It will give Lydia and Bethany time to make more tools, and Tamar and I can gather more supplies. I shall give you what you need so you have a chance to make it across the chasm."

In the few days before the brambles crumbled to dust and the seeds disappeared from their foray through the wind, Winkle learned the basics of anatomy and medicine, and toxins and potions, but she spent most of her time sitting with Judith, whose face and chest were made of paper.

Judith read a lot, and she kept a collection of books and drawings in a bag that she scavenged from her caravan. When she didn't read, Judith taught Periwinkle how to use a spear. And when they finished their practice with the spear, they sat in silence and drew. Judith mostly drew the sky and the bridges. Periwinkle preferred to draw the tents, and the day before they left, Periwinkle finally heard Judith speak.

"I need to practice," Judith said. "I am embarrassed by the way my voice sounds now after everything the girls here have done for me. I used to sing, but I do not think that I will ever sing again. In the least, one day I want to show them that I am as strong as they are and that their work has helped me recover."

Periwinkle nodded and felt that she should have said something important, but she could only think of asking if Judith really was a noble because Aster was curious.

"I am," Judith said. "Like Miriam said, I am a Vizconde's daughter. My father owns lands and many towns throughout those lands. He wanted to own more lands in the south." Judith held her throat and looked down.

"It's ok, you don't have to."

Judith waited. She drank some water and waited again. "I need to practice, or I will never heal the way that I want. Can I read something for you? My family never thought too much of reading and writing for pleasure, but it has always been my favorite thing to do, even more than drawing. Before I met you, I never had someone who would sit with me to just draw or read."

Periwinkle put down her pencil and her sketch and smiled. "I shall do my best to be a good listener."

"I wrote this after Bethany and Lydia attached new vocal cords and made my new eye and taught me to see. It was when I first saw my new skin." Judith held her throat until the pain subsided, then waited to catch her breath. Once she looked ready, she read a short poem to Periwinkle, stopping every two or three lines to rest her voice:

> I had no answers near the Whimsy Woods
> After blue blooms blossomed through early dew,
> Why rows of gravestones colored my childhood.
>
> We departed home where memories stood
> Beside remnant voices that never knew
> I had no answers near the Whimsy Woods.
>
> Then I deplored myself: answer—if you could,
> Without the quibble or the ballyhoo
> Why rows of gravestones colored my childhood.
>
> My remarks burned like dust off blistered wood
> For blistered voices that lead me askew.
> I had no answers near the Whimsy Woods.
>
> The delusion of harmony precludes
> Life's dolorous blow of lies that value
> Why rows of gravestones colored my childhood.
>
> Now—on this bridge, I never understood
> Amidst feasts of dust I always consume;
> I had no answers near the Whimsy Woods
> Why rows of gravestones colored my childhood.

The poem made Periwinkle feel a little sad, but she clapped quietly once Judith finished so as not to alarm the others in the camp because she learned Judith liked to keep to herself. "I like your poem and your voice very much. It's about how you came here, isn't it? At least partially. I think it will be no time flat when you can read it straight through."

Judith started to laugh but again grasped her throat. "I use that poem to practice. Someday, I hope to recite the entire thing without stopping, and I will read it for all the girls and tell them thank you for what they've done for me all in one breath."

Periwinkle decided that when she leaves, she would miss Judith the most.

***

Periwinkle helped Aster fill her small backpack with compote from the berries, and Hooyip honed her newly formed paper sword. They spoke about its weight and strength with Lydia and Bethany until Miriam, with the aid of a stick as a crutch, once again returned to her feet, and it was time for well-wishes and goodbyes.

Wells of tears formed in Aster's eyes. "We learned so much from them," Aster said. "But I don't think they really learned anything from us."

"Well, maybe there was some novelty in our companionship," Hooyip replied.

"That's not what I mean." Aster's hands fell to her knees as she doubled over. "I was a burden here. I was a burden before…"

"You're not a burden, Aster." Periwinkle said.

"I don't contribute. I'm not like you, Periwinkle. I'm not

like Hooyip. Everything everyone's done for me. I don't think I matter."

Winkle held her sister, and she wished she were strong like a parent. Winkle heard Tamar's voice, and she turned to wait for the youngest member of Deborah's group.

Tamar carried a fearsome helmet under her right arm. "Please take this, Winkle," Tamar said, who unlatched the knife from her belt. She handed Winkle the knife and its sheath. "It was the first thing Lydia and Bethany made for me. It's a good knife. I know yours broke when you helped us. Maybe it can help you get home."

"Home," Periwinkle said. "You have that here. I'm not sure if that really exists for us. Every time we try to get closer to a way back home, we just find another way to say goodbye."

"It does exist." Tamar said. "I guess that I felt that way, too, when I lost my mom. I don't know. I don't know what I felt. Only that I was sad. I still am, but there are good people that help. Deborah and Miriam. You and your sister. You're like that too. And you have Hooyip. All of you are a home." Tamar scratched her head and huffed. "Ahhhh. I don't know. I don't know how to describe it. It doesn't get any better losing people, but we move on because we have relationships, even if everything's awful for all of us. We're all the same sort of horrible."

Tamar rubbed her forehead. "Anyway Just take it. It's not as strong as the sword they made for Hooyip, but it's perfect anyway."

Periwinkle strapped the sheath to her belt and slid it to the small of her back. She let her shirt hang over the knife. "There," she said. "Now it's hidden a little."

Tamar nodded. "You know, there aren't too many people worth knowing out here." Tamar thought for a second. "Hey before you go, what do you think of my new armor?

Lydia had enough material after finishing a new arm and leg for Miriam. Hooyip was better at collecting those brambles than any of us. She brought back so much of it."

Tamar donned a bull shaped helmet. The horns were larger than Deborah's, and the snout tapered into a needle-sharp point. The eye sockets slanted toward the nose in a portrait of anger and rage.

"It is absolutely terrifying."

"That's scary," Aster said. "It fits you."

Tamar nodded. "Goodbye Winkle. I hope you make it home."

"Thank you," Periwinkle said. She felt a twinge pluck at her spine, and it felt different from the Berberoka. It was something sprouting and reborn, and it called to her. Periwinkle rubbed her back and looked ahead of the bridges. She knew the manananggal was far ahead of them.

Aster waved to Tamar, and Periwinkle thought the clouds made her sister look a little gray, almost like a shadow entwined along the ropes. Periwinkle's own shadow cast itself in front of her on the planks.

She took Aster's hand, and they followed Hooyip northward across the silver thread bridge.

Chapter 16
Alliteration

The floorboard planks looked like all the others, and the trio clip-clopped along to Aster's maniacal elementary school beat of singing and stomping and slapping her hands and knees.

"Is everyone in elementary school these days as wild as you, Aster?" Periwinkle asked.

Aster stomped, stomped, stomped, and spun and stomped some more. "High-five me bros! That's alliteration! Waaaaaaaaaah! I have to continue my education."

"That's not alliteration, Aster."

Aster ran in front of them, then ran back, then she ran ahead and returned again. "Waaaa waaa wuu wooooaaa! That's alliteration! Ooooo yoouuuu shooo shiii mah shooooooe. And that's assonance!"

Periwinkle held the sides of the rope and recounted Aster's words. "That is alliteration and assonance. Good job Aster!"

Hooyip tossed the bridge hook and grappled the next bridge. "I learned a-lit-er-ashun. Shaaaaa. Shoooowww. Shooooon. That's alliteration," Hooyip said.

"Shaaa. shhhhoowww. Shooooooooooooooon!" Aster repeated and threw her arms up. "Bridge bash consonance!"

"I feel like the bridge hook makes this like finding the secret shortcuts in video games and we're jumping down warp pipes," Periwinkle said.

Hooyip unhooked the rope rails and sent the bridge flying. "What's a video game? What's a warp pipe?"

"Hmm," Periwinkle said. "It's kind of like updogs."

"Updogs?" Hooyip asked. "What's updogs?"

"Nothing dog! What's up with you?"

Aster giggled.

"I'm not sure I understand," Hooyip said. "Is that a warp pipe?

"No," Aster said. "It's updog."

"That's what I asked," Hooyip said again, a little frustrated. "What's updog?"

"Nothing dog! What's up with you!" Aster said.

Periwinkle and Aster laughed again.

Hooyip growled. "I still do not understand what is updog."

Aster held her sides. "Oh no no no. It's too funny."

Periwinkle stretched, then looked around. "This one's a little different."

Aster started her full body run, staying in place and pumping her arms. "I'm going to make a big sign and post it right here. I'll make it red and neon yellow and everyone will see it!"

"Why would you do that?" Hooyip asked.

"Because this is our last bridge, and we can finally get off these wriggle ropes that make my stomach full of butterflies! Yesssss!"

Periwinkle and her companions walked for an hour. However, there were no more crossroads and no more twisted paths until they saw the cliff side loom in front of them. The bridge sloped up, which seemed to Periwinkle a fitting end to the frustrating Broken World Chasm. "Do you think some people made it this far and failed this last climb, and then they just slid back off and fell into the chasm?"

Aster wailed and took off running up the bridge. Periwinkle and Hooyip followed, and not one had any problems with the near vertical ascent at the end of the bridge.

"If we tried this when I first met you," Hooyip said, "neither of you would have made it."

Periwinkle caught up with her sister, who sat down to catch her breath.

"This part of the Ember Lands does not look like the other part," Aster said.

The trees beyond the trio looked dead. Jagged plateaus cast their jagged shadows over the ash-colored land.

Periwinkle looked for some living point of interest, but she only saw patches of gray grass. "It looks like a world that's had enough of the things who live here."

"This has to be the result of those who've entered the Ember Lands," Hooyip said. "They come from their own world and consume or destroy everything in ours, and once they've finished, these are the smashed-up bits left behind. If this is the part of the Ember Lands where most of them congregate, then the Abyssal Vine must be here in the north."

Periwinkle wondered what they could do against hordes of creatures with the ability to decimate a world; she was just a kid trying to keep her little sister safe, and she hoped Hooyip didn't expect too much from her or Aster. "No. Wrong answer," Periwinkle mumbled.

Winkle heard a whisper from her thoughts. "Wrong, indeed." Winkle shook her arms as Stay awoke inside of her.

Hooyip looked at Periwinkle. "Answer what? I didn't hear. Anyway, there's smoke, and a town. Can you see it?"

Aster stood on her toes and shaded her eyes. "I don see

nothin!"

"It's there," Hooyip said. "And it's a place to start."

Periwinkle batted her finger against her lips. "The place depicted in the book I found, will it even be recognizable? The pictures and descriptions had to have been from a different time."

"If my ancestors knew of the same place, then it can't be much further because I don't think the alakdans have ever traveled to the ends of the Ember Lands in the north. It still exists. The sylphs still exist. I know they do."

Winkle wanted to believe what Hooyip said because without the promise of hope, she could never return Aster home, so she nodded because nodding meant that Hooyip's dale of sylph's existed and she believed her and Aster could be safe.

Her arms and ribs ached from the customary twinge of the Berberoka's awakening.

"I think this is where we should tell Aster to go back to the bridge. Maybe she can find the wayward women and live with them." Stay whispered.

"That's a silly idea," Periwinkle thought back. "Why even suggest such a thing? I think we're closer now than ever. If we turn back, then we'll never get home."

"I did not say we. I said, Aster."

"If she did that, then she'd never make it home. I would fail."

"Yes," Stay said.

"No." Periwinkle looked at Aster running ahead of her. "Hey Aster, what do you think? Why have we come all this way again? Remind me so I can keep going."

"We're going to make it back home so we can see mom again. We're going to help Hooyip chase all the baddies from this world. You will get me home, and I will get you home."

"I'm not sending her back on the bridge by herself. That's a ridiculous idea. She would never make it. I'm not going to abandon my sister," Periwinkle whispered to the Berberoka.

"Things get sadder from here. They get more difficult."

"So help me, then, and make sure we keep her safe."

Winkle felt cold inside her arms and chest as Stay receded. "Ok Winkle, we'll do it. Just remember that I'm still here, ok. Remember that I am with you, and I can exist."

The entryway to the town was abandoned and only the smoke remained as its resident. Aster picked up a chunk of broken wall from one of the homes and turned it in her hands.

"You shouldn't touch that," Winkle said. "Maybe it has mold or fungus or bugs or something."

"Bugs or mold? Yuck." Aster threw the chunk of wood on the ground. "So, should we go to the smoke or look for supplies? Maybe there's something left in this place. Smoke doesn't just come from nowhere."

Periwinkle shrugged. "Maybe we should just avoid the smoke altogether. I really don't know. If we don't look for trouble—"

"It's better to know what's up there," Hooyip said. "We'll stay quiet. We can decide what to do after we know what's ahead of us."

Periwinkle winced. Hooyip's expression looked stern, almost like Deborah's the first time they met.

"Maybe you two haven't learned enough out here in the Ember Lands. I might be better off alone," the alakdan said. "I told you we're getting close. I need you to be better at this by now."

Winkle's stomach turned. She wanted to respond, but instead she just took her sister's hand and followed behind Hooyip, who already prowled into the abandoned city.

When they made it near the smoke, Periwinkle saw a horse with a bandaged knee tied to a hitching post outside one of the smaller homes. A wooden wagon resided near the snuffed-out fire, and two metal cages, some rope, and a large burlap sack rested inside the wagon.

Periwinkle stayed with her sister hidden behind the corner of one building while Hooyip retreated to tufts of overgrown grass next to the girls and allowed her two tails to poke above the surface of the stalks.

Aster strained her neck around the corner. "I'll go look,"

Before she even moved, Hooyip yanked her to the ground. Aster's elbow banged against a rock.

"I guess we should wait," Periwinkle said.

Aster rubbed her elbow. "It hurts."

They waited until the black fires at the edge of the world declined. Periwinkle managed to keep her sister still.

A girl, not much older than Winkle, if even older at all, returned to the makeshift camp carrying a cage. The girl had shaggy gray hair and powder white skin that might have made her look older if not for the softness of her face. The creature inside the cage, except for the gray fur and charcoal rings around its eyes, looked almost like a baby red panda. It mewed as the girl put it into the cart. She pulled bits of leaves from her pocket and fed the animal.

"Oh, she's fast," Aster said.

Periwinkle blinked. Hooyip had the girl subdued, and the alakdan held both of the girl's wrists behind her back.

"Where are the others you're traveling with?" Hooyip asked. "What's happened to this town?"

The girl let her body go limp. "I am here alone," she said. "I have one sack of food. The horse is lame. Please take whatever it is you need and let me work. If you take the horse, then please do not ride it because its knee might get worse."

"She seems nice," Aster whispered.

"Quiet," Winkle said. "What if she's lying?"

The girl looked over at the house where Winkle and Aster hid. "I'm not a liar. I already said take what you need and leave. Just leave me the animal and one more cage. They can't be useful to you anyway. I need to return them to our troupe. I work for the Wonders."

Periwinkle saw Hooyip's tails swirl and twitch behind her.

"She's right, no one else is around," the alakdan said. "Except for us, nothing else around here is moving. Periwinkle, tie her hands."

Winkle took some of the rope from the girl's wagon, and she bound the girl's hands using a knot that Hooyip taught her. She pulled the rope tight around the girl's wrists.

"Winkle?" Aster asked.

"It's ok, Aster. I think this is appropriate for a time like this."

"Ok."

Periwinkle sighed and sat down in the grass.

"You haven't told us why this place is abandoned," Hooyip said.

The girl turned around. "You're an alakdan. And you two look human, but not like any humans I've ever seen."

"We're human, same as you," Aster said, creeping from around the building. "You are human, aren't you? You look like us."

The girl waited. "I am a human."

Periwinkle felt uneasy. The girl's gaze remained on her and Aster more than Hooyip. Even with Hooyip's twin tails and her carapace body, the ashen haired girl looked more bewildered by her and Aster.

"Are you here to rob me?" the girl asked.

"Why is the town like this?" Hooyip repeated. "Is it

because of the creatures from the Abyss, the ones that come from the black fires?"

"Partially," the girl said. "Yes, those creatures you talk about have been to this town. I've traveled through most of the cities in this area. It's what we do."

"What is that exactly?" Hooyip asked.

The girl took a deep breath, then tried to arch her head off the ground. "I am a Wonder. We bring entertainment and curiosity. We provide experiences. We show people mystery and relics to bring joy into their lives."

"And still, you haven't said why this town is abandoned and burned." Hooyip left the girl's hands tied behind her back, but she let her stand.

Periwinkle considered the town. The town looked less burned than dilapidated from time, and what they thought was ash from further away, had a different texture entirely; dust covered the ramshackle buildings and the ground.

The girl sat on the edge of her cart. "One of those dark visitors came to this town. Its face and body looked human, but it was much more than that. It was always in flux. The creature looked older and younger all at once, like time kept changing for it. I do remember its hands. They were orange and red; the color of sand blown across the beach. I guess that's the color of it. The visitor asked for soldiers."

"The color of time?" Aster asked.

The girl looked at Aster, then smiled. She shrugged. "I think maybe you're right. The hands were the color of time."

Periwinkle looked at the girl's hands, and they looked normal. Maybe a little callused and pale, but normal nonetheless.

"Oh, I think I have heard of that one," the Berberoka whispered to Periwinkle. "Must be careful if he's entered the realm. I suppose I'm glad that I shall not have to face him."

Hooyip yanked on the ropes that bound the girl's hands and the girl tumbled into the cart. "What did it need soldiers for?" Hooyip asked.

The girl sighed. "The stranger told the townsfolk that it was on a quest. It made promises of treasure and power for anyone who would help find a certain type of vine or plant. It was terrifying to tell the truth, much more terrifying than you three. Things around it stopped living." The girl fidgeted a bit with her hands bound behind her back. "Oh, there was something else. Well, two somethings. Its eyes had flecks of green. I could see them. It was real vibrant, not like most of the plants here."

"Not like the color of pickles," Periwinkle said.

The girl looked up. "I don't think I know what that is." She waited but still seemed like she wanted to talk, like figuring out some riddle without giving the wrong answer. "It offered immortality, and that's what did it to this place. Oh, some men did try to stop it. They had weapons, but the creature was fearsome. It turned them to dust. It wasn't fast, and I've seen nothing like it. When the visitor touched them, their bodies caved in on the spot it touched. And the skin, it was like soot in a fire—so slow. They were still moving while it happened. Well, once people saw what it could do, and the visitor reiterated the offer, then just about everyone joined and they left to the north. No one stayed to watch our shows or explore our displays."

"Then if no one is here, why are you left?" Hooyip asked. "You said you have a traveling group."

"Well, I returned because we lost something. Some of our creatures have a way of slipping between places. I need to bring some of them back. That's what I do. I look after them. If you are not thieves, then you could travel with me, if you like. Maybe at least until I can catch up to my troupe. It does get lonely in the wilderness by myself."

Periwinkle watched Hooyip tie the girl's legs together. "Stay here," the alakdan said.

Hooyip joined her and Aster by the corner of the abandoned home and crouched beside them.

"What do we do with her?" Periwinkle asked. "If she's telling the truth, then that's a lot of people looking for the Vine. Maybe traveling with her to the next town isn't such a bad idea, especially if she knows the area."

Aster nodded. She looked over her shoulder at the girl. "Yes, and maybe she knows someone who could tell us about the sylphs. She takes care of animals. Anyone who cares for animals can't be all that bad. I've always wanted to take care of a pet one day. Maybe she can teach me how to care for them. She is an expert."

"And it might be safer to travel with more of us," Winkle said.

Hooyip scratched her neck and looked to the north. She shook her head. "Human girl, what's your name? How long have you been with those Wonders?"

"My name? My name is Esa Noche," the girl said. "And I told you. I am a Wonder. I'm not with them. I am one, and I have been one since I could remember, so whatever you decide, please do it soon. I still have one more of these critters to track down, and it's getting late. It'll need to eat and who knows what it'll get into in this place."

Hooyip shrugged. "I don't know humans."

"You didn't know us!" Aster said. "Or the women on the bridge, and we're friends."

"But she's not like you two. She's a real human."

"Do you think we could ask her about the sylphs?" Periwinkle asked. "She says she's traveled a lot."

Hooyip rubbed her eyes and temples, then shook her head. "I've never met a human before you two, but you're not like the humans from the pictures I've seen in our books, and the women we met on the bridge, they were different too—scarred, or more themselves than human. They were just trying to survive." Hooyip's mouth twisted, and she looked at the girl. "I'm afraid of her."

"Then it's settled," Periwinkle said. "We'll untie her and go on our way. We'll stick together and keep each other safe. We will only trust each other."

Aster's stomach growled, and she worked to carve something into the side of one of the homes.

"It's getting late, and she hasn't eaten," Periwinkle said after Aster's stomach grumbled again.

Aster continued to scrape something into the house. "I'm sorry. I can't make it quiet."

"You must be hungry," Esa Noche said. "I have plenty of food, and now it's almost dark. You can join me if you want. I couldn't do anything to you anyway. There are three of you, after all. If you want, you can even put these ropes back on me after we eat."

Periwinkle looked at Aster's work on the wall. "Hooyip, do you think we should let her go?"

"Ok, we'll untie you," Hooyip called to the girl. "You said you can take us to the next town? We are also trying to find something." The alakdan grit her teeth and took a deep breath. "We're trying to find the sylphs. They might know more about the creatures coming through the fires."

The girl stayed quiet. Then she nodded. "I know someone who could tell you about the sylphs. I have even met one. I know someone who could tell you all about them."

Hooyip untied the girl, then backed away. She looked to the fires at the edge of the world.

"It'll be too dark for me to find the missing panda," Esa Noche said. "I'll have to do it tomorrow. Tonight, we can eat, and after I find Lenny, that's his name. The one that's still missing—they are pretty rare. They're hard to come by, but the one that's still missing is Lenny." Esa Noche reached her fingers between the small bars of the cage to pet the captured panda. "This one is Bill. Lenny will probably look for her. So maybe by tomorrow, he'll be closer and easier for me to round up. Once I find him, we can catch up to the Wonders. I know someone you can talk to about your syl—"

"There we go!" Aster said, then backed away from the house where she worked. "Someone wrote something on the wall, so I left them a note."

Periwinkle read the message on the wall: "There is no hope anymore. Everyone has gone, and I am alone." Then she read Aster's response: "Do not give up. I will help you."

"Do you think they will see it?" Aster asked. "I should have written, my sister and I will help you." Aster twisted the corners of her mouth. "I'm stronger now. Not as strong as you or Hooyip. Maybe you and me together are like Hooyip. But I've seen it, Winkle. You can help people too, now. That's what I'm going to keep doing.

"That was really nice of you, Aster. But I don't know if the person who wrote it will ever be back here. Someone else might see it, though."

"I hope it makes them feel better."

Hooyip tapped Aster on her shoulders. "If we're going to eat, then let's eat something.

"Ok. Hey Hooyip. When did you decide you were a hero?"

Esa Noche watched the three girls from her cart.

Hooyip smiled but gave no answer, and then she swished her two tails against Aster's back before untying their captive.

Esa Noche shared food with everyone. Before she ate, she tended to her horse's bandages, and she cared for the small panda-like creature in the cage. She even let Aster feed the panda, and both tried their best to keep Bill comfortable.

Esa Noche's conversation was polite and pleasant, but Periwinkle thought there was a coast of loneliness in her actions, too—like a harbor no one ever visits. Periwinkle helped Esa Noche clean up the bowls when they all finished eating. No one talked anymore, not even Aster, and once they finished cleaning and they cleared out spots inside one of the abandoned homes to sleep, Esa Noche sat down and gazed toward the open grassy plains and sparse trees.

"I guess you three can tie me back up now if you want. Just untie me in the morning so I can look for Lenny and I can make sure my horse is ok. I shall have to change his bandages."

Periwinkle looked to Hooyip who shook her head no, and Winkle let herself feel at ease and stretched out next to Aster, where she felt safe. Tomorrow, maybe she would help Esa Noche find Lenny before they parted ways.

"We're getting closer, aren't we, Winkle?" Aster asked.

"I think we are. I think mom would be proud of you, Aster."

When she awoke, Periwinkle found some writing scrawled in the dirt which had one short sentence:

Take Care of your sister   -H

Winkle knew she didn't need to trouble herself looking, because the alakdan had left them. She left just as quietly as when she found them in the woods when she and Aster first entered the Ember Lands. Periwinkle brushed her little sister's hair from her cheeks, which were the most pale and the most colorful red in the entire world.

Chapter 17
Horse

Finding Lenny the panda was easy. In the morning, Esa Noche found the creature curled up against Bill's cage. She returned him to his carrier and asked Winkle if she was ready to depart.

Winkle didn't really know what the right move was, if she were being completely honest with herself. And being completely honest with herself, she's relied on Hooyip for direction almost since they've arrived. For now, she resolved to keep her sister distracted from any conversation about Hooyip's disappearance. Not that Hooyip disappeared at all. The alakdan left by her own choice, and Winkle decided to travel with the gray-haired girl to the next town. Who knows if that was the safest decision for her and her sister? She seemed safe enough, but once they embarked from the abandoned town, she realized just how little the girl talked, and Winkle hoped to use Esa Noche to keep Aster occupied. Aster always had lots of questions about everything. She's had even more questions since arriving in the Ember Lands, and Periwinkle knew that her little sister stirred with all sorts of questions about why Hooyip decided to leave.

Periwinkle didn't have a single definite answer to give

Aster, other than Hooyip, just wanted to leave them. Maybe she thought they were both too weak. She avoided looking at Aster.

"I don't understand why she had to leave," Aster said. "We're supposed to be friends. We said we would help her." Aster's face tightened, and she kicked the grass and uprooted a path of destruction as she walked. She balled up her fists. "She promised she'd help us. I don't understand. We need to go find her because she said she would help us get home. Hooyip made a mistake. We need to fix it, Periwinkle."

Periwinkle rubbed her temples and covered her face.

"I have a question."

Aster always had a question.

"Did she tell you why she left? Are we supposed to meet with her in the next town? Periwinkle, why aren't you looking for her? Periwinkle, this isn't right. She probably did not leave too far. Do you know where she went?"

Winkle closed her eyes and, with one hand, continued to squeeze the sides of her head. She patted the horse beside her and used it for support. It was the first time she's ever walked beside a horse like this. She's seen them up close, and she's petted a horse when her mom would take her and Aster to a local farm where they'd buy a small bag of brittle grass and fresh carrots. It cost a dollar a bag. She liked to pick out her own bag. Aster just grabbed the first one available, and they used the contents to feed some of the animals. She's only seen a horse from the other side of a fence. This one was so gentle. Esa Noche held its reins and walked beside it. Maybe the horse had an answer for her sister. "Esa Noche, does your horse have a na—"

"I have a question. Winkle, maybe I can find her! If we stop here, I can figure something out and see the threads, and maybe I can find Hooyip's threads. It works like that, you know." Aster moved her arms and hands in patterns. "The Kapre taught me that we all have our own threads, and I can find hers and we'll follow it to her, then we'll all be back together again and won't be lost or missing, then we'll be safe and we can go home and see our house and see mom again…" Aster rubbed her eyes and grabbed Winkle's arm. Tears welled in Aster's eyes.

Periwinkle pulled her sister close. "Hey Esa Noche, what's the horse's name?

"It's only ever been called horse. I've never named this one. It's always been with me, but I guess I've never thought to give it one."

"Hey, I have an idea, Aster. Maybe we can give it a name. All good horses need a name."

"No Winkle. I have an idea about Hooyip."

Periwinkle wanted to change the conversation. She wanted a distraction for her sister. Her fingers tightened against the horse. "See," Periwinkle said. Her mouth quivered. "We need to name this horse…"

Esa Noche ran her hand through the horse's mane. "You can name him if you like."

Periwinkle's throat tightened when her sister yanked at her wrist. Her head throbbed. Aster's weight felt like an anchor about to bury her in the dirt.

"I have a question about why she left."

Periwinkle snatched her arm from Aster, and she dropped her head in her hands. "I wish you would stop, Aster. Stop talking. If I could leave so I never had to hear you talk again, then I'd do it too. Just stop talking to me."

Tears welled.

Winkle stared at the ground. "I can't listen to it anymore." She felt Aster's warm hand on her shoulder. Aster's palms were wet both from tears and sweat, and Periwinkle slapped her hand away.

"Your sister," Stay whispered. "She makes so much noise. When will you take her home?"

"I can't listen to it anymore."

Periwinkle watched Aster tremble, and she wished she cared. She wished that she cared about Aster or Hooyip, but she only hoped for quiet.

The cold of the Berberoka spread across Winkle's back and crept through her arms. "Do you resolve to stare at the ground until your sister disappears? Or do you wish to make everything disappear entirely?"

"Shut up," Periwinkle said.

"You can still walk. Can't you? Is this what it is like when you give up?" Stay asked.

"I'm not angry." Winkle closed her eyes. She felt another hand on her shoulder. This time the hand was stronger, and it pulled instead of patted. Was Esa Noche trying to calm her? Periwinkle's face flushed with heat. The hand felt tighter. Did Esa Noche plan to leave them both here in the open plains, or did the gray-haired girl plan to leave just her?

With her eyes still closed, Winkle saw two colors form into shapes; one a perfect rectangle of white like a misplaced movie screen, and on that movie screen, the second color wavered into place—this one darker. It had the ooze of a shadow and cast four limbs and a head against its backdrop.

The hand released her shoulder. Periwinkle's face remained hot. Boots shuffled away from her. She pitied Aster for having a sister like her. Someone better would have gotten them home by now. Aster alone would have found a way home by now. The shadow on the screen tried to tell her something. Periwinkle did not want to listen, so she opened her eyes.

Periwinkle slumped forward, and she watched Esa Noche take Aster to the two pandas where Aster used two of her fingers to reach through the cages and pet the small animals across their brow. Esa Noche talked about their care and where they live in the wild and why their habitat makes them rare and that most people in the Ember Lands will never see creatures like these if not for the Wonders.

Aster, in turn, told Esa Noche about her journey across the Broken World Chasm and the strange plant that grew in the sky and cut through her skin. Aster told her how toxins from a worm that lived in the plant plunged her into a fever and how she felt ill and fell asleep and only had memories again after she awoke and saw her big sister.

Esa Noche listened. "That is something I've never seen," she said. "Maybe sometime the Wonders can make it as far south as that bridge."

"Oh, I do not recommend it," Aster said. "It was extremely dangerous. I was scared most of the time, and the bridges moved back and forth, and there was a monster, but my sister and Hooyip kept me safe."

Aster talked about Hooyip while Esa Noche gave water to her horse.

"I keep hoping his leg will heal before we return," Esa Noche said. "I think it will. It's not broken. It's got a cut and his leg swelled, but the swelling's going down. If I can get him better by the time we return, no one will know any different and I can keep him."

"I hope you can keep him," Aster said. "He's a very nice horse. He doesn't kick me or anything."

"He wouldn't kick you, Aster. He's gentle, and he's a draft horse. He's not as strong as some horses we have that pull carts and equipment, and he isn't as fast as some horses they use for the jumping or equestrian shows, but he gets things done. He's always my first choice because he's just pretty good at everything."

Aster returned to the pandas. "I was always told by my mom that horses kick. My sister promised that she'd ask if we can have our own pet to take care of when we return home. It'd be my first one. I hope they're as nice as the animals you look after."

"Well, promise me you'll pay attention to what the animal tries to tell you. They can't talk to us the same way you and I can talk, so you have to look for signs of their own language. Some of it is simple. Like if they pull away from you, then they need some privacy. If they move toward you, they want attention, or if they look at something they want, and look to you, then they're asking for help."

"Mmm," Aster nodded.

"People don't always realize what animals are trying to tell them because they just think about what they want for themselves. If we're given time enough to pay attention, then I'd bet there's all sorts of ways people could communicate with other creatures."

"I hope I'll be a good caretaker."

Esa Noche sparked a torch. "This is why this type of panda is so hard to keep alive." Esa Noche walked toward Aster and the caged animals while holding the burning torch.

"What are you going to do to them?"

Periwinkle saw the girl bring the fire closer to the face of the animals and closer to Aster's hand. "Hey! Stop it. Aster, get away!" Winkle ran to her sister and yanked her from the cages. She pushed Esa Noche aside. "You'll burn them!"

"I won't burn them," Esa Noche said. "If I don't do this, they won't live. They need the fire just like we need water or food."

Periwinkle pulled back. Esa Noche was the expert, not her, but did the animals really need fire the same way a human might drink a glass of water?

Esa Noche looked at Winkle, and then brought the

flames of the torch to the bars of the cages. "We've tried to keep them before, but it wasn't until I saw them eating in the forest after a thunderstorm when I realized why they perished with us."

The two pandas sniffed the flames and meandered closer to the bars. They both bit chunks from the torch, then flicked their tongues to expel the wooden remains after consuming the fire.

"I think there are other animals like this, too," Esa Noche said. "It's why they're so hard to keep alive, and I'm not completely sure if it's the heat they need or the fire itself, but I saw them eating one day in the woods. I saw one move into the path of a lightning bolt. I thought it was dead, but after the lightning hit, the panda just sat there cleaning its face with its paws. It ate the fire. Maybe one day, after I've been around long enough, I'll figure all this out—this and a lot of other things here in the Ember Lands."

The pandas continued to eat, and they bit the flames the same way a human might try to eat grapes from a vine. They finally stopped once the fire was pulled from the torch and only the chewed-up wood remained.

"I've never seen anything like that," Periwinkle said. "I…I was wrong."

Aster pushed her way between Periwinkle and Esa Noche. "Me neither! That's crazy. How can something eat fire like that?"

"I don't really know," Esa Noche said. "But they definitely need it. At least once a week, otherwise they get too skinny, and that's not good for anything."

Periwinkle watched the animals clean their fur and tails. "Is it ok if I pet them?" She reached her hand out slowly.

"Go ahead," Esa Noche said. "They seem to like it. They're friendly. Both of them are. They like to be scratched behind their ears and on their cheeks."

Periwinkle pet the two pandas on their cheeks and they strained their heads to rub against her hand. "When we get back home Aster, I'll talk to mom and I bet she'll let us get a cat or a dog. You can pick it out."

"We can both pick it out! And we'll both take good care of it because we'll learn to pay attention."

"Hey Aster, I really don't know why Hooyip left us. I wish she didn't, and I still think she's our friend."

Aster rubbed her nose. "I know. I have ideas why she left, and I even think I would understand, but she should have told us first if she had something to do."

"I don't think we should change our plans, though. We'll still try to find the dale and hills where the sylphs live, and maybe they can help us."

Aster nodded, and a smile returned to her face. They made camp for the night. It was the first night in the Ember Lands without Hooyip and the first time they slept when Periwinkle didn't listen to Aster bombard the alakdan with questions.

"Tomorrow," Esa Noche said. "We should reach the town tomorrow. I hope the Wonders are still there, but if it's cleared out, then they might have moved on already."

"What if they have moved on?" Aster asked. "What if the entire town is empty again, or what if the manananggal is there from the fire? Then what will you do?"

"I don't know." Esa Noche considered the question. Then she looked at Aster and shrugged. "I guess I shall move on to the next town."

"What if that town is empty?"

Esa Noche cleared her throat, scratched through her ashen colored hair and went to sleep.

Periwinkle closed her eyes as well, and she listened for the Berberoka. She still did not entirely understand its nature.

"Will you ever tell your sister about me?" Stay asked. "Or will you still keep me a secret?"

"Goodnight, Aster," Periwinkle said. "Let's try to get up early tomorrow."

"Oh, I see then," Stay whispered. "Well, remember what I said about you being appealing to my kind? That alakdan who went on her way was right. We must be getting close. The further north we get, the closer I think we're getting to the Vine. There will be more like the ones from the chasm. Maybe the alakdan was afraid, and she was right to leave. Maybe she was a coward."

"You know she's not a coward," Periwinkle said.

"Maybe," the Berberoka said. "But maybe we should give up this quest of yours. You and your sister could find a pleasant home here in the Ember Lands. I would help you. You're about to meet more humans. You are like them. They might accept you."

"Like they accepted Tamar and Miriam and the others who fled to the chasm?"

"Ahh, you're probably right. You and your sister are more like the ones on the bridge and less like the others, I suppose. You'll see that Esa Noche is not the odd one."

"What do you mean?"

"She is quite normal, but she seems more hospitable than the townsfolk that the wayward women told you about. Perhaps there are more like her."

Periwinkle drifted off to sleep. Dampness and cold blanketed her, and the cold no longer felt as awkward as when the Berberoka first revealed herself.

"Periwinkle?" Stay asked. "Do you dislike that I'm here?"

"No," Winkle whispered.

"That's good. You keep me from feeling alone. Maybe in that way I'm different from the others."

The next morning, Winkle helped attach the harness to

the horse and cart, and she and her sister walked beside Esa Noche, who continued to teach them how to lead the horse.

"You might like this town," Esa Noche said. "They have all sorts of shops. Nothing that compares to what the Wonders can offer, but they have toy makers, and seamstresses, and this one has a castle and tower and a drawbridge to enter."

Periwinkle had never seen a working drawbridge before. She wondered if there were guards at the bridge and if they wore suits of armor kind of like her idea of knights from Arthurian legends. Her father read her books about knights when she was young.

Drizzles of rain splashed upon them as they walked. Esa Noche's hair soaked with the moisture and it hung about her face in thick tufts. Periwinkle thought it looked a little like a mop and made her seem even older. She still was unsure of Esa Noche's age. Periwinkle wanted to thank her for taking Aster and her to the next town, but she always had trouble starting conversations with new people. It was especially difficult in school because she was one or two years younger than her other classmates after she skipped a grade just before attending high school.

The other kids in school joked around a lot and made fun of the way each other looked or acted. Esa Noche was maybe a year or two older than her—maybe. So she was about the same age as the other kids in her class. What if kids here treated each other the same? It was not uncommon for students to make fun of each other's hair. At home, this would be normal.

Periwinkle smiled at Esa Noche. "You look like an old lady in the rain because your hair is so gray!"

Esa Noche looked at Periwinkle. Her eyebrows pushed together, and she tried to wipe the rain out of her face and the dirt from her hair.

"That's not a very nice thing to say," Aster said.

Winkle read a memoir by a comedian once, and the comedian asserted that a way to get other people to laugh when everyone is quiet is to smile and start laughing, and then the laughter would spread. Periwinkle pointed at Esa Noche's hair and laughed.

"I was just saying, Esa Noche's an old lady because her hair's strange and gray, but she's like a nice old lady, I mean. Not like the angry ones, but she just looks like she's old because her hair is so weird. It's a joke."

"Stop it, Winkle," Aster said. "That's not a nice joke."

Esa Noche pointed in front of them, seemed confused and dropped her head, then twisted her lips. "I'll check the back."

Aster jabbed Winkle in the side. "That was really mean, Winkle."

Periwinkle's stomach turned, and she kept hold of the reins. She led the horse without looking at her sister or looking at Esa Noche, who let the horse and cart pass her by, and tried to straighten her hair.

Aster sighed. "A joke is like, knock knock, who's there? A door hinge. A door hinge, who? Door hinge rhymes with orange."

"Ok," Periwinkle said.

Dirt turned to mud as the rain increased, and Winkle slipped in the amalgam of grass and unearthed rocks.

"It's ok. It won't be long now," Esa Noche yelled from behind the cart. We'll probably see the town soon."

The castle took shape in the distance, and Periwinkle and Aster worked to keep the horse walking straight. Winkle's sleeves and mud-covered hands looked bedraggled in the rain, and though the castle and town waited in the downpour, the rain obscured the path in front of her. Periwinkle wiped her eyes and heard a clunk, then a thud, before sliding to the ground with her sister.

She sloshed through the mud on her knees, and she heard the horse neigh and huff as it collapsed. Its left front leg dangled at an awkward angle. She saw Esa Noche working to unlatch the horse from its harness. Periwinkle scrambled on top of the capsized cart to help undo the buckles and relieve the pressure of the straps from the horse's body.

"His leg gave way!" Esa Noche yelled as she forced her arm under the horse to remove its straps. "We have to get him back up. He can't stay down like this." Esa Noche pushed at the horse, coercing it to stumble back to its feet.

Periwinkle fidgeted with the harness, and she removed the last buckle to release the horse. It trampled back up but had difficulty maintaining its posture as it limped in a circle.

"He won't put his leg down," Esa Noche said. "This is bad." The girl started pacing. "I can get the cart up and pull it in myself. I can pull it back to town. He hurt his leg." Esa Noche sat down next to the horse.

Winkle felt Aster tug at her arm. "Did he break his leg?"

"I think so," Periwinkle said. She retrieved the cages with the pandas, and then she and her sister sat quietly with the girl in the rain.

Rain continued to pour for what must have been an hour. "I have to let him go," Esa Noche said. "They won't let me keep him if he can't work. This isn't the type of thing that heals right. Maybe he can live out here. Can you help me lead him away from the town? If someone finds him, they'll just try to take him and sell him. Once they realize he can't work, they'll put him down. I wanted to watch this one grow, Periwinkle."

Periwinkle nodded. They carried the two cages and took the horse to a sparse clutch of trees out of view from the trail. A stream trickled nearby and spilled over its banks because of what had now become a torrent of rain. It took a few tries before Esa Noche could make the horse stay, and they left it behind, then returned to the cart.

The three heaved the cart back onto its wheels. Then they used a blanket to cover what was left of their food and pulled it toward the castle.

"You know, I have very few friends among the Wonders. None if I were to be honest," Esa Noche said. "There just aren't any who are much like me in the troupe. There aren't any who would have helped me with these animals. That is why I had to stay behind by myself. It's nice to spend time with someone who feels more like a partner than a worker." Esa Noche shaded her eyes with her hand. "If they are here, we will find them on the outskirts outside the town gate. It is where we always set up."

They muscled the cart along and barreled it through the soft earth. Winkle saw hills with jagged bushes that looked as if she had visited them before. She also saw three large circles formed by various cages and giant wooden wagons, most of them covered from the elements.

"The Wonders are still here," Esa Noche said.

As they drew closer, Winkle noticed a set of chains larger than she thought imaginable. They were the largest chains she's ever seen, and the animal they bound was the saddest creature she's ever seen. It was someone she never thought to meet again.

"Look at the hills," Aster said.

Winkle remembered now. The hills and the shrubs outside the town were like those in the book. They arrived at the dale of the sylphs.

Chapter 18
Esa Noche

When she visited the circus with Aster, Aster was four, and it was the circus's last tour before the owner's went out of business.

Once the show ended and they left the auditorium—they were one of the last people to leave the auditorium—they took the long way around the building. Her dad said he wanted to wait for the traffic to clear out, so he did not want to rush. He bought each of them cotton candy. She wanted pink. Her sister had blue. They glimpsed all the large carts behind the building that housed the animals. The animals looked very old because their ears drooped. A milky haze covered most of their eyes, and flies picked at their skin. The animals did not even bother to use their tails to swat the flies away, and most of them were chained to cages or cars or other heavy things.

The chains she saw now were larger than those. There were more flies today than the day she saw those.

The last time they met, Periwinkle figured the relationship had ended. After all, the thing was stuck. The point of ever crossing paths again was moot. She wondered if she used that word right. Was the creature moot like she thought?

Periwinkle held Aster's hand. They saw Nephthea shackled to iron pegs. Its massive slug foot undulated over dirt, having already smothered and crushed any live or dead object that had the capacity to be smothered or crushed.

One manacle bound its stem. The body of Nephthea wept forward—or backward, thought Winkle—since direction did not matter to such a thing. The Not was there, too, but only The Not. The No and The Sweeping, Winkle deduced, were the flesh stump remnants, now a pockmark at the base of Nephthea. The Not looked much worse than a stump. The skin over his eyes grew into his face and remained shut. Feathers of hair remained, as did his half agape mouth. Nephthea looked somehow smaller than it did back in the old ruins of the buried city.

"That one is new," Esa Noche said. "We caught it maybe a week before I left to find the pandas. It's one of the biggest ones we've ever had. It's about as safe as they come, though, and a bit of a pushover. We found it washed up in a stream."

Periwinkle brushed her hair from her forehead. "I guess that makes sense, then."

"I'm going to look for the caretaker to let her know I'm back. They'll need the pandas for the display tonight. You can look around before the crowds arrive. I'll find you. If anyone bothers you, you can give them my name and let them know I found you."

Periwinkle tapped her sister's shoulder. Aster was folding the hem of her pants and fussing with her shirtsleeves. Aster rolled both sets so that her pants were cuffed even with each other, and her sleeves were rolled even with each other as well.

"We should stay away from her," Aster said. "She's baaad news that one. I'm glad she's caught. She deserves to be trapped for what she did to us."

"I don't know," Periwinkle said. "She was just trying to survive. Same as us. I want to see her."

"You can go see her. I'm going to do the alternative to go see her, which is not to go see her. I'm gonna go see something nicer. Not like her. They are called the Wonders, so there's got to be something here to make me wooonder. Maybe they have—"

"Wait. Aster, what are you going to see?"

"I don't know—I said I'm going to see something else. They are the Wonders." Aster used her index finger to measure the folds she made to both shirt sleeves to make sure they were even.

Periwinkle smiled. "Your I's and R's, Aster—the impediment. Your speech is better. It happened just now." It was like her sister grew up in just that moment. Winkle wished she had her colors so she could draw the way her sister looked just now—Aster was a snapshot of color introduced to the Ember Lands, the likes of which it had never indulged. If she were home, she would use her best pencils. Here, she had nothing of the sort.

"I said it right? It sounds right when people hear me? I feel the same, though."

"It sounds right, Aster. Ok, you can look around on your own to celebrate, but the rule is you can only go as far as you can still see me and I can still see you. This is a milestone for you. You deserve some freedom."

"So like on a tower I'd be really tal—"

"Stop it. Freedom, but you don't want to get separated here, right?"

"No, I don't."

"Ok, then. Let's think about this first and make sure we're safe."

Aster smirked. "Okay." Aster grabbed her sister's head, and Periwinkle and Aster put their foreheads together and closed their eyes so they could both concentrate on their situation.

Aster giggled.

"Ok!" Periwinkle said. "Any ideas?"

"Yeah, we should stay in places where we could see each other. That way we'll both stay safe, and you should not get too close to Nephthea."

"Good ideas."

Aster did her stationary run and chugged her arms to limber up before walking off toward a booth labeled, "This is it."

Nephthea remained gigantic, but also not. She stood as tall as a house, but Winkle remembered her even larger, and seeing her in the open somehow diminished her presence. Periwinkle took a deep breath.

"Are you afraid of it even chained up like this?" The Berberoka whispered.

"Yes, I think so," Periwinkle said.

"You should not be. This poor creature is over. I can feel it wither. There is no place for it here."

"I want to talk to her," Winkle said.

"It is strange," Stay whispered. "You can save it if you wish, but I do not think even the creature knows what has to be done to make that happen, and I am not sure I want to help you do such a thing without a compelling reason. Ah well. Maybe you can figure it out on your own if you feel it is necessary. You are a smart bird, after all."

Winkle walked toward the creature. She saw Nephthea's head rock upward, then swing to face her. Periwinkle took a step back. "Do you remember me?" Winkle asked.

"Have fun with your conversation," Stay whispered. "I think I am going to rest now."

Nephthea swayed and stared at Periwinkle with her large black eyes. "Yes, I remember you. You showed me light filtered through glass and it looked like snow. I languished. Then I thought of that night and it gave me hope, and the hope brought me here to my end."

"It's not my fault you ended up here. You hurt my friend, but I never wanted you to end up like this. I just did not want to be food, either."

Periwinkle saw the tan and wrinkled face of The Not waver toward her, as if straining to hear the conversation. "I know that voice, even though I cannot see." Two of the featherlike extensions unfurled from The Not's neck. "I still kept it, and I understand more of it now." He produced the fire hydrant nut from before, and he held it between his two delicate feathers. "I aspire to be more like this treasure, but the light in this world is not enough to sustain me—not even as part of a whole. I have lived so long, but soon I think I might be reabsorbed to where I began."

Periwinkle touched The Not's neck. Even his flesh felt weak, and his pallor faded. "What will happen to you?"

"He will wither. I will reabsorb him like I absorbed The No and The Sweeping to prolong my life as much as possible. He can no longer maintain his purpose in this place. The light here is too dim for him to absorb. I tried to at least save him. It is one reason we drifted from the cave. The light you created gave me hope that there would be enough to sustain him if we moved higher, so I detached myself and we floated. For a while, I consumed enough in the rivers to nurture us both, but I am such that I must grow or go dormant. The creatures in this land are not rich enough for me to flourish. No matter how much I ate, we failed to thrive. These humans found me washed up on a bank. I could not even fight back. I did wonder though, if eating you would have been different. You are not like the denizens that live here. There is a color to you."

"Well, you do not get to consume me," Winkle said. "But

I am sorry you ended up like this. Maybe there is still a place here for you. A place you just haven't found yet. The people who caught you travel to different spots in this world. Maybe there's somewhere habitable and you can escape."

Nephthea smiled. "You are the only thing I have met here that has felt like some place better. Maybe it is your youth and your naivety. Even if there were a place to go, I do not think I am fit to find it." Nephthea rested her head on the ground. "And your friend and sister, where are they? Has everyone you met in this nightmare of a world left you?"

Periwinkle did not want to answer her question. "What if…" Periwinkle's voice shook, and she felt her breath catch in her throat. "What if I help you? What if I help both you and The Not?"

"I am exhausted." Nephthea strained her snakelike body to try to hold herself up. "I am so enfeebled that my place in the future is to perish."

"We follow the rules," said The Not. "I can only arrive from below, and there is no longer a below from which I could travel. The beginning can only arrive from the sides. She still has the sides from which she can move. Maybe there is a way."

"That's silly," Winkle said. "What is there to make you follow those rules? Have you even tried to move from a direction other than below? What would even happen to you?"

Nephthea swung her head and pushed Periwinkle from The Not, knocking her over. "We have our nature, just as you have yours. He could not arrive from another direction, just as you could not expect to plunge to the bottom of an ocean and presume survival."

"I don't understand." Periwinkle said.

"It is ok," said The Not. "There are always rules and you

do not always get to understand, but I am just this fastener. Same as you." The Not's feathered appendages bent, then cracked. The hexagonal nut fell from his grasp and rolled across the ground. He positioned his head over the top of it and strained to open his eyes. The wrinkles across his brow and at the corners of his eyes pressed into folds and his eyes crept open. The nut continued to roll through the dirt, then roll into the grass, and The Not wormed to follow, and then he halted.

"I will not stop you," Nephthea said.

The Not's body pulled away from the base of Nephthea. He split from her as a singular wormish creature, and he hovered above his treasure as it rolled further and further through the grass.

The nut bumped over a rock, then its pathway curved. The Not continued to follow and slithered on the ground to keep pace with his treasure. It continued in an infinite circle and The Not continued as well, coiling around himself over and over. The gash in his skin where he separated from Nephthea withered into powder. He looked back toward Winkle and Nephthea, and he frowned. The corners of his mouth twitched, then he continued in a spiral until the dust of his body crept along itself from his tail end up and he teetered over his treasure and he dispersed atop of it.

Winkle scrambled to her feet. She wiped the dirt from her face. "Why didn't you stop him? He is part of you!"

"He has never had the opportunity of self-determination before. He wanted to experience the freedom to make a decision all his own, and I wanted to let him have it. I would have absorbed him soon. He pulled away from me to follow that object of his." Nephthea smiled. "I suppose life decided that it was my decision, after all, to let him go. There is cruelty even in that."

"You're next then," Winkle said. "You said you needed

to absorb him to prolong your life. Without him, you'll die next."

"Yes, without some food or light, I shall disappear as well."

"I don't want that to happen. I'm going to help you whether you want me to or not!"

"Then that is your choice, but think, my little piece of debris. What in this world is left to sustain me even if you manage my freedom? But I shall be here waiting if that is what you choose, because I am part of their show. Look around and see how different these people are from yourself, and when you return, I think I shall not be hard to find. Many people in this town will come to look at me."

Periwinkle did not want to believe that Esa Noche had any part in Nephthea's treatment. She spent so much time teaching her and Aster how to care for creatures. How could Esa Noche allow this? Maybe she had no choice; she was just a worker here.

Periwinkle looked for her sister. She saw a woman setting up a booth who had the same gray tinged hair as Esa Noche. Behind the booth was a man with inky black hair and with a similar pale and washed-out tone to his complexion. Every member of the Wonders was working or setting up attractions, and every town member visiting the attractions had the same washed-out complexion and some shade of gray, white, or black hair.

This must be normal for them, Periwinkle thought. She felt even more awkward about her comments to Esa Noche. If she wasn't suspicious about her origins before, her comments must have shown that she and her sister arrived from some place strange.

She saw Aster near a white booth holding a fruit that looked like a washed-out pear covered in gray syrup. A glob of syrup stuck to the corner of Aster's mouth just under her cheekbone. Aster jumped and waved.

"Periwinkle! I found him! We're going home!"

Winkle shook her head. "Quiet!" What was her sister talking about?

"No, here! Over there!" Aster said, pointing.

Aster ran toward her, and Periwinkle grabbed a hold of her sister's arm. "Calm down. Everyone's staring."

"Look what he taught me how to do! He's a sartor just like me." Aster wove her hand as if stitching a hole in a worn shirt. Her pear on a stick floated upwards. "I can keep it here! Look at what else he taught me. It needs to be natural, though."

Aster scoured the Wonder's encampment. "There." She pointed to a wagon with various flowers and plants. Some flowers spiraled like a corkscrew. Others drooped with elongated petals that hung from their stems. "Watch this." Aster concentrated. "It's almost the same as the Kapre taught me."

The corkscrew flowers unraveled and separated into their petals, then burst apart and floated toward Aster.

"No Aster, wait!" The crowd stopped, and everyone watched the petals float toward Periwinkle's little sister.

"Aster, stop it!" Periwinkle slapped Aster's hands. The petals floated to the ground, and Winkle pulled her sister behind one of the larger trailers. "We shouldn't do things like that out in public. We still don't know how safe it is here." Winkle wished Hooyip were with them.

"You don't understand, Periwinkle. I found someone who can tell us where the Vine is and get us home. His skin was the color of nighttime, and his hair the color of the sky in summer. There are others like him, and he knows about the creatures that look for the Vine. He's one of the sylphs. We can try to find the Vine before they do and use it to go back home!"

"I… I have to talk to him." Was she telling the truth? Was this one of her stories? The crazy description seemed to match what Hooyip had told them.

"We'll have to help him get out of here. He does a show from one of the cages. There are more of them here, too."

"Take me to him, Aster."

Periwinkle heard someone round the trailer. "I thought that was you." Esa Noche slouched against one of the enormous wheels. She rubbed the back of her neck. "I told the caretaker how you helped me when I was away. She said she might repay you with food and a horse." Esa Noche frowned and started looking through the crowd.

"We have our theater show. I'd like you to see it, but our vocalist isn't doing well. I think we'll have to change the performance, and it's sort of our marquee production."

Aster stepped in front of her sister. "Winkle can sing. Is it really like a play? I've always wanted to see one in person. It'd be so much fun. My sister has a magnificent voice."

Periwinkle's face flushed. "I don't know the songs. They can't put me on a stage. That kind of thing takes practice, Aster. I'm not that good."

Esa Noche stretched, put her finger to her chin, then shook her head. "No, no. The vocalist doesn't have to go on stage. Not in front, anyway. She stays behind the curtains. You could read everything and sing it from there. The caretaker, she would give you anything you would need for sure if you did something like that."

Winkle looked at her sister. "We could use a horse, maybe, to help us travel."

"Come on, Periwinkle, it's music! No one will even know it's you behind the curtains. We haven't done anything creative and fun for so long."

Winkle nodded. "Fine, let's go. I did say that you deserved to celebrate. But Aster, we have something to take care of after this.”

“I know that, and we will. I think I have an idea. If we can get their help, it’ll be even easier. Maybe Esa Noche can help us, too.”

Esa Noche led them toward the stage for the performance. Their encampment bustled as more people arrived to see the oddities offered by the Wonders. They passed Bill and Lenny, the two pandas that had an entire glass-screened cart dedicated to a makeshift forest habitat where patrons could view the two creatures as they ran and rummaged about. Inside the cart, a mock thunder storm rumbled, and the cart shimmied when rain dripped in from some mechanism built into the cart’s ceiling.

“Hey Esa Noche?” Periwinkle asked. “How long has this town been here? Is it one of the older places?”

Esa Noche shrugged. “Maybe you two don’t travel much. It’s closer to the edge of the territories. This is one of the newest towns. We just added it to our route. Before the people, it was nothing but hills and twisted plants. The people here tried to harvest the plants, but they were more of a weed. The ground has greater value without them. Why do you ask?”

They passed another animal that stood as tall as Aster and looked a bit like a kangaroo with an anteater’s snout. Its arms were trunk-like things that hung to the ground and terminated into three smaller tentacles that explored the floor of its enclosure.

“I just wondered, I suppose.” Periwinkle looked at the tracks made by the various wagon wheels in the grass. “I guess this is progress.”

“Look at some attractions we have, Periwinkle.” Esa Noche said. “Maybe you and your sister could stay with us. We could travel to so many places and have so many adventures. We could go even further than where the

Wonders have traveled. There are a lot of places for us to see, but time always gets in the way. There's always some responsibility or some schedule to follow. What we've done here with the Wonders stops time; it places everything on hold and we show people the way things appear as they were meant to be in and of themselves."

"What happens to some of these creatures when they get too sick or too old and can no longer be on display? The horse you had, maybe it could have had a place in this town."

Esa Noche furrowed her eyebrows. "We release them and replace them. We show people the way everything *should* be."

Aster tried to stop them at a booth that used miniature rivers to allow participants to change various water pressures to flood a model of a small village or make fake crops grow or shoot boulders high into the air.

"I want to try that," Aster said. "How'd they make the water-pressure that strong?" The entire booth shook with a whoosh of water. "The rocks rumble just by pressure, then the plants grow bigger, kind of like we do. I think I've been growing bigger since we've come here. I can feel it."

"We will come back," Periwinkle said. "Maybe they'll have something you can do in the play, Aster."

"You can help me manage the animals that we use in some of the scenes if you want!" Esa Noche said. "I guess I should try to explain some of the story."

Esa Noche grabbed a stick to use as a pointer and tried to explain the plot: "The narrative encompasses the meeting between a young warrior named Brulon and a townswoman named Dulsinee. At the start of the play, Dulsinee gathers food and collects her animal traps from the forest, but then she is shunned because she tries to warn the other townsfolk about an impending attack by a forest keeper she meets called the Grandaloo. The Grandaloo plans to unleash horrors and shades on the town so he can absorb the area back into the forest and expand his realm. In act two, Brulon tries to help Dulsinee and they fall in love."

"It's a love story?" Aster asked.

"It is," Esa Noche said.

"Awww, they fall in love. Will Periwinkle have to sing a love song?"

"She will. It's one of the most popular songs. It happens right when Brulon and Dulsinee are at the edge of town stuck between the forest and the last sympathetic farm. They look at each other and realize they share the same thoughts; that even though what they are about to do will be dangerous, they must continue to the forest and vanquish the Grandaloo to save the town. Dulsinee feels that Brulon is a proper hero, and your sister's song echoes in the background as they walk silentl—"

"Silently, but full of feelings." Aster said.

"Yes, silently, but full of feelings into the forest to find and confront the Grandaloo. Once your sister starts singing, we release some of the forest creatures. You can help with that. They're trained and go into the crowd. We use the smallest and cutest ones we have. The crowds like that."

Aster smiled. "This sounds fun."

Periwinkle smiled as well. Her sister had a way of doing that to people—making people feel the way she felt. Maybe Aster was right. Maybe it was okay to turn tough situations into games. They'd be here regardless of how they felt. What's wrong with feeling excited as opposed to frightened or morose?

"But what happens to the Grandaloo?" Aster asked.

"Like I said, he's vanquished. He's not the hero, but he is very important. He's there so Dulsinee and Brulon can fall in love."

Aster pursed her lips. "Ah, I see. But he's the hero to someone."

"No, I don't think so. Not in this story."

"You said he wants to make the forest bigger."

Periwinkle shook her hands. "How many songs will there be?"

"Seven," Esa Noche said. "One of them you just hum, though. It's still one of my favorites."

"I think I like the Grandaloo," Aster said. "Maybe we can rewrite the ending."

Esa Noche smiled. "No, Aster. He's the villain. He looks quite monstrous—you'll see once the actor is in costume. The Grandaloo has these sharp teeth, and he looks real serious all the time." Esa Noche curled her fingers into claws and rumbled a play-growl at Aster. "The Grandaloo is a monster. He doesn't even try to change his ideas, so he can't be the hero."

"Ah, I see," Aster said. "But why do the townsfolk have to—"

"Will I have time to practice?" Periwinkle asked.

Esa Noche nodded. "Yes, of course. I'll have you work with someone." Esa Noche pointed at the stage. "Come on Aster. I want you to see this! It's going to be a lot of fun. The creatures they use for this show are trained so well. There's so much we can learn from them."

The stage was larger than Winkle expected. They took a short stairway up behind some of the constructed scenery and behind a scrim and a backdrop. The wooden boards creaked, and the wood and metal smell of the stage almost smelled like the piers on the beach at the ocean. Esa Noche dug through a prop chest, pulled out a book of papers, and tried to straighten them before handing the script over to Winkle.

"You can practice back here. Our first show starts soon.

Then we have one more when it gets dark. It is one of our grandest attractions." Esa Noche motioned to a white-haired girl surrounded by instruments. "This is Cruces. She will help you with the music."

Cruces kept her head down, and hunched her shoulders together, then raised her hand to wave. "Hello." She continued to look at the ground.

Periwinkle wondered if this was how most people got their start in the theater. She looked at the wrinkled script and began to dog ear all the music. She thought for a second that this world had to have been somehow connected to their world. The music used staves, notes, and measurements similar to theirs. She put the matter out of her mind.

"Too much to learn, Winkle," she whispered to herself. It looked like her part was bigger than Esa Noche let on.

"Hello," Cruces said. Cruces stared at her and seemed unsure of how to start a conversation.

Periwinkle wondered how someone so shy could make it in a performing troupe like the Wonders. The girl picked up a flute, then pointed to the first song while Esa Noche and Aster left to ready the animals.

"So, this is like what I've learned in my own town," Periwinkle said as Cruces tried to coach her through the music. "Our symbols for depicting the notes are different, but the beats and positioning are the same. I think I can do this."

Cruces twisted her mouth and nodded. Winkle talked through the songs first, and as they practiced, Cruces switched out instruments appropriate to the song. Sometimes Cruces switched out instruments mid song as the musical numbers continued.

"Are you the only musician?" Periwinkle asked. "Does anyone else help with the music?"

Cruces nodded. "He's ill." She tapped on the paper for the current song, indicating for Periwinkle to continue.

Winkle tried to concentrate on the music, and she ignored the stage actors and costuming that carried on around her. The production overwhelmed her; everyone looked and acted like an expert. Her stomach turned. How could they just trust her to do her part? Because Esa Noche said so? They trusted her judgment that well? She expected a small production. This theater did not look like that at all.

A woman in a brown costume-dress rested her hand on Periwinkle's shoulder. "You're the one who Esa Noche said could handle the vocals? Listen, we need you to do well. We need this so we can stay." The lady walked off and adjusted her hair and makeup in a mirror.

Even backstage, everyone's movements looked rehearsed and precise. Periwinkle heard someone shout, "It's almost time. The seats are full and it's almost time."

A tall man walked up the stairs and pointed at Winkle. Everything went silent.

She saw Cruces staring at her and holding a knobbed mallet for one of the instruments. Cruces scrunched her lips and turned her head to the side. "You're ok," Cruces said.

Periwinkle took a breath. Her voice shook, and she started the introductory ballad that brought about Dulsinee's trek into the forest. Periwinkle felt so nervous that she dropped the last words from the song into an inaudible mumble.

The lady with the brown dress shook her head and scowled. Periwinkle clenched and opened her fists to try to calm herself as she followed along with the script.

"Come on, Periwinkle," she said to herself. "This isn't so bad." She shut out the noise from actors and technicians who shuffled backstage, and she quieted the murmurs of the crowd. The play continued, and Winkle started to get a headache from following everyone's lines on the crumpled script. Another song: "The Meeting with Grandaloo."

Cruces picked up a large stringed instrument that looked like a cello with three levers attached to the strings and waited at attention while staring at Winkle. The girl's straight-faced visage looked like either the mark of professionalism or the mark of death.

What would Bob Ross do? What would Hooyip do? Periwinkle mimicked people tougher than herself. Control, she thought. Happy little trees. Beat the devil out of it, beat the devil out of the song. The words and notes felt easier this time, and she limited her thoughts to the world of the paper and the world of time scales and music, and she matched pitches with Cruces' perfect matched counts.

Once the music ended, Winkle lifted her head up. No one moved. The murmurs in the crowd disappeared. The lady with the brown dress dropped her comb and her mouth rested open.

Cruces looked at Periwinkle. "You're good."

They heard the Grandaloo growl out his lines from the stage. Cruces picked up her flute and pointed at Winkle's script. The play continued. Winkle's voice and Cruces's instruments carried the mood of the entire show, and no one backstage dared to give Winkle a mean look again.

When she finished the last song, the two heroes, Dulsinee and her warrior beau, Brulon, finally defeated Grandaloo. They returned to the town and fell in love and the town prospered. At the end of the play, the curtain dropped, slowly falling to the prompter's call. Winkle heard the shuffle of velveteen curtains finally close, and Esa Noche returned. She removed a blackened mask the same color as the theater curtains that concealed her face from the crowd.

"That was an amazing performance," Esa Noche said.

"The crowd loved the show. I saw all of it. You and your sister could have a home with us if you want. Stay with us. Travel with us. We could put on performances like that every day and every night—even until the end of it all if we wanted."

Periwinkle fidgeted. *Would it be so bad?* Aster might enjoy traveling with the Wonders and moving from town to town and putting on shows for everyone. What was there for them in their own world, anyway? Once they returned home, she would return to a bunch of desperate kids and weary adults, and waking up on time to sit in classes so she could eventually sit in a job somewhere as an adult.

"You would be great with us and the Wonders," Esa Noche said. "This could last forever."

Would it be so bad even though Periwinkle wanted to see her mom? Was this the only place that Winkle could become something useful or something great? And what of Aster? Her little sister has an entire lifetime of potential back home in their own world.

"Thank you, but no. My sister and I have to find something and go somewhere first. It's important."

"You have a brilliant talent, Periwinkle Dalisay," Esa Noche said. "It reminds me of home somehow. It's a comfort. But I have someplace to go as well. Your sister, too, is a find. Sartors are rare here in the Ember Lands. She can even see the threads to help us end what needs to be ended."

Aster? Periwinkle looked. Her little sister fiddled with the lock on a cage at the opposite end of the stage. Esa Noche returned the mask to her face. One of her hands looked like sand blown across a beach, and she held her other arm behind her back. Then she disappeared.

"I like you, Periwinkle. Maybe someday you will change your mind, and we can try again. We are good people," she said.

"Run, Winkle!" a voice whispered.

Periwinkle grabbed the back of her head. She saw a flash of light and felt pain and dizziness, like she was thread being spun from straw into gold.

Chapter 19
A Tarp in the Chain

When Periwinkle recovered, she smelled sugar and corn, and she crawled across the trampled grass and the torn cloth from the tents.

She kneeled against a tree and tried to pull herself up and tried to listen for anything in the abandoned field. Opened doors swung on hinges of empty homes. Aster? She saw a gray mound in the distance and trailing from the mound was a dark chain that attached to the ground. A red string floated in front of Periwinkle. She opened her hand. The string connected to her palm, but she felt nothing. Her stomach growled and hurt. Her head felt worse. Periwinkle rubbed her temples, and the red string mimicked the movements of her palm and stretched itself toward the mound in the distance. She followed it as it increased its length and wafted in front of her. The string beckoned her past the rubbish, around the abandoned wooden booths, and beyond any obstacle between her and the gray heap which heaved and deflated like a balloon.

When she arrived at the thread's terminus, she found Nephthea in the grass, still chained to the iron peg. The ancient creature coughed and opened her eyes when Winkle approached.

"I hoped you'd return somehow. I'm all that's left. I'm too weak to move and was no use to them anymore, not worth the cart I traveled in." The muddied face of Nephthea still looked beautiful, and the creature turned her neck to look upwards. "They took your sister, I'm sorry to say, and everyone followed. They said there was something resplendent about her that could help make things grow." Nephthea tried to hold her head steady to look toward Winkle, but it wavered, then lolled about her neck.

Periwinkle felt a bruise on the back of her head, and she had trouble concentrating. Was Nephthea talking? Or did she imagine a conversation with Hooyip or Aster? Pressure in her head felt constant.

"I must smell like death by now," Nephthea said. "Like a fish too long in the sand. I've never been alone this long before, but there is nothing left for sustenance to regrow more of myself. Not those who come from below or even those who can hunt from above. I suppose this is how we are all left at some point."

Alone? Without her sister, it's how Periwinkle felt. Bits of brown tarp that wedged between the chains rubbed against Nephthea's neck and left an indent in the ancient creature's skin. Winkle, confused, pulled the scrap of tarp from the chain.

"Thank you," Nephthea said. "A constant source of discomfort, that was."

Periwinkle nodded. She felt empty. She saw a half-smashed barrel that still contained some water. The Berberoka remained distant, but Winkle was getting better at using its gifts on her own; she understood more of what the Berberoka offered—more of a feeling than a matter of intellect, and Periwinkle held her hands toward the barrel and inhaled. The water pooled into itself until it disappeared.

Periwinkle slowed her breath and touched Nephthea's

wound. She controlled her exhalation in a long and slow breath, and water cleaned away the dirt and blood from Nephthea's body, washing away more of the brown cloth that had wound itself into the creature's skin. "When I was younger, I had my own room," Periwinkle said. "It was always my own place to sleep. It had this brown fibrous carpet. I spent most days in that room, and I didn't know why. I didn't really like it there."

Nephthea smiled. "Conversation? I have not had one in so long. You were the last, actually. The last to try to speak with me. You always have reminded me of someplace safe. Maybe you can do that again, and we can talk a bit. What was it like where you came from? I imagine, like me, it was a place different from this."

Periwinkle nodded. "Outside where Aster and I lived the grass has always been like green emeralds, except for—I guess except for when it's not. The sky in our neighborhood was clear, and we lived—we live in a friendly spot by the park with the yellow swing sets." Periwinkle continued to expel water and coat Nephthea's bloodied skin.

"When I was little, I don't know why I stayed in that room so much. No one told me to do it, but the colors of that carpet—it made everything look small and dirty. Finally, my parents replaced all the carpeting with plastic gray laminate. My mom and dad did it themselves, and my bedroom looked brighter then. It was like my lights worked better, and I went outside more, too. It was when I found the cubby in a bush in our front yard, my favorite place. Maybe that was my only Spring—it was January then, and I was the hedges and the wind. It was the same year Aster was born, and I got to be a big sister. The place we're in now. This entire place is like the time before my sister was born."

Nephthea squirmed to try to coil around Periwinkle. Her flesh looked supple and alive where her skin absorbed the water. "Yes, the Ember Lands are like that. This place is loneliness and a brown carpet. And what are you now, Periwinkle?"

Periwinkle shrugged. "Maybe I'm a spirit and the host. I don't think I know anymore—or maybe I'm just an anchor. Did you see where they took my sister?"

"No, I am sorry, strange one. I did not see, but I know nonetheless. It is a place I am drawn to as well, even though I am in no shape to compete with them or the others." Nephthea rolled a red fruit to Winkle. "You may as well have this. I had an idea to keep it for myself, one last hurrah to stumble myself away, but I imagine I'll be gone in a day or two."

Winkle frowned. A round bit of split fruit rolled from one of Nephthea's unfurled feathers and wobbled in the dirt.

"It's a pomegranate," Winkle said. Its dull red looked hand drawn and unreal, like a page from a coloring book. "Nothing much has color here. It's beautiful. Where did you find something like this?" The pomegranate felt smooth against her palms, and she brushed off the dirt, then used her small knife to break it in half. Winkle handed one half to Nephthea and kept one half for herself.

"That girl with her mask, the caretaker, really has all sorts of strange collections. She threw it to me before she left. Her way of mocking a rival, I suppose, but no thank you. I think I'll just wait here for the end. All things end, and I think I am finally learning that life at the end is ok."

"Take it, or I will make you eat it. I'm going to free you so you can help me find my sister. She wanted me to find you, and she has a knack for knowing the right thing to do, so you are going to survive and come with me."

Nephthea smiled, then laughed. "Oh Winkle, when we first met, you were always shying away. You're different now. I wonder if you even see it. What are you going to do? There will be armies and warriors. How will you deal with those? The time is almost up. I can feel the Abyssal Vine growing somewhere out there. We have already lost. The girl who convinced everyone to leave here must have felt it too, and I suspect your sister can somehow make it easy for her to harvest.”

Periwinkle stared at the ground. “It’s what we need to go home. That was the idea anyway. My sister probably has a plan already. I’m letting her down.” Winkle shook her head. She tried to clear the fog from her thoughts. “If I have to, I’m going to travel at the speed of light until I get her back. They’ll call me Mrs. Fahrenheit, and I’ll burn through them all. You’ll help me.”

“What a strange response. I’m not sure I understand, but ah well.” Nephthea bit into her half of the fruit and tried to right herself. Her face looked smoother. Leaves shook free of her silver hair, and her rough snake body slithered forward. “You will have to break these chains, of course. Once we get there, do you think we’ll be able to see the snow again?”

Winkle concentrated. I need you, she thought. You have to wake up. Wake up! Winkle felt cold liquid push through her veins, then creep down her arms, and twist through the arteries in her neck that heralded the awakening of the Berberoka. Black liquid cut outward through Winkle’s wrists and hands and poured into the puddle that Winkle used to wash Nephthea’s wound. The black fluids desiccated the liquid from the mud.

“I am here,” Stay whispered to Winkle from beyond the dark doorway where she resided. “You can help this one in much the same way that you helped me if you like. You are like a receptacle for us and you need only to make the offer to those of us who cannot find their own way to exist in this world."

Winkle grabbed the chain and the black fluids entwined through the links and forced water into the metal until it cracked and burst.

"There were whispers like thoughts," Nephthea said. "A portion of you invited me to persist like a changed mind. Something younger than me and alluring. I think I might not take the offer, though. I have kept my own company for so long. It is that I am, but maybe along with you, I can remain here."

Nephthea unfurled one of her feathery appendages and entwined it around Periwinkle's hand. "I can feel their prize budding through. Your sister will be there."

Periwinkle walked and Nephthea slithered. Even with her diminished stature—Nephthea remained too grand for Winkle's interpretation. She held the feather of a hand which felt like thorns.

"You are more like me than different now," Nephthea said. "I can feel a kinship with you. The humans here might think of you as a monster."

She was right, thought Periwinkle. The Berberoka felt like it was a part of her now, too. She felt as close to her as someone might feel to an arm or a tongue, closer even because its voice had become a nuanced facsimile of her own. Were they even separate anymore? The dialogue that persisted between her and the uncanny spirit felt no different from an interior monologue with herself. "I can help keep you safe." It told her. "We can find your sister. We will return home." Periwinkle was unsure which of them thought or spoke.

They followed the trampled ground and followed footsteps that converged from a multitude of directions, not because they wanted to see where they led, but because Nephthea felt compelled toward the direction. Winkle heard it too—just as before, over the Broken World Chasm. They walked until the air turned humid, and they found themselves in a world of stems and leaves where shadows cast from objects made her feel no more significant than the dust from the bark on a tree. Within the thorns and humidity, the wetness of the air precipitated on Winkle's nose, and droplets of water languished on her cheeks. Her hair curled tighter, and strange gray trees with gray thorns and crumbled leaves clung to her neck and clothes like dead silkworms stuck in their thread.

"If any place were to grow an infinite vine, then I suppose this is it," Winkle said. "If you were to have arrived here instead of the forest, then maybe things would have been different."

"No, Periwinkle. I do not think it would have mattered. Everything native to the Ember Lands feels empty. There is no sustenance for me here."

Periwinkle leaned against a cluster of white vines which grew upward and curled back toward the ground like an alabaster fountain. "Have you noticed that the mass of footsteps disappeared?"

Nephthea nodded. She coughed, and her flesh looked pallid. "It was not the footsteps that led us here, and we do not need them to find our way to the end." She slithered around the eruption of vines and disappeared behind the plants.

Winkle sat and waited for her companion. "For being so much larger than me, you can be amazingly difficult to find sometimes." Winkle heard Nephthea's body pull along the ground.

"Do you remember what she wanted with you and your sister when you first met?" Stay whispered. "That vine will bring immortality for those like us. She just needs to survive a little longer to find it."

Periwinkle thought of her sister. She wished Hooyip had stayed with them. Maybe she and Aster would still be together. "And you, Berberoka?" Winkle thought. "Are you sure it isn't what you want? Isn't immortality and the Ember Lands as a gift, enough of a prize for you to leave me?"

"Ah Winkle. I have told you. I like it here. With you, experiences have texture. They are electricity that buzzes from hand to hand. That is not something we can ever have, even if we were to last forever. We do not feel things or know things the way you do. But I have explained the best I can, and your companion is missing. Should we be wary of that one, Winkle?"

"Are you there, Nephthea?" Periwinkle asked. "Where did you go?" Periwinkle circled the cluster of plants and saw nothing. "Have you finally left me, too?" She kneeled and touched the ground, which felt tender and soaked with moisture. Her hand pushed into the earth, first to her flattened fingers and over her knuckles, then over the knobby bones of her wrists. She always did have skinny arms, even with all the training from Hooyip, and she pushed further still, down to her forearm and then to her elbow. The dirt crumbled around her, and she went further still, deeper and deeper into the fallow earth. "There is water here." Periwinkle said. "I can see it. I can hear it."

Nephthea disappeared to hunt. Soon, maybe the creature would devour her, Periwinkle thought. Periwinkle imagined becoming part of the black soil and helping the white vines grow. Whatever was left of her that came from Earth, which came from her neighborhood back home, was so far away she may as well be born to the Ember Lands.

Her arm melted through the loam to her shoulders and chest now and she felt it—a stream of water that ambled under the soil.

Periwinkle sank. She felt the fluids bubble up through the

dirt and around her hands. Her knees sunk, and her boots felt stuck.

"There is water here," Stay whispered.

"Maybe this is where we'll stay," Periwinkle said. "I can't sense your Abyssal Vine. Not anymore. I don't hear a battle. It must be over. And Aster."

"Is this what we want?" Stay asked. "I can help you remain in the Ember Lands. There might be some excitement in it."

The ground gave way. All around her, the earth crumbled and replaced itself with the buried water, but Periwinkle did not follow it down. She felt herself yanked upwards. Then she floated and felt squeezed within Nephthea's coiled body and transferred to her companion's back.

Nephthea plodded through the swamp, and her back wobbled. The enfeebled movements felt close to a collapse. "I left only for a moment to find nourishment so I could last to the end, but it was tasteless and empty like all the rest. This place erases even the memory of life. It has its own erosion, and there is no life to the water here."

"Can you feel it again?" Stay asked.

Periwinkle rested against Nephthea's neck.

"We are almost there," Nephthea said. "It feels like a way back home." Her body shuddered from coughs. "My strange girl. Maybe you and yours have made me persist."

Periwinkle looked for signs of life. "My sister Aster would have made this a game."

***

There were the dead. Periwinkle wanted to see solace in the jungle, and her eyes found the memory of a battle:

shattered swords and axes, trails and footsteps in the mud, and helms loose among the leaves. All the accouterments that departed from their owners seeped into the ground. The water receded behind her, and Nephthea's body tethered her to land.

"From here, I think it will be up to you," Nephthea said.

Periwinkle slid from her companion's back. Nephthea's head rest on the ground with the rest of her body partially on land and partially in the water. Winkle stroked Nephthea's hair. "Don't leave us."

There was silence.

Periwinkle's throat went dry. She stroked Nephthea's cheek. Periwinkle's eyes widened. She grabbed at the water and sloshed it over her companion. She tried to press the water into Nephthea's skin and imagined rivulets of water seeping through the minute cracks of Nephthea's pours and then into her flesh and running beneath her neck, then dripping across Nephthea's veins and arteries until it eventually coated the entire inside of her companion.

"Wake up, wake up, wake up, wake up, wake up," Winkle said. She continued to grab at the water and try to force it into muscle and skin. With enough water inside her, I can control her, she thought. I can bring her back. I can make her move again. I can get her home.

"Stop it, Periwinkle," Stay said. "She is gone, or almost gone. Get up. We have to move from here."

Periwinkle checked for the sheath on her lower back which housed her paper dagger. It remained concealed under her shirt. "Keep the brush moving, Winkle," she told herself.

"Yes," Stay said. "We will see it soon. Please keep going."

Periwinkle picked her way across the swamp. The vines smelled of peppers and wet tomato plants doused in rain. She slipped in the mud and crawled herself through the collection of muck and the failed weapons and armor of the dead. Seeing no person left, she moved quicker. She heard the call of the Abyssal Vine. Was it calling for her or the Berberoka? Its song played through the jungle. How many others remained to listen?

A dead gray light shone ahead of her in the dead gray jungle. Her sister stood in the center of it with both her arms outstretched. Aster looked as if she were trying to hold something. Winkle ran toward her. She felt Stay surge inside of her as the strange spirit propelled her forward, and she saw shimmers in the air. They webbed through Aster and entwined around a pair of arms made of orange sand, as well as a strange black vine that arose from the ground.

"I can see it, too," Stay said. "That is what it means to be a sartor. Those are the threads that connect us all. That is what the world looks like to Aster, an amalgam of thread and string, with hardly any space that separates one from the next. But she can separate them. She can make them unravel and knit and reconnect ways she sees fit. Aster is like you and I, but she is more than either of us, too. We have to help her."

"We have to help her," Periwinkle repeated. She saw splotches of blood trail from Aster's nose. Her sister's little fingers worked in endless patterns as threads continually wrapped and re-wrapped themselves around the black vine and around her enemy—her enemy. She had hands that looked like sand and dust. Her eyes were emeralds. Her enemy, the girl, Esa Noche who escorted them through the town of wonders, who introduced them to the other humans of this world. The entangled strings dissolved from Esa Noche's hands and arms just as they reformed and wove between her and Aster to bind her in place.

"She is one of you?" Periwinkle asked. "She is one of the things from the Abyss trying to return the Vine?"

"It appears so," Stay said. "I could not see it before. She is an old one, then. She is like the Pillar with the duendes from the forest. If she claims and returns the Vine, then she will persist and be reborn as a true companion of Time, and the Ember Lands will be her land to explore, reshape, or destroy. She will live forever."

Periwinkle saw another creature on the ground beside Esa Noche. Its body partially dissolved and collapsed into a pile of soot. It was the sylph with the night-colored skin and hair that looked like the sky. The same one Aster wanted to help. Periwinkle unsheathed the dagger from its place against her back.

"He is not the only one left," The Berberoka said.

"Aster! I'm here." Periwinkle's voice trailed off. "Don't get hurt. Please."

The wind screamed. Periwinkle felt the wail above her and saw the last of the manananggal dive toward her sister. Hooyip held on to the creature's chest and raised the sword made for her by the papersmiths, ready to slash at the monster's chest, but the manananggal caught Hooyip's arm and dropped the alakdan from the sky, then continued to dive toward Aster. Threads materialized from the ground, trees, and wind, all originating from Aster as a locus, and the threads stopped the manananggal mid-flight. Esa Noche, Aster, the manananggal, and the Abyssal Vine were all connected, as if knit together into a tapestry on the verge of shredding apart. Periwinkle saw the strings around Esa Noche dissolve faster and faster.

"You will not hold both of us," Esa Noche said. "What will you do, Aster? The manananggal is a monster. If it wins, it will return and feed on these people forever. That is its nature. We can stop it, you and I. Then I will take you and your sister home, if that is what you want."

"That is a lie," Stay whispered to Periwinkle. "Only one

of us can ever return with the prize. She could not use it to find your way home. Maybe in the next passing in another world when the remains of the Vine migrate somewhere else and regrows, but by then, I'm afraid you and your sister will have long passed on."

"I can help her," Periwinkle said. Moisture seeped from the ground and surrounded Periwinkle in a thickening fog.

"Winkle!" Aster said. "The manananggal. I can't hold it. I can feel it ripping the threads."

Hooyip stirred on the ground. "Go, Periwinkle, help your sister. I never left you, but I never trusted that girl, either. When she took Aster, I followed so she wouldn't be alone. You can see it, can't you? That's the Vine your sister holds back. I'll destroy that thing, and none of those creatures will come back here again. We're all that's left."

Periwinkle sent the fog to surround the manananggal. She pressed her hands toward each other and directed the vapors into the creature's nose, mouth, and ears, all the while forcing the mist to return to liquid. "Drown won't you," Periwinkle said.

The manananggal sputtered and choked, and Aster released it to focus her attention on Esa Noche who inched closer to the black vine that continued to sprout.

Aster's ears bled, and she began to cry.

The vaporous cloud all but disappeared; Periwinkle flooded all of it into the manananggal and the creature plummeted to the ground. Winkle felt the water surge through the manananggal and she tried to direct it to the monster's lungs.

The manananggal spat and growled. A flame formed around its arms and snaked around its chest.

"Just stay down," Periwinkle said. "Please, just stay down." She watched the half-bodied creature drag itself toward her. The manananggal moved faster and faster until it launched itself back in the air.

Winkle tried to move aside, but the creature was so large and moved so fast that it crashed against her and slammed her head to the ground.

"I have to end it, Winkle," Hooyip said. In a flurry, the alakdan sped by her almost too fast to see as the manananggal clawed at Winkle's arms.

The manananggal's teeth looked like shards of glass and they filled its mouth like some predator from hidden ocean depths. Periwinkle's muscles burned from trying to hold the manananggal back.

"I'm not alone," Periwinkle said. "You will help me, won't you? You're here with me, too. I think that you were here even before I entered the Ember Lands. You're here with me now. I know you are."

When Winkle grabbed the monster's wrist, darkness coalesced between Periwinkle and the manananggal. The shadow enveloped her attacker and shielded Winkle from its claws and flames.

"You've saved yourself for this. Help us then," the Berberoka said.

Periwinkle felt a rush of air blast by her, and her hair swept across her face. She saw the blurred form of Nephthea plunge into the manananggal, biting it across its neck. Stay's vague shape responded the same, and the two creatures tore into the monster. Once it was down, Nephthea and Stay started to consume the bloodied manananggal.

"This one is unstable," Stay said. "I can taste it. It did not enter this world by choice. It is lost."

Periwinkle felt as if the manananggal called to her and pleaded for help. "Lost?" Winkle asked. Periwinkle approached the creature. Nephthea and Stay continued to feed. "I can bring it inside. Would that be some sort of penitence for all that it's done?"

Stay halted the consumption. "Penitence? I am not sure spirits like us can ever feel remorse or understand concepts like shame and atonement. Is this a sort of revenge? Are you trying to set the world in order for the destruction this thing caused?"

"I think so," Periwinkle said. The remains of the manananggal continued to call to Winkle, and it clawed at the dirt to try to reach her.

"We have room still to let this one in, and it is important for me to keep you happy. You are more welcoming and agreeable that way. After all, I dislike instability. I do not enjoy it. Not one bit."

"Then this one will be invited in. Manananggal, this is your only chance to persist."

Periwinkle reached toward the creature. Its broken chest continued to heave on the ground. Its eyes widened, then its body relaxed.

"Fine then," Periwinkle pressed her hand against what remained of the manananggal, and the creature's body ceased its movement. Periwinkle felt a stab in her back and a sudden weight puppeteer'd her spine like being tethered to the sky. She doubled over and leaned against Nephthea, whose body quivered, then went lifeless and still.

Periwinkle looked to her sister and to Esa Noche. "We are almost done, Aster."

Hooyip collapsed on the ground beside the vine, but the alakdan had done enough. Her sword left a cut in the Vine, and Periwinkle saw Hooyip's chest continued to move.

In the end, Hooyip remained their friend. She was the first real friend Periwinkle ever had, and she realized she wanted to protect Hooyip and protect Aster. She was ready to take her sister home.

Threads around Aster and the Vine fell like cinders as

Esa Noche continued to move toward the prize, but Aster, too, had done her part and pulled the vine further away even as Esa Noche's strange sand-colored hands pressed forward.

Periwinkle gripped her knife, then released it to float in a contained torrent of water that took shape in front of her. She aimed it toward Esa Noche and felt Stay's strength well up inside her. "Together," Winkle thought.

Stay stood in the dark doorway inside Periwinkle's mind and frowned. "Together."

The knife propelled toward Esa Noche's chest. It moved faster than wind—faster than thought. It was time to return home.

Chapter 20
"Periwinkle, I'm sorry."

"It's finally time," her dad said. "Your new sister is born."

The baby was only big enough to fit in her mom and dad's palms. Her lungs weren't really developed yet, and her vocal cords were so weak. She never cried. She never cooed. She almost weighed three pounds. If someone were to be mean, they'd comment that it was almost as if she was never there to begin with, almost to say she had never been born. The baby was too small to go home.

They waited to see her.

Periwinkle's mom and dad showed her a list of names. "We've narrowed it down," they said. "She might like one of these."

All the names on the list were from nature. Her sister could have been a Fawn, she could have been Birch or Clementine.

Periwinkle was still little then, so she had to read about most of the names. When she looked at pictures, she liked blue asters the best, even though sometimes to her they looked purple.

The description in the encyclopedia said that it was a reliable growing flower that added color to a landscape and always attracted pollinators, which made other plants grow as well.

"Blue Asters," Periwinkle told her dad. "Can her name be Aster?"

She remembered her mom liked the name, too.

They waited.

"It's almost like the baby is not even there," said the NICU nurse. "Sometimes it's better if they're just let go."

Periwinkle's dad heard her. Periwinkle heard it, too, so she knew it really happened—the nurse really said that. She remembers how angry it made her mom, and after that Aster was moved into the hospital room where her mom and dad stayed. They never let her out of their sight.

On the fifth day Aster weighed three pounds, and Periwinkle used all her Christmas and birthday money to buy her sister a green and pink stuffed turtle to keep her company in the medical crib. It had a nightlight that displayed a pantomime of stars on the ceiling. Aster could not yet control her neck, so it was dangerous to leave it with her because she could suffocate, so Periwinkle set it up on the table across the room. The turtle had quite a long neck. Its legs and arms hung out, and it had a smile on its face, which Periwinkle pointed toward her sister's crib, so maybe the baby would see it. Winkle was too young to know that eyes didn't work that way yet.

When her parents fell asleep, she sang to the baby, too, and if Winkle were older, she would have read that babies can remember voices and it is in this way they form their first relationships.

Despite her weight, Aster had chubby cheeks, and Winkle decided her sister was her favorite person in the world. She wanted her to have fun, so during hospital lunches, Winkle played peekaboo with the baby because that's what she's seen other people do with newborns. When Aster did not quite respond the way babies do on television,

Winkle decided that she did not like the idea of her little sister disappearing from view—or worse—the entire world disappearing from her little sister just by pretending it wasn't there; she never played games like that again.

Instead, she read her sister stories of inventors and scientists like Marie Curie, or authors like the Bronte sisters who created an entire world of stories when they were young. She read to her about each sister, but mostly read about Anne, who Periwinkle liked the best because she used words like Wildfell, which had a strange mystery to a 5-year-old girl.

She read to Aster about cats and horses, and they waited.

***

Periwinkle looked at the gray jungle that somehow looked vibrant. The dark trees shone darker. The white and ashen vines had lines and definition that she could have traced and translated to an ink and pad back home. She heard her little sister call to her again.

Hooyip lay across the base of the Abyssal Vine, and a gouge split through her back. Her paper sword remained embedded into the flesh of the plant, and a miniscule fracture branched out from the blade.

"I liked that one," Esa Noche said, whose orange and red hand pulled away from the alakdan at Aster's command. Esa Noche broke free, then thrust her hand toward the dagger that sped at her chest.

Winkle's dagger dissolved and fluttered to the ground. Aster struggled for control.

Esa Noche moved toward the Vine. "It's not your fault, Aster. Right now, you're too little and too new. You might have won this in a year or two." Esa Noche tore her hands through the air, and the surrounding trees turned to dust.

Whatever threads of reality Aster maintained started to fade, and she held her stomach and cried.

Esa Noche frowned at the girls. "Sometimes, this is all there is."

Periwinkle saw Aster curled on the ground. She looked the same as when they entered the Ember Lands. Winkle felt cold and started to shake. "Aster?"

"Periwinkle, I'm sorry."

Her little sister grabbed hold of the Vine. Periwinkle ran toward her. She saw Aster pinch her fingers into the wound created by Hooyip's sword and pull out a brittle thread. Aster wove it between her fingers.

The string formed into a little black flame, and the Vine started to unwind. Aster's small body shimmered. It started at her legs—she was smart enough to give herself as much time as possible—and Aster unwound as well. She became a willful blue thread that overtook the dark thread of the Vine, and she wove herself with the Vine to help the flames grow.

"If you do this," Esa Noche said. "You will lose this type of gift forever. Do you think your world is unique in this life or that you are unknown to us or those like us? You have gained the attention of Great Ones and they have shared this attraction to those even greater. And that will be horrible for you. You have a choice not to fight, Aster. We can explore and persist. If we return the Abyssal Vine together, then nothing will be a danger to us. You and your sister can come with me."

Aster wove her away, too. She pulled on the threads of whatever made Esa Noche unique and entangled her with herself and the Abyssal Vine because Aster knew that if she didn't do something to help her sister and Hooyip and remove the promise of the Vine forever, then someone else would find some way to do them harm. So she had to spin all of it away, and her threads followed both of them to make sure she left none of it behind.

Periwinkle grabbed for her sister. "Stop it, Aster. I'm here. You're safe." She saw Aster's stomach and chest billow faster and faster.

"She was bigger than us," Aster said. "But I can weave all of them away. I just have to follow to make sure none of it returns. Thank you for staying with me. Thank you for singing to me. Thank you for giving me my name."

Periwinkle grabbed for Aster's insubstantial body. Aster slipped through her fingers more than once. She tried to take her sister's hand at least six times before failing to hold on to her fingers. Periwinkle lay down next to Aster where her fingers held the sky instead of her sister's hair because it was all she could do as Aster continued to unwind until the last dark cinders burned an exit way open.

"You have to go," Hooyip said. "It won't open like this forever."

Periwinkle felt herself lurch to her feet. "Do you really want to remain here?" Stay asked.

She stepped forward. It felt rather simple, and it even tingled like a mint or tea-tree shampoo. She did not belong in that world. Maybe her sister did; her sister, who was too magical, too creative, and too much and too grand for their own world of colors. Was that place somehow better than where she lived? In the end, she didn't even have an answer for that. Winkle knew that she wanted her sister back. All she had left was the imperfect memory of her sister's voice and everything she should have been.

Periwinkle felt her body compress into itself, then disappear and reform. She was only thought. She was an idea of form.

She held on to one recollection, which helped her return;

she learned the color of her sister's name. She learned how to define the colors in the dark when she closed her eyes too tight. It was in the way she learned to listen to her sister talk. It was the way she learned to watch for the details of how her sister wore her clothes.

It was the last color Periwinkle saw before she returned. The color of her sister's name was a brilliant phthalo blue.

Chapter 21
The Houses Outside

The houses outside the hospital were on fire. News reports stated the fires were less frequent and less severe and fewer homes burned. The monetary loss to the city was minimal, the news reports stated. The third thing Periwinkle remembered after the news and after a hug from her mother, was a note from her high school that said "thank you" printed on school branded stationary and some dried flowers with a certificate for being student of the month.

Once she was well, the hospital and the police released Periwinkle to her mom and they visited her sister in the burn unit before they tried to return home.

"You escaped with a few burns on your arm and some on your back. It's miraculous," the nurse told her.

Aster looked small in her bandages, and Winkle's mom could only cry. Periwinkle did not know if she was allowed to touch her sister. She wanted to pick her up. She wanted to take her home. Digital lights from the medical machines illuminated her sister's hands. "Can I just stay here?" Periwinkle asked, barely above a whisper.

Her mom shook her head no.

"Can we come back?"

"Yes. We will come back."

Winkle left her "thank you" card and certificate on the nightstand in Aster's room. She hoped they would somehow help her sister find a way back home. She made promises, too.

By 9:00 pm, Winkle's mother rushed her through the cops, who tried to wish her well as they left. Winkle's mother told the police to leave her daughter alone.

The car door shut. "They suspected you of the fires," her mom said. "They found you with the old lighter your dad gave you. I hate them. I'm sorry, Periwinkle. Sometimes things are too much."

It was too much.

When she was ready, she walked to school. On her way to school, she heard neighborhood boys beat the ground with their sticks. There were three of them. They smiled when they saw her.

"You were on T.V.," one of them said. "You're that girl in that bush that caught on fire and spread to other houses."

Periwinkle saw a litter of strange animals curled beside the hedge where the boys used their sticks. They looked like cats with brown-black mottled fur. Two of the babies tried to move, and the boys beat the creatures again with their sticks.

"Hey let's go," one of them said, and he threw his stick on top of the animals.

"Yeah, if my parents find out I'm late again, they'll freak."

"Hey Winkle, you should hang out with us sometime. You're like famous now. It's a miracle you survived that."

Periwinkle kneeled beside the creatures after the boys left. The animals had faded gray tails—it was the only portion of their bodies that had a solid color. They looked like kittens, but their combination of colors weren't like anything she's seen on earth, which made them wondrous.

She's seen the creatures before, and Periwinkle tried to nudge them and get them to move. She tried to give them water and nuzzle their heads. None of them moved.

The bushes shook. A creature a little larger than the babies, and which couldn't have been more than a year or two older, darted from the hedge and pulled an electrical box with wires that shot off sparks and electricity. It must have traveled far, because it looked winded.

When the creature saw its babies, it lunged at Periwinkle and bit her arm. Then it ran to the litter, smelled the bloody sticks, and pulled the electrical box to her babies. The creature chewed back the wires and created more sparks along with a small black fire wherever she bit off the casing into the wires. The mother consumed some of the black flames and sparks to show her kittens what to do, and then she butted the box closer to her babies. None of her kittens moved, and the small creature collapsed beside them and yowled as the bush caught fire.

"You're right, kitten," Periwinkle said. "It's a wonderful world. Let's go, get up, girl." Periwinkle picked the animal up to keep her from burning, and the creature held on to Periwinkle and cried.

Winkle and Aster

***

www.ingramcontent.com/pod-product-compliance
Lightning Source LLC
Chambersburg PA
CBHW020653120726
47906CB00001B/256